BADLANDS
A Sheriff Lansing Mystery

Books by Micah S. Hackler

Sheriff Lansing Mysteries
Legend of the Dead
Coyote Returns
The Shadow Catcher
The Dark Canyon
The Mutes
The Weeping Woman
Moon of the Blue Mustang
Badlands

Coming Soon!
A Sheriff Lansing Mystery
Cerro Grande

BADLANDS
A Sheriff Lansing Mystery

Micah S. Hackler

SPEAKING VOLUMES, LLC
NAPLES, FLORIDA
2020

Badlands

ISBN 978-1-64540-235-0

For
Don and Robin Perrero

Acknowledgments

Thank you, Olivia, for the daily encouragement, for a comfortable home to work in, and your love. Thank you, Dan Baldwin and George Sewell, for the decades of support and your valuable friendships. I want to thank my Pulmonologist, Dr. Ragiv Agarwal, for his invaluable medical expertise used in this novel.

Thank you, Kurt and Erica Mueller and all the staff at Speaking Volumes for your continued faith in me.

Prologue

The three figures in the rocky, dusty yard sat motionless, staring at the cabin.

Tina Morales jumped when the door slammed behind her. Charlotte "Charlie Brown" Etsitty, Tina's best friend since second grade, quickly locked the door. This had been her second trip to the generator shed to restore power to the isolated dwelling. Despite her best efforts, the Briggs and Stratton engine wouldn't start, even though it was new.

This was Tina's first trip to Tuba City, Arizona. The two fifteen-year-olds had travelled the 200 miles from Phoenix to attend the 17th Annual *Western Navajo Fair*. It was an excuse for Charlie Brown to visit her extended family on the rez. She worked full time during the Summer and hadn't seen her grandparents since the Spring. This was the first time either girl was able to travel anywhere without their younger siblings tagging along.

An involuntary shudder wracked Tina's entire body. She had been warned, the high desert was already chilly, even though it was only mid-October. It had been 90° when they left Phoenix the afternoon before. By the time they left the *Fair* that evening it was near freezing.

"Are you kids all right?" Charlie asked her three, younger cousins. She was frustrated with being saddled with babysitting. Now, suddenly, she realized the responsibility she had to face. Turning her flashlight in their direction, the two youngest, William and Jennifer, clutched each other, as far away from the window as they could get, but still be in the room.

At 12, Walter was the oldest and the spokesman. It was his job to protect his brother and sister. "Yeah . . . Are those dogs still out there?"

"Yes, but don't worry. Grandpa said he would be here soon." Un-owned, ungroomed, underfed dogs were common on the Navajo Reservation . . . but Charlie knew they weren't dogs.

The window shade had been raised 3 inches . . . just enough to give the two high schoolers an unrestricted view of the darkened yard. They watched from the black interior of the cabin.

Movement caught their attention. One of the "animals" stood on all fours and trotted to a derelict truck a few yards away. First raising its snout to smell, it jumped into the bed of the truck, then onto the cab.

A second creature stood and started toward the house.

Tina's eyes widened. What she thought was a coyote went from approaching on four legs to standing upright on two. It disappeared from their line-of-sight.

A second later, something on the outside began rattling the front door latch. Then whatever it was began pounding on the door.

Five-year-old Jenny whimpered and buried her face in her brother's arms.

The two friends looked at each other. The fear was overwhelming. "What could they do?"

The pounding stopped suddenly. Then came the distinctive crack of a rifle being fired.

The "coyote" at the front door began running. Tina and Charlie watched as it quickly dropped to all fours and disappeared into the darkness . . . joined by its two companions.

There was a gentle knock. "*Dáádílkaał ąą dinít̨įįh.*"

Charlie recognized her grandfather's voice. She rushed to the door and opened it as he requested.

"Come," he ordered. "Everyone, into my truck."

One of Charlie's uncles stood next to the cab. He was armed with a rifle, scanning the darkness, making sure the intruders didn't return.

The two youngest rode in the cab. Walter, Tina and Charlie huddled in the truck bed, bracing themselves against the rush of freezing air. The twenty-minute ride from the top of Preston Mesa was miserable. The road was rutted with deep grooves. The occupants in back were bounced mercilessly.

Charlie's grandmother admonished her husband for letting children stay at the remote cabin with no adult supervision . . . no protection.

It was well past midnight before everyone was settled in for the night. Tina and Charlie were allotted sleeping bags in front of a wood-burning stove in the kitchen.

In the darkness, Tina finally worked up the nerve to ask. "What were those things?"

"They are called *yee naaldlooshii* . . . Skinwalkers . . . and they are evil."

Chapter One

Johnathan Akee stood at the open doorway and ushered the sheriff in when he arrived.

The body lay face up. The eyes were open . . . as was the mouth.

As he knelt next to the dead man, Lansing couldn't decipher the expression. Surprise? Fear? Pain? Shock? He wasn't sure.

There was no sign of a struggle. The body had no visible wounds. The powder on the corpse's face told him they were probably dealing with drugs.

"Heart attack, maybe?" the sheriff suggested.

"I don't know," Johnathan Akee admitted, shrugging. "I think he was only, like, forty."

Lansing stood, removing the white, latex gloves. With the dawn of the 21st Century just a few months away, Cliff Lansing wanted the San Phillipe County Sheriff's office prepared for the future. He needed his personnel up to speed on the most current law enforcement policies and techniques.

DNA evidence was an increasingly hot topic. A conviction in court could hinge on even the smallest bit of DNA material found at a crime. Conversely, contamination of a crime scene could result in a guilty person walking free. The sheriff was shocked to learn how easy it was to transfer his own DNA onto evidence. It was now office policy all personnel wear latex gloves at crime scenes, especially if they were gathering forensic evidence.

"You didn't touch anything, did you?"

"No." The Pueblo Indian shook his head. "I was driving to Santa Clara . . . Susan and me. We saw the door was open. Been a lot of break-ins around here. Thought maybe Juan was off on one of his runs, so we stopped."

"One of his runs?"

"He was a truck driver. He might be gone two, three days at a time."

Lansing stepped through the front door, into the bright sunlight. Akee followed.

The small adobe house was one of a dozen along this stretch of County Road 2. Every other dwelling had bars on the windows. Juan Pedro's house was no exception.

"This is a hell-of-a-way to start the week . . . Did he have any family?"

"Not around here."

The yard . . . mostly dirt, gravel and the occasional, hearty weed . . . had a chain-link fence with no gate. The only vehicle was Lansing's Jeep.

"He owned a car, didn't he?"

"A truck. But it ain't here now. That's why I thought he was on a run."

"Probably stolen," the sheriff nodded. He was starting to think in terms of foul play. "Where's your car?"

"Susan dropped me here. She had to be at work. I stayed." Akee looked up and down the Old San Ildefonso Highway. "Segovia Police said this part of the road wasn't theirs. It doesn't belong to Santa Clara Pueblo, so I didn't call them."

"Yeah, I have a quarter mile of road all to myself." The short stretch of the old highway belonged to the county . . . sandwiched between Segovia city limits to the north and Santa Clara Reservation to the south. "How long have you known this Juan Pedro?"

"Couple of years. We live two doors down. He used to have a dog we took care of when he left town. That's how we knew him."

2

"Did you hang out with each other?"

"What do you mean?"

"Go out for a drink . . . something like that?"

"I don't drink no more. I got a good job at the Pueblo . . . me and Susan both. She works at the Adult Day Care. I work out at Puye Cliffs . . . maintenance, clean up . . . stuff like that."

"So, you probably didn't know any of his friends."

Akee shook his head. "We were just neighbors. That's all." He hesitated. "Can you take me to the Pueblo Offices? It's only a couple miles. I can get a ride out to the Cliffs from there."

Lansing hesitated. He was thinking more and more he was at a crime scene . . . a dead body, a stolen truck. He was reluctant to leave the area unsecured.

He still held his latex gloves. He gingerly pulled the door shut, making sure he didn't leave his own prints behind. He had Johnathan help him stretch yellow Crime Scene tape across the door.

"Get in the Jeep."

"In front?"

"Sure. You're not under arrest." Lansing had known Johnathan Akee and his wife Susan for over a decade, though he hadn't seen either in nearly two years. For a long while they were the Las Palmas town drunks. Drifting back to their native Santa Clara Pueblo in the south of the county, they had turned their lives around.

Akee allowed himself a rare, crooked smile. "I never rode in the front before."

"It's a brave new world, Johnathan."

Chapter Two

"So, no one's seen Harry this morning?" Chaco Canyon Park Superintendent Michael Quijano asked. He didn't sound angry or upset, but there was an edge of concern in his voice.

"No, sir." Jackson McKee was Chief Ranger for Chaco Canyon National Park. Harry Miller was one of the full-time rangers who worked for him. "He signed out Patrol Truck two about nine o'clock last night."

"Why?"

"The last few mornings maintenance crews have been finding trash around Pueblo Bonito . . . near the western kiva. Stuff dropped during the night."

Pueblo Bonito was the largest of the dozen major Puebloan sites in Chaco Canyon. With an estimated 650 rooms at the height of occupation, it held 2 great kivas and 20 clan kivas. The kivas were the round ceremonial structures, used for religious and cultural activities. The great kivas were used for mass gatherings. The smaller clan kivas were used by the different religious "societies."

"After sunset? Even though everything is supposed to be shut down?"

"Yes, sir."

"It's not just because of extra visitors over the weekend, is it?"

"No, sir. It's trash from night activities."

"I've been gone a week. How long has this been going on?"

"At least two nights in a row . . . Friday and Saturday. Probably again last night. Harry was hoping to catch the culprits."

"What are we looking at? Beer cans? Teenagers up from Crown Point?"

McKee shook his head. "I wish."

"What then?"

"Bones . . . I'm not sure, but they look like human bones."

Quijano's brows knitted into a scowl. "And now Harry's missing?"

The Chief Ranger nodded. "The truck he checked out isn't in the park."

Chaco Canyon was relatively small . . . only 53 square miles. Essentially 5-miles by 10-miles, there was nowhere to hide a white, park service truck . . . no hidden arroyos, no groves of trees . . . just barren cliffs, rocks, scrub desert and, of course, ancient ruins.

"Then start looking outside the park."

"Yes, sir. I'll call Aztec. See if we can get help from the San Juan Sheriff's department."

"What about McKinley?" Chaco Canyon National Park straddled the border of New Mexico's two northwest counties.

"If we need to, we can call Gallup . . . but I think our best bet is to the north."

Quijano nodded. He understood McKee's logic . . . unnerving as it was.

"The State Police have search-and-rescue aircraft," McKee suggested. "I'm sure they can help."

"Yes," Quijano agreed. "Have you talked with any of our visitors? Maybe they saw something."

"It's the end of September. Right now, we only have campers at twenty sites. I can ask, but Gallo is five miles from Pueblos Bonito. I doubt if anyone heard anything. Besides, after dark they're not supposed to leave the campgrounds."

"Ask anyway."

"I will . . . Anything else?"

"No . . . Just find that truck . . . and, of course, Harry."

Chapter Three

Charlotte Etsitty stood outside her grandparents' house, still holding the carbine rifle. Dawn was breaking to the east. The cold, high desert air was invigorating, but what she really wanted was a cup of coffee.

She had been up since 2:00 a.m. That's when she first heard the whistling.

They were back again . . . the second time in two weeks. Sightings of *yee naaldlooshii* were rare, but common enough that most Navajo knew Skinwalkers truly existed.

Charlie Brown Etsitty hadn't seen them the night before. She only heard the whistling, a warning that they were near. When she stepped outside, she yelled for intruders to leave. She thought she heard something scraping against the ground. To demonstrate she was serious, she fired two shots into the darkness.

After that, there was only silence. Charlie kept her vigil anyway. Daylight would keep her and her grandmother safe.

Stepping inside, she could smell the coffee brewing on the wood-burning stove. Her grandmother, Sarah, was busy preparing their break-fast of Blue Corn Mush. The recipe was simple: roasted blue corn flour, a tablespoon of juniper ash and water. With just the two of them on the ranch, an elaborate meal of frybread, beans, bacon and eggs would have taken too much time.

Her *análí* had to feed her animals before they could head into town. The three sheepdogs needed their morning meal. Her thirty sheep got oats to supplement their sagebrush diet. Her dozen cattle were fed hay since there was little for them to graze on. *Análí* also had to make sure there was enough water in the trough.

"You fired the rifle last night." Her grandmother only spoke Navajo.

"I did."

"What did you see?"

"Nothing. I only heard them whistling." Charlie paused for a moment. "Do you know why they keep coming back?"

"No, *shidibé yázhí* (my little lamb), I do not. Maybe I should talk with Billy Nez."

"Yeah . . . Billy Nez." Charlie tried to hide her disdain. Not raised on the reservation, she had less esteem for medicine men than other Navajo.

When her grandfather started feeling ill early that summer, he went to Edgar Chee. Chee used the traditional Navajo trembling hands technique to diagnose his ailments. His conclusion was Nathan Etsitty had bad blood.

Nathan and Sarah, both in their late 70s, scraped together $1,000 by selling two heads of their cattle . . . enough to hire Billy Nez to cure the ailing man. He made a sandpainting in the family hogan located behind the house. Nathan had to sit on the painting until the songs were finished. The medicine man chanted the Enemy Way and Blessing Way Ceremonies. It took nine days.

Nathen didn't get better.

Charlie's mother, Amanda, and her Uncle Benjamin finally convinced her grandparents that Nathen needed to see a doctor. He went to the Tuba City Regional Health Clinic where he was diagnosed with stage-4 cancer.

When Charlotte heard the news, she knew her family needed help. She asked her boss, Roman Garcia, for an extended leave of absence. The lawyer told her to take as long as she needed. Her position would be waiting for her.

It took less than a week for her and her two daughters to sublet their apartment, pack almost everything they owned and leave Phoenix.

Though she was born on the reservation, Charlie grew up in Phoenix. Her father had been a mechanic. He could make more money in the big city than he could ever make on the Navajo Reservation. The family spent his two-week vacations at their grandparents' place far outside Tuba City. But that little bit of exposure hardly steeped her in Navajo traditions.

The summer before Charlotte's senior year in high school, her father was killed in a robbery in Tolleson where he worked. The comfortable life she and her sister, Emily, had enjoyed evaporated. They were forced to move to Tuba City . . . strangers to their own kind. Their only saving grace was their parents insisted they learn the Diné language, so the two girls weren't total outcasts.

Part of her was glad she hadn't grown up on the rez. But another part of her wished she had. It took her a long time to realize the importance of extended family and the need to know Navajo traditions. Her two daughters, Tina, 12, and Lizabeth, 8, were now enrolled in the Tuba City elementary and junior high schools. They were going to get a much richer experience than what the Phoenix school system could offer.

Charlie's biggest regret was her daughters were living in town, in a trailer, with her mother while she helped on the ranch. Nathan's chemo-therapy had taken a toll. Two weeks earlier it was determined no therapy of any kind would cure the poor man. The ranch was too far out of town for daily hospice visits, so he was placed in acute care at the regional clinic.

Every day after chores, Charlie and Grandmother Sarah drove thirty minutes into town.

Sarah stayed at the hospital while Charlie ran errands.

It was only a matter of time before Nathan passed. Charlotte wasn't sure what would happen after that. She would have to make a decision:

8

stay on the reservation with no work or return to the big city where her good paying job waited.

Chapter Four

Only two weeks into the fall semester and the newness of the school year had already worn off. Tina Morales guessed it was because this was the beginning of her third year at Las Palmas Middle/High School. With a student body of less than 200, most of the faces were familiar to her, though she didn't know all their names. The school campus and faculty were all part of her life now.

The seventh-grade class had 26 new students. They would take her eighth-grade science the next year. In a few weeks, their faces would be as familiar as all the others.

On a truly positive note . . . at least, to her . . . she was no longer the new kid on the block. Susan Bustillo finally followed through on her threat and retired. Marta Gomez was the new High School "Language Arts" teacher. (The title of "English Teacher" was passé now.)

Marta was also the youngest teacher on the faculty. At 23, she was 7 years younger than Tina. However, the Chemistry teacher was closer to her age than anyone else at the school. Gomez was grateful when Tina offered her friendship and guidance.

Tina sat at her desk while her 10 Chem II students finished reading a chapter in their books. This was double her normal attendance for the class. Chem II was pretty much a prerequisite for college. Morales didn't think all 10 were headed for higher learning. When asked why they were taking such a difficult class, most said it was because she was their favorite teacher.

Maria Alba, now a senior, looked up from her text and raised a hand. "Yes, Maria?"

"I was curious, Miss Morales, did you go to *St. Anthony's in the Canyon* this past summer?"

"I did," Tina admitted. "I got to spend a week there."

"Did you go anywhere else?" Rob Sanchez asked, grateful that the oppressive silence of the classroom had been broken.

Tina hesitated. There was supposed to be a wall, of sorts, between student and teacher. Too much familiarity eroded the authority teachers needed to maintain discipline.

"I visited family," was all Morales said. No one needed to know she was from Phoenix or that she had grandparents in Mexico. Other students had looked up from their reading, enjoying the distraction.

"Apparently, everyone is finished reading," the teacher observed. "Rob, what is an exothermic reaction?"

Sanchez blanched. "It's a . . . uh . . . uh . . ."

"Maria?"

"It's a chemical reaction that produces heat."

Morales nodded. "Good . . . Can someone else give me an example?"

A single hand was tentatively raised.

"Juan?"

"Copper sulphate mixed with water?"

"Actually, anhydrous copper sulphate mixed with water. What does 'anhydrous' mean?" She waited. "Anyone?"

"Something that doesn't have water?" Rob Sanchez offered.

"Was that a guess?"

The student reluctantly nodded. "Yes, ma'am."

"Well, that was a good guess . . . and you are correct." She hoped he guessed that well on his next test.

The questions and answers continued for another 15 minutes, when the school bell rang, announcing the end of class.

Chapter Five

It was after 10:30 before Lansing was able to leave Juan Pedro Garcia's hovel. He borrowed forensic personnel from the Segovia Police Department to collect evidence and take photos. His own specialist, Deputy Wilma Estrada, was working a crime scene in Cohino, a hundred miles north. He also had to wait for an ambulance to retrieve the body for the Medical Investigator in Albuquerque.

The sheriff, then, was not surprised by Police Chief Solano's request to visit another crime scene in Segovia. The two departments cooperated often. Lansing didn't see a problem, provided it was still in San Phillipe County. Segovia straddled the San Phillipe/Santa Fe county line. Even though this was just a consult, he didn't want to step on someone else's toes.

He only had to drive a mile north. After passing *Santa Maria Catholic Church*, he turned onto Calle Carmen. Five hundred feet west was the gate to the church's cemetery. Beyond the gate, the road continued for another 400 feet. The road ended at a circular, turn-around for convenient departure. A civilian car, a police cruiser and a hearse were parked next to the graveyard. The same forensics van that visited his crime scene was parked there, as well.

Lansing found a knot of people gathered around an open grave at the edge of the cemetery. Something didn't look right. The grave interior didn't have straight, vertical walls. The hardpan soil had been scraped away, as if someone had been using their bare hands. The coffin had been partially pulled out. The lid was open. The body of the occupant had been vandalized. The forensics team was dusting for prints.

"Excuse me . . ."

The small group turned their attention to the new arrival.

"I'm Sheriff Lansing. Chief Solano asked me to stop by and see if I could help."

"I'm Officer Delgado," the policeman said, nodding to the sheriff. "This is Father Ortiz. This is his church's cemetery."

"I'm Fred Holloway," another man said as an introduction. "I'm from the funeral home. These are my assistants." He gestured to two men standing near the coffin. "The good father asked if we could assist in some way."

"Does anyone know what happened?" Lansing asked.

"Isn't it obvious?" Ortiz asked in a thick, Hispanic accent. "This grave has been desecrated." He made the sign of the cross.

The sheriff stepped closer to the open coffin. From the clothing he could see, it was the body of a woman. The head had been removed, as had an arm and a leg. The torso had been splayed open, allowing the removal of some of the organs.

The woman had been interred long enough that the body had become desiccated.

"How long does it take for a body to dry out like this?" Lansing asked Holloway.

"I'm not used to disinterring bodies," the man from the funeral home admitted. "Evidently about a year. According to the grave marker, that's how long Mrs. Caldera has been in repose."

The sheriff noted the quiet, soothing way the funeral man couched his words.

"Have you ever seen anything like this?" Officer Delgado asked.

"I'm not all that familiar with grave robbing," Lansing said, for the moment ignoring the fact that he dug up and destroyed the body of a suspected witch the winter before.

"Why didn't they take the entire body?" the priest asked. "This mutilation . . . it doesn't make sense."

"It may not make sense to us," the sheriff agreed, "but whoever did this knew exactly what they were looking for." Clean, straight incisions had been made with a very sharp instrument.

"Should we close up the coffin and just rebury it?" one of Holloway's assistants asked.

"My God, NO!" Ortiz nearly shrieked. "This ground has been defiled . . . it must be re-consecrated. I must perform a mass . . . And the poor woman . . . we can't bury half a body."

"Maybe you should talk to the family," Holloway suggested. "I would think they would want to know what happened . . . let them make the final decision regarding the body."

The priest looked at him disapprovingly but said nothing.

"Has this happened around here before?" Lansing asked.

"Not in MY cemetery!" Ortiz exclaimed.

"Not in the rest of Segovia," the police officer said. "At least, not that I know of."

Holloway shook his head.

Lansing shook his head as well. "This is the first I've ever seen. My guess is the vandals are Devil Worshipers of some type." He knelt and examined the grave. "I can't figure what they used to dig up the corpse." He made a mental note about the apparent claw marks . . . and the possible paw print of an animal. "It doesn't look like they used any tools."

"What did they use?" Delgado asked.

"Have you ever seen how dirt gets piled up when an armadillo digs a burrow? It looks something like the pile of dirt around this grave."

"So, you're saying an armadillo dug this up?" Ortiz asked, sarcastically.

"No," Lansing said as he stood. "Something bigger."

14

Chapter Six

"I am so happy with the girls living with me," Amanda Etsitty said, handing her daughter a cup of coffee. "It's like when you and Emily were here. How is your grandfather?"

"Still the same, I guess. I didn't go in today," Charlie said. She doctored the brew with sugar and milk.

***

It had been 7 years since Charlie Brown Etsitty left the reservation. Lizabeth was only a year old. The young mother was excited with the idea of moving back to Phoenix. It was the last place she was truly happy.

Raymond Johnson, her husband of two years, told her they needed to get away from the poverty of the reservation. He had talked to friends who said if you wanted a job, Phoenix was the place to be.

Charlie couldn't believe her luck when Raymond proposed. She was a single mother with a three-year-old daughter. (Tina was the result of a rape. Her father, Ricky Lapahie, fled the reservation before the authorities could arrest him. After that, he seemed to disappear off the face of the Earth.)

Phoenix wasn't the Nirvana Johnson had promised. Charlie wasn't carefree like when she was in high school. Embarrassed over having two kids and no education, she refused to call any of her old friends. The one exception was Tina Morales. She talked to Tina's mother and found out her former best friend had finished college and was teaching in New Mexico. The young mother didn't pursue the issue further. Their lives had taken different paths. They had nothing in common.

Living out of their car, it was a month before Johnson found a job at a warehouse. Making little more than minimum wage, Raymond soon came to resent his family. He hated the fact that he had to share his hard-earned money with a nagging wife and two snot-nosed kids . . . one of which wasn't even his.

The husband and wife fought constantly. He was often drunk when he came home to their shabby apartment. Arguments eventually morphed into violence. Charlie accepted the beatings for a while, but when he began threatening their children, she had had enough. He was finally arrested for domestic abuse and she told him to never come back.

Within a week, Charlotte Etsitty found herself in the law offices of Roman and Roberto Garcia. A social worker had recommended that she seek legal advice if she wanted to be free of her husband.

Roman, the older brother and senior partner, took pity on her. He not only offered to handle the divorce pro bono, when he found out she could type he offered her a position as a clerk/receptionist. She suspected it was because she was still young, still pretty, and had kept her figure after two pregnancies. Charlie wasn't in a position to turn anything down and soon discovered Mr. Roman had no ulterior motives. She was hired because he was a good man.

At first only typing letters for general correspondence, she soon found herself producing wills, affidavits, partnership agreements, prenups . . . anything the law firm handled, she did too. She found she had a knack for legalese. After six months, her boss insisted she started taking classes. Within a year she had her paralegal certificate.

The shame and embarrassment over the life she had lived was gone. She had a job. She had a career. The first Christmas after she became a paralegal, she even wanted to reach out to an old friend, Tina Morales.

Tina was overjoyed at hearing from her old, best friend. She was even more thrilled that Charlie had named her first daughter after her.

During the next six years, they talked often and got together whenever Tina was in town.

Life was good.

***

Charlie looked around her mother's trailer. Amanda Etsitty had lived there for 13 years, ever since the family left Phoenix. Only 14-feet by 48-feet, the two-bedroom, one-bath abode was crowded after leaving a 1500 square foot house. Charlotte had to endure the small space through graduation and her pregnancy. It became more crowded after Tina was born.

Surprisingly, no one complained. Her mother and sister loved the new addition to the family. It was almost like Tina had three mothers. With all the help, Charlotte was able to work as well.

Emily was eight years her junior and always idolized her older sibling. (Her mother got their first names from the Brontë sisters . . . not that she ever read their books.) Charlotte was always very protective of her sister and the two were close, despite the age difference.

"Is your car working?"

Amanda shook her head. "Not this week. Your Uncle Jerry thinks it needs a new battery."

Her mother drove the same Oldsmobile as when they left the big city. The new town was only two miles by two miles. Not having a car in town wasn't a major inconvenience. Yellowman Trailer Court was on the west side of town. Charlotte got used to walking the nearly two miles to Tuba City High School on the east side. All the kids in town had to hoof it to school . . . unless they owned a car. (Few did.)

Now her own daughters walked the mile from the trailer to the schools. They had always taken a bus in Phoenix. Their complaints fell on deaf ears.

Even her mother walked the half-mile to work every day. She had been a housekeeper at the Navajo Inn since moving to town. The two sisters were embarrassed that their mother worked such a menial job. They soon discovered that kind of work was more the norm than the exception on the rez.

"The girls should be home from school in an hour," Amanda observed.

"Good, if *Análí* Sarah isn't ready to leave, I thought I'd take them for ice cream."

"You know, they miss you."

"I miss them, too. I call them every night."

"That's not the same as being with them. As much as I would love it, I don't think they want to stay with me forever."

"I know . . . and they won't. I'm just here to help out until . . ." She couldn't bring herself to say, "until my grandfather dies."

"And he will . . . soon. What then? Are you going to stay on the ranch with Sarah?"

"No. I can't raise my daughters out there. No running water, no indoor plumbing. My God, the twenty-first century is going to start in three months. No one should have to live like that."

"Many Navajos do. Your grandmother does."

Charlie shook her head. "But I don't know how much longer she can stay out there. It takes the two of us half a day to get the chores done. She can't do it by herself . . . and besides . . ." She stopped herself.

"Besides what?"

"She can't be out there alone."

"Why?"

18

"Skinwalkers are coming around. Ever since Grandpa Nathan went to the hospital. At least once a week. *Análi* wants to talk to Billy Nez. I don't know what he can do."

"You both should move to town. I don't want you out there with those creatures."

"She's not going to leave her animals. Don't worry. We're safe. I have a rifle and I know how to use it."

She paused for a moment. "Before the girls get here, do you mind if I take a shower?"

Chapter Seven

Back at his offices in Las Palmas, Lansing began searching for information on Juan Pedro Garcia. He did possess a Commercial Driver's License, which made sense. Akee said he was a truck driver. But the man's wallet yielded little else. There was no business card to indicate who he drove for . . . no gas receipts to indicate where he had driven.

Garcia's small house had no landline, so he had to be using a cell phone. However, no cell phone was found. It probably had been taken along with the truck.

The sheriff asked Clem Montoya, the Desk Sergeant, to check the state law enforcement network for outstanding warrants or any record of traffic stops. A ticket might, at least, show who his employer was. Garcia's record was clean.

Johnathan Akee said he thought Garcia's truck was a 1995 Chevy Silverado, dark blue. The San Phillipe Sheriff's office wasn't prepared to issue an APB for a stolen truck yet.

To be honest with himself, Lansing wasn't convinced a crime had been committed. Not every dead body was an indication of foul play. Until he heard differently from the Medical Investigator's Office in Albuquerque, Juan Garcia could easily have died of natural causes. He might have loaned his truck to a friend.

Lansing wasn't interested in dedicating resources to a non-crime.

He was, however, curious about the open grave at *Santa Maria Cemetery*. A very short conversation with Chief Solano indicated there were no suspected Devil Worshipers in Segovia. Not for a long time. The incident might be nothing more than a prank . . . a prank in extremely poor taste . . . but still, a prank.

Lansing needed to confer with his "expert," Tina Morales. Over the past two years, she had become his go-to source for all things occult, other-worldly or just, plain weird. He checked his wall clock. It was 1:30. School wouldn't be out until after 3:00.

He hoped she would answer when he called. They hadn't talked in the past five weeks, ever since she moved back to her little house in Las Palmas.

***

Tina had taken a two-week trip to visit family in Phoenix and Nogales, Mexico. That worked out fine. Cliff, Jr. came for a visit. He was getting ready to start his senior year and the two needed to discuss his future after high school. (That would be a continuing conversation.)

The sheriff wasn't surprised that he missed the schoolteacher. She had become a large part of his life. But when she got back in the middle of August, she was aloof. He wasn't sure what she discussed with her family during her trip. Whatever it was seemed to sour her attitude toward him and their relationship.

When Tina returned to New Mexico, she went directly to her place in town. Her visit to the Lansing ranch was to gather the belongings she had left there. He had been in the barn and didn't know she was there until he saw her car.

"What's going on?" the sheriff asked, standing in the bedroom door-way.

Morales stopped her packing and turned to him. "Cliff, I've been do-ing a lot of thinking this summer . . . ever since my week at *St. Anthony's in the Canyon.* What are we doing?"

"What do you mean?"

"Our relationship . . . where is it going?   Or is it going anywhere? Are we going to just shack up for the rest of our lives?"

"I didn't think you had a problem with that."

"I don't . . . I didn't . . ." She sat on the edge of the bed. "I don't know what you expect of me . . . long term."

Lansing was tempted to sit on the bed and put his arm around her, but the tone of Tina's voice told him to keep his distance. "I don't expect anything from you!" he blurted, defensively.

"That's the problem, Cliff: No expectations. That's worse than 'low' expectations."

"What do you want me to say?"

"I don't want you to say anything!" She paused. "I think we need to spend some time apart."

"You were gone for two weeks," he protested. She gave him an icy stare, indicating he had just said the wrong thing.

"We need a time-out . . ." She stood to resume her packing. ". . . until the two of us can figure out what we want from each other."

"How long are we talking?"

"As long as it takes!"

***

When Carolina left him eight years earlier, Lansing promised himself he wouldn't beg her to come back. He never broke that promise.

When Margarite Carrera took up her new position at the University of New Mexico Medical School, he refused to try and contact her. She had made it clear she was moving on to bigger and better things.

Lansing knew he had a stubborn streak . . . and promises were easy to keep when your "exes" were 150 miles away. There were only 15 miles between him and Tina Morales. He had managed to resist the urge to call her . . . not even drive past her house. If this was going to be a test of wills, he could last just as long as she could. Besides, he hadn't figured out what she wanted from their relationship. Even worse, he hadn't figured out what he wanted.

When he called her up, he would keep it professional.

Chapter Eight

Lansing wasn't surprised that Tina Morales said she was too busy to talk when he called her. He was surprised when she suggested that they meet for supper at *Paco's Mexican Cantina.*

Tina's car was already at the restaurant when he arrived. That was encouraging. Maybe she was anxious to see him, he thought.

Paco's 14-year-old daughter greeted him when he entered. "Can I get you a table, Sheriff?"

"No thanks, Maria. I'm meeting someone."

"Miss Morales?" the diminutive hostess guessed. "She's right over there." She pointed to the far side of the room.

When he saw her, Lansing felt a pang of disappointment. Tina wasn't alone. Another woman, younger than the chemistry teacher, sat with her. The two were so engrossed in conversation, they didn't notice the sheriff until he reached their table.

"Hi, Tina," he interrupted.

"Oh, hi! I didn't see you come in." She gestured to her companion. "Sheriff Lansing, this is Marta Gomez. She's new to the school. Marta, Sheriff Cliff Lansing"

The teacher extended her hand and smiled. "Please to meet you, Sheriff. I teach English."

Lansing shook the offered hand and quickly sized her up. Gomez was in her early twenties. She was short, but hard to tell how short because she was sitting. Her hand was pudgy, and he guessed she was almost twenty pounds overweight. But her smile was bright, and he soon found she was a pleasant conversationalist.

"Nice meeting you." He returned the smile, then looked at Morales. "Should I sit down?"

"Unless you want to eat standing up."

The table had four chairs. Lansing sat across from Gomez, next to Tina. His cattleman's hat occupied the empty seat.

A very pregnant waitress approached. "Can I get you anything, Sheriff?"

He noticed his companions were drinking margaritas. "A *Dos Equis*, please."

Lansing sipped his beer. The two teachers sipped their drinks. Pleasantries were exchanged. When dinner was ordered, he made sure everything was on one check so he could pay. The women were grateful for the gesture.

It wasn't until the food was delivered that Tina finally asked, "What did you want to talk about, Sheriff?"

He was taken aback by how formal she addressed him. He ignored it for the moment. "I'm not sure this is an appropriate subject while we're eating. Besides, this involves your . . ." He struggled to find the right word. ". . . You know . . . your avocation."

"If you're talking about me being a *curandera*, Marta knows all about that," she reassured him.

"Oh, really?" He wiped his mouth with a napkin. "In that case . . . This has to do with a grave I saw today. Someone . . . or something . . . dug up the coffin, then mutilated the corpse."

"Was this a fresh grave?" Tina asked.

"No. The woman had been buried a year ago. Her body was pretty much dried out."

"You said the body was mutilated. How?"

Lansing hesitated to answer. He saw the distressed look on Gomez's face. It was obvious she wasn't used to people talking so casually about grave robbing or a body being desecrated. She wasn't aware of Morales' and Lansing's shared experiences . . . or how unremarkable the conversation really was. He pressed on, anyway.

"The body had been cut open . . . some organs removed. Also, the head, an arm and a leg were taken."

"Who was this woman?" Marta asked incredulously.

The sheriff shrugged. "As far as I know, just some poor old lady . . . The case really belongs to the Segovia Police. I'm sure they'll find out who she was."

"So, if this is a matter for the Segovia Police, why are you getting involved?" Tina asked.

"It's still in San Phillipe County. I'm afraid this might not end up being an isolated incident."

"You wanted to see if I knew anything about someone disturbing a grave." It was a statement, not a question.

"Well, yes."

"I honestly don't. The only thing even close to my experiences is *Dia de los Muertos*, the Mexican Day of the Dead. Sometimes people remove bones from a crypt and parade around with their dead relatives. But I never heard of *brujas* or *brujos* digging up graves . . . even for evil purposes."

"You're sure?"

Tina gave him a hard look. "Why would I lie to you?"

Lansing shook his head. "Sorry." There was a tinge of disappointment in his voice. It barely masked his embarrassment.

"You said 'someone or something' dug up the grave. What did you mean by that?"

Lansing thought Morales was trying to sooth his ego a bit after her previous statement. He was regretting that he ever brought up the subject. "I didn't mean anything. Forget I even mentioned it."

The three finished their meals in near silence. As they left the restaurant, the teachers thanked him for the meal. He, in turn, thanked Tina for meeting with him and sharing her knowledge. She apologized for not being of any help.

There were no good-bye handshakes. No quick kiss on the cheek. No "see you later."

As the teachers drove away, Lansing's thoughts were interrupted by a call over the radio.

"Dispatch to any available unit . . ."

The sheriff picked up his mic. "This is Patrol One, dispatch. Go ahead."

"Roger, Sheriff. We had a call from the State Police. One of their patrols picked up a teenage girl on Highway two eighty-five, south of Ojo Caliente. She was covered in blood."

"Is she hurt?"

"I don't know. They took her to the Presbyterian Hospital in Segovia."

"If they call again, tell them I'm on my way. Patrol One out."

Chapter Nine

State Highway 15 split from U.S. 285 five miles north of Segovia.

The idea of a national road system emerged in 1912, 4 years after Henry Ford introduce the Model-T. The first effort was the Lincoln Highway, essentially a 3,400-mile gravel road that stretched from New York City to San Francisco. It was hardly practical. By car, from beginning to end, it took an estimated 30 days to make the trip. The same distance could be traveled by express train in 83 hours, less than 4 days.

The States requested the Federal Government create a unified, national road system in 1924. Legislation was passed the next year, and the first numbered, paved roads were laid out the year after that.

U.S. Highway 285 was commissioned in 1936. Designed as a secondary road to link rural towns, its 850 miles ran from Sanderson, Texas to Denver, Colorado. Used primarily as a truck route, Santa Fe was the only major city it passed through. State Highway 15 and U.S. 285 joined up in the state capitol, then separated north of Segovia.

Continuing north to Ojo Caliente, the highway followed the county line between San Phillipe and Taos Counties all the way to Colorado. With the creation of the interstate highway system, nearly all the older roads became secondary routes. U.S. 285 was still a truck route, providing links to smaller towns. (It was also considered a convenient way to avoid prying eyes and nosey law enforcement.)

Segovia Presbyterian Hospital was situated on Highway 15, ironically, a quarter mile north of the cemetery Lansing had visited earlier that morning. The Emergency Room was on the north side of the building. The State Police cruiser was still parked outside. The sheriff slid his Jeep into the slot next to it.

Officer Rich Hidalgo stood next to the registration desk sipping on coffee from a Styrofoam cup. He broke off his conversation when he saw Lansing enter.

"I see we're going casual tonight," the state patrolman remarked.

"I do wear something besides a uniform on occasion." He didn't feel it was necessary to explain he was at dinner. "Where's the girl you brought in?"

Hidalgo gestured with his head. "Exam room three."

"Was she hurt?"

"I don't think so. You'll have to talk to the doctor."

"But you told my dispatch she was covered in blood."

"It evidently wasn't hers."

"Where did you pick her up?"

"Highway two eighty-five, about five miles south of Ojo Caliente. She was walking along the shoulder." He finished his cup of coffee. "I was just waiting here till someone from your office showed up. I need to get back to where I found her. See if there was an accident."

"Did you ask her what happened?"

"She isn't talking . . . at least she didn't talk to me. I played hell trying to get her in my car. She was scared to death. I don't know if it was just me or if she's afraid of men in general."

Lansing nodded. "Okay, Rich. Thanks. Notify my people if you do find a wreck."

"I always do." Hidalgo headed for the exit, grabbing his uniform cap from the registration counter. "I'll check in later to see how the girl is doing."

As the patrolman left, Lansing headed for exam room three. Quietly opening the door, he evaluated the situation.

The girl was in a bed wearing a hospital gown. She had long, black hair. Her complexion indicated she was either Hispanic or Native

American, probably no older than fifteen. A nurse in green scrubs was taking her vital signs. A white, plastic bag apparently holding her bloody clothes sat on the floor next to a chair.

"How is she?" The sheriff tried to speak softly to keep from startling anyone. As soon as he spoke, the girl shot him a fearful glance. She started trembling but said nothing.

The nurse immediately turned to him. "Would you please get out?" she said harshly.

"I'm the sheriff. I need to talk to her about what happened."

"Right now, she shouldn't be disturbed! Can't you see you're upsetting her?" A privacy curtain hung from a track. The nurse grabbed it and pulled it across the room to mask the bed and its occupant.

Frustrated, Lansing stepped back into the hallway. If not the girl, then he needed to talk to someone. A male nurse was hurrying by. "Excuse me," he said insistently.

"What?" The man seemed irritated.

"I need to talk to the doctor treating the patient in room three."

"I have no idea who's treating her. Ask at the nurses' station." He quickly stepped away.

Lansing wasn't used to being dismissed so readily. If he was wearing his uniform, he suspected he would have gotten a little more respect. He found the nurses station where he explained who he was and what he wanted.

After several minutes, he was approached by a slim, dark complected man in scrubs.

"I am Doctor Garnepudi," he said with a thick East-Indian accent. "Can I help you?"

Chapter Ten

It was past 11:00 p.m. when Sheriff Lansing got back to his ranch. He was tired.

During the 30-minute drive from Segovia, he had plenty of time to review the day's events. It started out with the discovery of Juan Pedro Garcia's dead body. Everything for that case was on hold until he got the autopsy results. He hoped the findings would be that he died from natural causes. Even then, his office had an obligation to notify next of kin.

Judging from the light dusting of powder on Garcia's face, Lansing was convinced drugs were somehow involved. Drug overdoses were too common, not just in San Phillipe County, but through much of the state. He would have to wait and see.

The next issue he pondered was the opened grave and the mutilated body. He had hoped Tina Morales could give him some insight into what might have happened. That angle was a bust, though he had to admit he was happy to see her. He wondered if she returned his feelings.

The most disturbing case of the day was the teenage girl Officer Rich Hidalgo picked up on the highway.

***

"I'm Gloria Sanchez," the rolly-polly social worker announced when she arrived at the Emergency Room nurses station. "I'm with the State Child Protective Services." She tapped the nametag on her chest. "My offices got a call. An underage girl picked up on a highway. I need to talk to whoever is in charge."

"Dr. Garnepudi is the senior Emergency Room Physician this evening," the charge nurse explained.

"I've made arrangements for the young lady," Sanchez announced. "I need this Garne . . .?"

"Garnepudi," the nurse completed.

"Well, I need him to sign some forms so I can get her into a more appropriate setting." The social worker began pulling papers from a slim, leather folder. "I understand she wasn't injured."

"That's not completely true. She did have some injuries, and he hasn't released her from his care, yet."

"That's what I need his signature for." Sanchez was all business. "So, she can be released."

"I don't think he's finished with her," the nurse protested.

"I can wait. I'll start on the paperwork. What's the girls name and age?"

"We don't know."

"What do you mean, you don't know?"

Lansing had listened to the conversation from a distance. He'd dealt with the state Children, Youth and Family Department before. They claimed, particularly the CPS division, to have the best interests of children in mind. Too often bureaucratic regulations dictated their actions, rather than common sense. He thought he should step in and arbitrate before an argument ensued.

"Is there something I can help with?"

Sanchez coldly eyed the man in blue jeans and flannel shirt. "And just who are you?"

"I'm Cliff Lansing, San Phillipe Sheriff."

"I suppose you have I.D."

A little ticked, Lansing produced his wallet which, among other things, included a badge with a seven-pointed star. The social worker gave a slight nod, acknowledging her acceptance.

"They don't have any information on the girl because she hasn't spoken to anyone," the sheriff explained.

"Maybe she can't speak," Sanchez countered. "Have they tried sign language?"

"We did." The charge nurse was tired of being bullied. "We also tried English, Spanish, even Tewa. So far, nothing's worked."

Dr. Garnepudi approached from one of the exam rooms. "Is there a problem, here?"

"Yes, doctor," the nurse said. "This woman wants you to release the girl the State Police brought in."

"Release?" The Indian doctor sounded shocked. "To where?"

"We have foster homes for temporary placement. I've made arrangements for this evening."

"No," Garnepudi said with finality.

"What do you mean, no?"

"I am admitting her to the hospital for observation. We need to keep her . . . maybe for a few days. We need time. Perhaps we can get her to speak."

"I am not happy with that response, doctor." The social worker turned to Lansing. "Sheriff, you will back me up. My offices have the ultimate authority for child disposition."

"In the great scheme of things, I believe CPS responsibilities fall somewhat below the courts and law enforcement," the sheriff observed. He wasn't going to be intimidated by a state official. He was also curious about why the state was in such a hurry to place the girl in their custody. "And as far as this Emergency Room is concerned, I think your authority stopped at the door."

***

After his shower, Lansing laid in bed, staring at his cell phone, debating if he should dial Tina's number. The report from the doctor was disturbing. The young patient had been molested . . . possibly raped. Her refusal/inability to talk might have been the result of that trauma. Then there was the issue of the bloody clothes. The blood wasn't hers, so, whose blood was it?

Tina dealt with teenagers all day long. He was sure she could offer some insight about the patient in Segovia Hospital.

Before their separation, Tina asked what he wanted from her. He realized he wanted her in his life because she was a good sounding board . . . and more than a lover, she was his friend.

Before he could make the call, he fell asleep.

Chapter Eleven

No Navajo owned land on the reservation. It was communal property belonging to all members of the tribe. The houses, hogans, corals and pens could be claimed by the families who built them and were handed down, one generation to the next.

The frame house Grandfather Nathan had built stood just a few feet away from the cedar log cabin he had grown up in. Behind the house was the eight-sided hogan that predated the 90-year-old log cabin by 10 years. It had been repaired and rebuilt dozens of times. Once the Etsitty family dwelling, it was maintained as the ceremonial and religious heart of the homestead.

Nathan Etsitty made improvements beyond a new house. He drilled a better water well, added a generator and had a phone line installed. The line was extended all the way to the hunting cabin on Preston Mesa, 5 miles away.

Despite these luxuries, none of Nathan and Sarah's 5 children chose to stay at the ranch. Two of their 3 sons had already passed. Uncle Benjamin, the youngest son, was a supervisor at the Navajo Generating Station 3 miles east of Page, AZ. Living over an hour away, Benjamin tried to get down to the ranch at least twice a month, but there was no way he could stay for an extended time.

Charlie's two aunts were married and lived near Farmington.

Guilt over not growing up close to her extended family is what spurred Charlotte Etsitty to volunteer to help her grandparents. She might have left her daughters in Phoenix if she knew someone who could stay with them. However, with the two girls living with her mother, she could see them often. It wasn't going to be ideal to move them back to their old schools in the middle of the year, but Charlie knew Tina and Lizbeth would survive the ordeal.

It had warmed up nicely that morning, reaching 75°. Only half finished with their chores, Charlie had removed her jacket and was inside the house getting a drink of water when the phone rang.

"Etsitty *dá'ák'eh hazá* (farm)."

"Hey, Charlie!"

"Emily, when did you get back from Window Rock?"

"Last night. I've been gone a week and I was worried about grandpa."

"Have you seen him today?"

"I got there right when they called a Code Blue on him. . ." Emily's voice started quavering. "That's why I'm calling. Grandpa died this morning."

Charlie felt the sting of tears. She cleared her throat. "I'll tell *Análí* Sarah. We'll be in town in about forty-five minutes."

"Good. There's a lot we need to discuss."

***

Sarah said nothing as they rode to town. Her only outward emotion was the trickle of an occasional tear. Crying and other depictions of grief were avoided by the Navajo people. It was believed such emotions hindered the departed soul's journey to the underworld.

Nathan and Sarah had been married for nearly 60 years. Charlie couldn't help but wonder how much longer her grandmother would survive, especially if she was forced to leave the farm and her animals.

Amanda and Emily stood in the waiting area, talking with three tribal elders from the Tuba City Chapter House. Edna Claw, Charlie's maternal grandmother was also there. (Edna had been a widow for almost twenty years and still remembered the pain Sarah now was going through.)

Nathan Etsitty had told his family what he wanted for his funeral . . . a Christian burial along with Navajo prayers. The service would be conducted at the Church of Christ in one of the hogans located behind the church proper. He would be buried in the graveyard just west of town, only a few hundred yards from Amanda's trailer.

When Sarah Etsitty reached the waiting room, one of the nurses asked if she wanted to see her husband before he was sent to Valley Ridge Mortuary. Sarah shook her head violently. Fear of the dead was common with the Navajo people.

Reverend Hodges had already been contacted. The funeral would be in two days, long enough for family to be notified and allow them to make the trip to Tuba City. Phone calls were already being made, as were reservations at the Navajo Inn.

Charlie stood away from the group. She knew none of the men talking to her mother and didn't want to interrupt. When Emily saw her, she immediately came over and the two embraced.

"What time did you get in?"

"I left right after the conference was over," Emily said. "But I still didn't get in till nearly midnight." She studied her older sister for a moment, then whispered, "We need to talk." She looked around. "But not here and not now."

Chapter Twelve

"Why didn't you tell me you and Sheriff Lansing used to date?" Marta Gomez whispered. Gomez had joined Tina Morales in the teachers' lounge. Both had second period free.

The chemistry teacher shrugged, taking a sip of coffee. "I didn't think it was important. Where did you hear that?"

There were no other teachers in the lounge, but Marta kept her voice low, as if someone might be eavesdropping. "I was in the front office before classes started. Mrs. Basa asked what I did last night. I said we had dinner with Sheriff Lansing. That's when she asked if you two got back together again." She looked around to make sure they were still alone. "What happened?"

"What do you mean?"

"Between you and the sheriff . . . why'd you break up?"

"We didn't really break up." She paused, looking for the right words. "I guess you could say we're taking a vacation from each other."

Gomez couldn't hide her surprise. "You're taking a vacation from him?" The emphasis was on "him." "He seems like a nice guy . . . I haven't been here long, but there don't seem to be that many eligible bachelors in Las Palmas."

"There aren't," Tina admitted.

"I mean, you treated him like a casual acquaintance yesterday. I couldn't tell you two had ever been together. Who decided you needed a vacation from each other?"

"That would be me."

"What did he do?"

"He didn't do anything."

"Did you do something?"

"Nothing wrong . . . I went to Phoenix to visit my folks. My younger brother is married and has a daughter. I ran into a classmate from high school. She's married and has a couple of kids. I kept getting asked when I was getting married, or why wasn't I married yet. Didn't I want any children?

"It's a nine-hour drive from Phoenix to Las Palmas. I had a lot of time to think about our relationship. I want something more than the two of us shacking up."

"He isn't married, is he?"

"Of course not. He's been divorced almost nine years. That happened before we ever met."

"He has kids? Are they a problem?"

"He has a son, and we get along great."

Marta shook her head. "He didn't slap you around or anything, did he?"

"No. No, he didn't. My ex-boyfriend in Albuquerque did. That's how I ended up here. But Cliff Lansing is one of the most decent men I've ever met."

The English teacher leaned back in her seat. "I don't get it then. Why the sabbatical from him? I know he respects you. Why else would he come to you with a work problem? I'll admit it was a weird problem . . . but still . . . he needed your help. How many men do you know who ask for help?"

"I suppose."

"Is it because you want children? You think your biological clock is ticking louder every day?"

"No, it's not that," Tina admitted. "I don't think I want any."

"Has he been bothering you a lot . . . calling you up all the time?"

"Yesterday was the first time he called me since I moved my stuff off the ranch in August."

"He has a ranch?"

"Yeah. About fifteen miles south of town."

"Tina, I haven't had that many boyfriends. The few I've had I was glad to get rid of. I don't know what you want from your sheriff, but it sounds like you have a keeper."

Morales nodded, but said nothing.

Gomez stood. "I need to go to class."

"Yeah." Tina stood as well. "I do, too. I'll see you later."

As she followed her new friend into the increasingly crowded hall-way, Tina wished she could tell Marta the truth behind the split-up, just like she wished she could tell Cliff Lansing.

Chapter Thirteen

Lansing started off the morning making phone calls. The first was to State Police District 7 office. Evidently Rich Hidalgo had not found a wreck along U.S 285. The sheriff requested a FAX of the incident report involving the teen age girl.

The next call was to Segovia Presbyterian Hospital. Lansing was transferred twice before he reached the nurse's desk on the third floor. "Jane Doe" still hadn't spoken. She slept fitfully and seemed afraid of everything . . . especially the male doctor who visited her during his rounds. The nurse would not release the girl's medical condition over the phone. The sheriff's department would have to send someone to talk to the staff face-to-face.

Lansing went to the front office and studied the county map on the wall. Hidalgo said he found the girl five miles south of Ojo Caliente. The incident report said she was heading south. There were no buildings within a mile of where she was found. Of course, there was no telling how long she had been walking. There was also the possibility she had been dumped along the highway.

He had the dispatcher, Marylin Bea, contact Deputy Willie Estrada, his only female officer. He needed her to go to Segovia and attempt to interview the girl, as well as take a photo for distribution. She would also have to talk to the nurses and doctors to find out the extent of the girl's injuries.

Deputy Clem Montoya was tasked with checking reports in surrounding counties, just in case their teenage patient had been reported missing.

His third call was to the State Children, Youth and Family Department in Segovia.

"New Mexico Department of Children and Families, Segovia Office," the receptionist said. "How can I help you?"

"Yes, this is Sheriff Lansing, San Phillipe County. I need to speak to one of your Child Protective Services Officers."

"I'm sorry, all of our CPS placement officers are in the field right now. Could I take a message?"

"No . . . Is your director available?"

"Yes, she is. Can you tell me what this is about?"

"This has to do with a teenage girl brought to Segovia Presbyterian Hospital last night."

"Okay, I can connect you."

A moment later a voice said, "This is Christina Archuleta. How can I help you?"

"Yes, this is Sheriff Lansing. I need to ask about a teen the State Police picked up last night."

"The young lady in the hospital?"

"That's the one."

"We got a call about her from the Hospital Administrator this morning. Our office hasn't had a chance to find a placement, yet. It sounds like she'll be under observation for a few more days . . ."

"Wait a minute," Lansing interrupted. "You didn't send someone to pick her up last night?"

"Of course, not. She has to be interviewed first so we can determine the type of placement she needs. And then, she can't go anywhere until she's been released by a doctor."

"I ran into a Gloria Sanchez in the Emergency Room last night. From your office."

"Excuse me, Sheriff. We're a very small operation. There is no Gloria Sanchez here. Maybe she was from Santa Fe. They pick up some of our load when we're overwhelmed."

"But you said the hospital didn't call you till this morning . . . They wouldn't have called Santa Fe first, would they?"

"No, I wouldn't think so. Would you like for me to ask Santa Fe about the woman you met?"

"Yes." Lansing provided the woman's name again and a description. Archuleta already had the phone number to the sheriff's office.

He didn't have to wait long. Director Archuleta reported back that there was no Gloria Sanchez listed anywhere in the Children, Youth and Family Department.

She asked if he could have been mistaken. Maybe this Sanchez person was from a different agency. Lansing assured her he had made no mistake.

After the call was finished, the sheriff was admittedly angry with himself. Sanchez, or whoever she was, had been brazen enough to demand to see his credentials. Why didn't he return the favor? He had accepted her identity based on a fake nametag.

His questions were mounting. Who was the girl in the hospital? Why was she walking down a highway at night? Whose blood was on her clothes? If there was a crime scene, where was it? Who was Gloria Sanchez and why was she trying to abduct the poor girl?

Those questions could be answered if the girl would only talk. Lansing wasn't sure that would ever happen.

Chapter Fourteen

It was lunchtime. There were few sit-down restaurants in Tuba City. Emily and Charlie opted for *Kate's Café*. The attraction was the umbrella-shaded picnic tables in front. They could talk without other customers listening to their conversation. Besides, it was late September, and this would be one of the last warm days of the year.

Emily knew the waitress from high school, having lived in Tuba City for most of the past 13 years. The only time she was gone was the two years she attended the University of Arizona in Tucson. She was there to complete her bachelor's degree in Information Technology. Being less than 80 miles apart, the sisters saw each other often during those two years.

Charlie was a bit jealous. She felt Emily was more Diné than she would ever be. Her younger sister had no qualms about returning to the reservation after getting her degree. In fact, she had a job waiting for her. The Housing Authority needed an IT Director and had paid for Emily's two years at college.

"Janice, do you know my sister, Charlotte?"

"I think we might have met." She set two glasses of water on the table and nodded at Charlie. "Nice to see you again."

"Same here," she replied, returning the nod.

The waitress handed them menus. "Can I get you something to drink?"

"I think we can both use coffee." Emily looked at Charlie who confirmed the order.

"I'll be back in a minute to take your order."

Once they were alone, Charlie leaned forward. "All right. What's going on? You said we had a lot to talk about."

"This has to do with Uncle Isaac and Aunt Jules."

"What are you talking about? They've been dead for what . . . seven years?"

"I know, but this goes back to what happened after they died."

When Amanda moved her daughters to the reservation, Charlotte was looking forward to seeing her three younger cousins, Walter, William and Jennifer, on a regular basis. That excitement was short lived. Uncle Isaac took a position working full-time at the Navajo Nation Historic Preservation Department in Window Rock. The family moved to Fort Defiance just a few miles north.

Four years after the move, Isaac and Jules were killed in a car accident. William was 14. Jenny was 12. One of the Farmington aunts offered to take them in. They were old enough they could decide for themselves. A neighbor and friends of the family in Fort Defiance said they would keep them so they could be close to friends.

Besides, Walter was 19 and still living nearby. He was apprenticing to become a medicine man and couldn't afford to move again.

After the encounter with pure evil on Preston Mesa when he was only 12, Walter decided he wanted to become a shaman. He was frustrated at how helpless he felt that night. His parents approved and he immediately began his studies under Billy Nez. Those studies were interrupted when the family moved. It took 6 months before he found another medicine man to apprentice under.

The death of Isaac and Jules was a shock to the entire Etsitty family, especially after the loss of Jacob, Charlie's dad. Unfortunately, with Fort Defiance being nearly 4 hours away, no one kept a close track of the three children. At first there were a few Christmas cards and family members tried to remember birthdays, but contact became less and less. Now, there had been no news of them for years.

"They gave us a day off on Sunday. I think they were expecting us to do some sightseeing. I had William's and Jennifer's old address, so I took a short ride to Fort Defiance."

"Did you find them?"

"I found where they used to live. I talked with Cecil and Marsha Duncan, the family they stayed with."

"What did they say?"

"It wasn't good news."

Chapter Fifteen

"By the time Uncle Isaac and Aunt Jules died, Walter already had moved out," Emily began. "He lived in a trailer in Window Rock along with a couple of friends from high school. He was still studying under a medicine man and working at a veterinary clinic. I guess he didn't have much time to spend with his brother and sister.

"The Duncans said they never had a problem with Willie. He wasn't all that good in academics, but he loved school sports . . . especially basketball."

"Did he at least graduate?"

"No, but I'll get to that in a minute."

Janice approached with two cups and a coffee carafe. She set the cups down and filled them. "Have you had a chance to look at the menu?"

Emily opened hers and took a quick glance. "I'll have the mutton sandwich."

Charlie shrugged. "Make that two."

"It'll be out in a few minutes." Janice turned and left.

Emily added a pack of sugar to her coffee and continued the story. "Marsha Duncan said Jenny was fine for the first year or so. The Duncans had raised four kids of their own and Marsha remembered how difficult teenagers could be. Especially the girls . . . in and out of love, weekly crushes on a different boy, raging hormones.

"At first, Marsha thought Jenny was just going through the normal phases girls go through. When she turned fourteen, she really started being secretive. The Duncans found all sorts of jewelry and new clothes hidden in her bedroom. When they confronted her, she became defensive

. . . almost, belligerent. She refused to tell them where these gifts came from.

"They put up with that for almost a year. Cecil said he was just about ready to hand her over to Family Services when Jenny disappeared."

"What do you mean she disappeared?"

"Right after she turned fifteen . . . she went to school one day and didn't come home."

"She ran away?"

"That's what the tribal police think. I guess they did a search . . . asked all her friends if they'd seen her. They even contacted some of the family to see if she showed up. Nothing.

"Willie didn't think she ran away. He even told the police she didn't leave on her own.

"William told the Duncans that Jenny made a confession to him a week before she disappeared. She went to the Navajo Fair in Window Rock right after she turned fourteen. She met a man who told her she was pretty. He gave her a necklace and told her to come back to the fair the next night, he would have something else for her. She caught rides with her friends and kept going back.

"When the fair was over, this new friend asked if they could meet after school. He wanted to give her more things, take her shopping, help her feel good about herself."

"Why did she make the confession? Was he molesting her?"

"It doesn't sound like it, but he was pressuring her to leave home. He told her she owed him for all the gifts. She talked to Willie because she was getting scared."

"Was this man she was seeing Navajo?"

"I don't know. The Duncans didn't say. I would think so."

"Did Willie have a name for this guy?"

Emily shrugged. "I guess not. Cecil and Marsha passed on everything Willie said to the police. They insisted Jenny was kidnapped and the police or the FBI needed to do something. An agent did come down from the FBI field office in Farmington and took a report, but he didn't offer much hope. He said dozens of Navajo citizens disappear every year and those disappearances never get solved.

"They explained Jenny had probably been groomed by this stranger. It happens all the time. Some teen is picked out by these crews and are lavished with cheap gifts. They invest time and money. When they're ready, they grab their victim and sell them into a kind of slavery. And it's not just girls. It can happen to teenage boys, as well."

"Damn!" Charlie swore under her breath.

Janice approached with their sandwiches. "Will there be anything else?"

"No, we're fine," Emily said.

Once they were alone, Charlie asked, "Walter and William weren't satisfied with that answer, were they?"

"Oh, Hell no!" Emily took a small bite of her sandwich and chewed while she talked. "Evidently, Walter had completed his medicine man studies. When he found out what had happened, he decided to find Jenny and go after the men who took her. Despite the Duncans' protests, Willie dropped out of school and joined his brother."

"Something like that takes money."

"There was some life insurance. I guess that's what they used."

Emily took another bite of her mutton, chewed and swallowed before continuing.

"Willie would call Marsha every month or so and give her an update on what was going on. She said that went on for over two years, then the calls stopped."

"Why?"

"They didn't know. They asked around. It sounds like the boys stepped on a lot of toes both here in Arizona and New Mexico. They not only pissed off law enforcement in both states, Walter got crossways with some Navajo medicine men.

"No one's heard from them in three years. Cecil said he thinks they're dead."

Charlie frowned. "What about Jennifer?"

"It's been five years since she went missing. They think she's probably dead, too."

Charlotte Etsitty stared at her half-eaten sandwich. She couldn't finish it. "What are we going to do?"

"About what?"

"About our cousins. We have to do something?"

"What can we do? I have to go to work tomorrow. After the funeral, you and the girls are going back to Phoenix. Life is going to go on."

"I suppose," Charlie said, shaking her head. Her sister was right. Life would go on, but the nagging thought continued . . . she needed to do something.

Chapter Sixteen

The Navajo medicine man woke with a start. He had driven all night. It was already past mid-day. The box-canyon where he had been sleeping ran from southwest to northeast. The walls were 400 feet high and the bottom of the gorge only got a couple of hours of sunlight in the summer. Now past the Autumnal Equinox, long shadows would bathe the canyon for the next six months.

At night, the high desert was chilly . . . even in summer. As he pushed open the door to the van, he kept his Navajo blanket wrapped around his shoulders. By walking around, he knew he would warm up.

His first meal of the day was venison jerky and a few swallows of water. A cup of coffee would have been nice, but he didn't have time to build a fire. The Lindsay Trading Post was thirty minutes away. The trading post café would have coffee. *Red Mesa Express* filling station was 10 minutes further west on Highway 550. It had better coffee, but it was too far out of his way.

The medicine man considered the canyon his private domain, though he didn't own it. The Jicarilla Apache Reservation was nine miles to the east. The eastern-most patch of Navajo Reservation Trust Land was just a few miles to the west, across the San Phillipe/San Juan County line. He had staked out the deep arroyo six months earlier. Hidden as it was, it had become a graveyard of sorts. Not counting his own, rag-top Jeep, the canyon had two "abandoned" trucks, a car, and now, a van.

Three vehicles were covered with camouflage tarps. He would have to drive 40 miles to Cuba in Sandoval County to find the nearest hardware store. He needed a tarp to cover the dark blue commercial van he had acquired the night before.

The trucks, car, and van were trophies . . . his "scalps" . . . though he didn't know exactly why he kept them.

The trophies and the canyon . . . they were the shaman's secret. Much of his life was a secret now . . . what he had done . . . what he was intending to do . . . even who he was.

It was June when he declared his war of retribution. He had been preparing for years and it had taken all those years to find out who should be punished. Unfortunately, his activities had not gone unnoticed. He found two recent bullet holes in his jeep. That was a warning to be more careful.

He had no reason to suspect otherwise, but the reprisals against him had begun in earnest. They would end up being much more than just random gunshots. His enemies' retaliations were already raging across the Navajo Reservation . . . and there could only be one outcome.

Chapter Seventeen

Lansing read through Juan Pedro Garcia's autopsy report twice. The FAX came in right after lunch. He had seen lots of such reports over the years, but he was unfamiliar with terms like Pulmonary Edema and Neutrophils.

Nicholas Picado, the doctor at the Las Palmas Clinic, didn't return his call until 2:30. The physician listened intently while Lansing read him the report.

"I know it may sound strange," Picado said, "but in layman's terms, the man drowned."

"How can that be? His clothes were completely dry."

"Drowning occurs when the lungs fill with liquid. That's called Pulmonary Edema . . . essentially, an accumulation of fluid in the tissues and air sacs of the lung. The fluid prevents the absorption of oxygen. In this case, the victim's body produced the fluid probably as a result of the individual's exposure to a toxic substance.

"There are five types of white blood cells in the body. Neutrophils refer to the most numerous. They are the first responders when the body is attacked by a foreign substance. It sounds like the lungs were full of them."

"Where did that 'toxic substance' come from?"

"I wouldn't have a clue. I'd have to examine the scene. Did you discover the body?"

"No. One of his neighbors did."

"Was this place dirty, dusty?"

"No, it was relatively clean. But the face looked like it had been covered with a fine powder."

"What was the time of death again?"

"I first saw the body at nine a.m. yesterday. The autopsy estimate he had died six to twelve hours before that."

"You say the location was clean. Could you smell anything unusual?"

"Like what?"

"Chemicals . . . gas . . . maybe something musty?"

"It was obvious the man had soiled himself."

"That was from him struggling to breath. He lost control of his bodily functions. Or, it could have happened after he died."

"Honestly, that was the only thing I could smell."

"If there was nothing obvious in the immediate surroundings, he could have died somewhere else. Did it look like the body had been moved?"

"It could have been. The Segovia Police took pictures of the scene. Maybe I can figure out something if I look at those."

"The report didn't identify anything toxic, did it?"

Lansing glanced over the report. "No, not that I saw."

"They probably sent tissue samples to a lab for examination."

"I'll call and check. With any luck, they're testing the powder on the face as well." Lansing paused a moment to think. "Does it sound like the man's death was accidental?"

"It very well could have been. The autopsy didn't say anything about trauma to the body. He might have just been at the wrong place at the wrong time."

"If he was exposed to a toxic substance . . . and it sounds like he was . . . how long would it take him to die?"

"It depends on the type and toxicity of the foreign matter plus how much he breathed in. It could take anywhere from a few hours to a few days to kill a person."

There was a rap on the sheriff's open door. Looking up, he signaled for Willie Estrada to come in.

"Doc, I need to get off."

"Yeah, I've got patients waiting."

"Thanks for the info."

"Any time."

Estrada stepped forward and handed her boss a manila folder.

"What's this?"

"Those are your crime scene photos. I stopped by the Segovia PD to see if they could get me multiple copies of my 'Jane Doe' pictures."

"And . . .?"

"I have a couple of dozen for distribution."

"Did you talk to the patient?"

"Oh, yes, I talked to her. She just didn't talk back. The doctors aren't sure if she will.

"There was chaffing on her wrists and ankles indicating she had been restrained.

"The staff confirmed she wasn't penetrated and there was no evidence of semen. A rape kit was done anyway and sent to the state crime lab . . . see if they could pull usable DNA. They were also able to confirm her clothes were covered with human blood. That's being checked for DNA, as well."

The sheriff shook his head. "We have to find out who this girl is. Post a photo on the visitor's board at the entrance. Make sure every deputy gets a copy.

"I hope you left a photo with Segovia."

"They have a couple."

"There are a string of ranches and homes on the north side of Highway two eighty-five between Segovia and Ojo Caliente. I want you and

Danny Cortez to do a house-to-house check, see if anybody knows something. Show them the girl's picture."

"Yes, sir." Estrada turned and left.

Lansing picked up his phone and pushed two numbers.

Sgt. Clem Montoya answered immediately. "Yes, Sheriff?"

"Any word from the surrounding counties about our mystery girl?"

"In the past month there have been eight missing persons reported . . . three of them teenage females."

"Willie has a photo of our girl in the hospital. FAX copies to the counties you talked to. Maybe they know who she is."

When he was finished, Lansing called the Medical Investigator's office in Albuquerque, hoping they had identified the toxic dust that killed Juan Pedro Garcia. And even if the man's death was accidental, it wouldn't explain the missing truck.

Chapter Eighteen

Surveying the parking lot from his window, Bud Baker chomped on his cigar and frowned. There was one paneled truck and one windowless van parked outside. Two vehicles in his fleet were on the road. One was missing. He kept his business under the radar. The low-keyed, Santa Fe hub was a small part of a much larger operation.

Smuggling humans was becoming as lucrative as smuggling drugs. It was much safer, as well. For one thing, dogs seldom sniffed out their cargo . . . plus there was no shortage of foreign volunteers who wanted to break into the United States.

Asian women were always a popular commodity. Especially the younger ones. Baker didn't think they aged very well, though, with a shelf-life of no more than ten years. After that, they were sold for work in motels or sweat shops.

In the American southwest, there was no need to cross any international borders. There were entire Native American reservations full of young girls. In some quarters, American Indian girls were more popular than Asians. If they weren't enticed to come peacefully, grabbing them off a street or a lonely dirt road wasn't a problem.

Baker had been in the smuggling business for almost twenty years. Human smuggling for the last ten. He had never had any problems to speak of. On Monday, however, he had two disruptions to his normally smooth operations in one day.

First, Juan Pedro Garcia, one of his most reliable drivers, didn't show up for a run from Santa Fe to Denver. Cell phones had become a necessity in Baker's business. When Garcia was late, Baker called him but never got an answer. There wasn't time to drive to Segovia to look for him.

The route was simple: Highway 285 to Alamosa, Colorado; U.S. 160 to Walsenburg; then I-25 to Denver. All the vehicles had the innocuous *Southwest Antiques* sign on their sides along with commercial license plates.

Local police almost never stopped his vans, especially on the back roads at night. State Police and Highway Patrol Units could be more curious, particularly on interstate highways. That was the rationale to avoid them.

The only reason for using I-25 this trip was snow squalls were forecast for the mountains west of Colorado Springs. He couldn't afford for his van to get stuck. Also, there was too much money involved. He needed the four Indian girls delivered as soon as possible.

Reluctantly, Baker gave the assignment to Roberto de la Cruz, his newest driver. The man had ridden "shot gun" to learn the routes. This was his first solo trip.

The boss noticed the leer on his driver's face when Roberto saw his cargo. Baker told him flatly, do not touch the merchandise. He would regret it if he did.

The van departed the parking lot at sunset, a few minutes before 7:00.

The second disruption that day came two hours later. A male nurse at Segovia Presbyterian Hospital, a part of his network, called. A State Police Patrol had picked up a teenage Indian, possibly Latino, girl on the highway south of Ojo Caliente. He would provide more information when he could.

Baker immediately called de la Cruz. He wanted to make sure things were okay. He was greeted with voicemail . . . something that shouldn't happen. Now, he was getting concerned. If the girl headed to the hospital was indeed one of his, he needed to retrieve her.

He called Wanda Florin. Florin was his go-to chameleon. She could be a nurse or a grieving mother or an officious pain in the butt. When he explained the situation, she suggested her alias of Gloria Sanchez, Social Worker. She promised she could snatch the girl out of the hospital before anyone knew what was happening.

Baker gave Florin the nod to go in after a second call from Segovia. The girl did appear to be Native American and seemed too upset to talk. She was also covered in blood that wasn't hers. He needed her out of there before she did speak.

Despite Florin's guarantees, the girl was still in the hospital.

Baker bit off the soggy end of his cigar and spit it out. He re-evaluated the situation. There weren't just two disruptions on Monday. There were at least four.

Juan Pedro Garcia didn't show up for his driving assignment and couldn't be reached on his cell.

A girl, probably his, showed up at a Segovia hospital covered in blood . . . most likely de la Cruz's . . . and appeared to have been raped. Baker was positive he knew who the rapist was.

Wanda Florin failed to spring the mute young lady from her doctor's custody. She complained she had been thwarted by the local sheriff.

And finally, his van with the three other girls was missing, along with Roberto de la Cruz.

Bud Baker had superiors he had to answer to. They wouldn't be happy over what was going on. He had to rectify the situation before they got wind.

He sent men out searching. They would spend nearly a week looking with no results.

He needed that van. He needed those girls. And maybe most importantly, he needed to make sure the girl in the hospital never talked to anyone.

Chapter Nineteen

"Well . . . where do we go from here?" Michael Quijano asked. The Chaco Canyon Park Supervisor had bags under his eyes. He had hardly slept in two days.

"The State Police have started their aerial grid search in McKinley County." Jackson McKee had been positive Harry Miller and the missing truck would be found north of the canyon. "That's still part of the Badlands."

Quijano nodded. He understood McKee's logic. A thousand years earlier, Chaco Canyon was the religious and cultural center of the ancient Pueblo people . . . people the Navajo invaders called Anasazi, sometime translated as "Ancient Enemy." The Chaco Canyon culture reached as far away as modern-day Utah, Arizona and Colorado.

The Athabascan migration began around 1200 A.D. As the Anasazi culture declined the Navajo and Apache became dominant . . . in many cases absorbing Pueblo customs and ideas. The vast, deserted desert around Chaco Canyon, though abandoned by the Anasazi, became integral to Navajo mysticism. A vague area of 6,000 square miles, it was unofficially known as The Navajo Badlands.

On a modern-day map, the Badlands were roughly defined by Highway 666 to the west and San Phillipe County to the east; Bloomfield to the north and I-40 to the south. The 216,000 acres had few towns, the largest being Crownpoint, New Mexico with 2,200 residents. There were few paved roads and the many dirt roads were often impassible after heavy rains.

The Badlands featured sagebrush filled deserts, occasional clusters of juniper trees, isolated/unexplored canyons and even more isolated farms and sheep ranches. With the exception of Chaco Canyon, the entire area was designated as Navajo Nation Off-Reservation Trust Land.

Bisti/De-Na-Zin Wilderness Area, 15 miles north of the canyon, was the geographical center of the Badlands. It had made sense to the Park Superintendent that they started looking in that direction. There had been an aerial search and a ground search. They found no white, National Park Service truck and no Harry Miller.

Miller had been posted at Chaco Canyon fulltime for three years. Being from New Mexico, he volunteered for summer internships at the park all through college. His goal in life was to be a Ranger at Chaco Canyon National Historical Park. He was fortunate to marry Jill, a woman who loved the Canyon as much as he did. Two years after they moved to the park, they were blessed with a newborn son. Neither thought life could get much better.

Jill's happiness evaporated rapidly when Harry went missing. She knew he was resourceful and could take care of himself. She tried not to be too concerned that he was going out that Sunday evening to look for intruders.

But Jill Millar had heard the tales about the Badlands . . . everyone in the Canyon had. The most persistent stories concerned Navajo medicine men who had turned to evil. They came to the Badlands to restore their strength. In some instances, the Badlands were where they were initiated into their wicked ways. Their rituals called upon the spirits of the ancient dead and they believed the holy kivas of the Anasazi instilled formidable powers. That was the reason for their presence in the ruins of Chaco Canyon.

The young mother sat outside the superintendent's office with her fussing one-year-old. It was Wednesday morning, and she was hoping for news of any kind. McKee opened the door and ushered them in.

"Jill, would you like to sit?" Quijano offered.

"Not really," she said, struggling with a cranky one-year-old. "It's been two days and three nights and you haven't found Harry yet."

"We know that! We have a police helicopter looking south of the Canyon today," the superintendent explained. "They searched 2000 square miles in San Juan and Sandoval Counties yesterday."

"We also have ground searches out, as well," McKee added.

"Why did you let him go out at night by himself?" She addressed the Chief Ranger.

"He was armed," McKee pointed out. "And there should have been no reason for him to leave the park."

"Well, he did! So, who took him?" She looked from one man to the next. Her anger was building. Her whining son didn't help matters . . . for anyone.

"We don't know that he was taken." Quijano tried to calm her fears. "He could have chased someone out of the Park."

"That's probably what happened," McKee said. "We've found no sign of a struggle anywhere."

"You won't admit it, will you?"

"Admit what?" the ranger asked.

"Harry told me things were going on at night in the kivas. I was afraid for him, but I didn't say anything. I should have . . . and now he's gone. Probably dead. You both know who killed him."

"Who?" the superintendent demanded.

"Those damned, Navajo medicine men!"

Chapter Twenty

The call came in before Lansing made it into his office. Cleo Valdez found a dead body and an abandoned truck on his ranch on the west side of Black Mesa.

Deputy Jerry Lopez was on the southern end of San Phillipe County already, but he had his hands full with a domestic battle. That was fine with the sheriff. He suspected the body and the truck were related to the silent girl in the hospital. He wanted to see things for himself.

The Valdez property bumped up against Highway 285. The access road was 4 miles south of Ojo Caliente, not more than a mile from where Rich Hidalgo picked up "Jane Doe."

Cleo was sitting in his truck, waiting for the sheriff, a quarter mile from 285. Lansing parked, then walked toward the rancher, surveying the scene. A dark blue Chevy truck was parked a few feet off the dirt track. Beyond the truck was a body lying face up. The man's pants and underwear were pulled down to his knees. The private parts were missing, leaving a bloody mess behind. Valdez evidently laid a towel or rag across the face, either out of respect or because of the horror of the sight.

"Señor Valdez?"

"Yeah, that's me," the man said, getting out of his truck. He had only the slightest hint of a Hispanic accent. The two men shook hands, then walked toward the body.

"Any idea how long the dead man's been out here?"

"I try to ride the perimeter of the ranch every two or three days. The last time I was on this side was Sunday morning. So, this happened some time after that."

Lansing stood over the body studying it. He could see the man's throat had been cut. On closer inspection, it appeared more like it had been ripped open. Blood had soaked into the shirt and dried. It wasn't a recent death.

"I covered the face," Valdez explained. "It wasn't pretty. The birds and coyotes had gotten to him."

Lansing lifted the rag. There could be no way to identify him by his facial features. The nose was gone. The flesh on the right side of his face had been stripped away exposing the teeth and jaw. The damage to the throat was even more pronounced than he first thought.

He replaced the rag and stood.

"The keys are still in the truck over there," Valdez observed.

"Thanks. I need to get on my radio and make a call," he said, excusing himself.

"Dispatch, Patrol One."

"This is dispatch," Marylin responded. "Go ahead, Patrol One."

"I have a DB here for the Medical Investigator's Office. Use one of our Segovia ambulance services."

He gave his location along with the license plate number to the truck. It took less than a minute for the dispatcher to pull an ID on the owner . . . Juan Pedro Garcia.

As he hung up the radio mic, Lansing tried to piece together the puzzle. He had the mute girl in the hospital. She was picked up approximately a mile from a dead body and a stolen truck. The girl had to be associated somehow with the dead man . . . she had been assaulted, probably by him.

Her bloody clothes were at the State Crime Lab in Santa Fe. He needed a DNA comparison of the rape kit, the blood on the clothes and the corpse. If there was a match, he had two pieces of the puzzle figured out.

"Mr. Valdez, I don't think you need to stay here any longer. We'll let you know if we need a formal statement."

As the rancher pulled away, Lansing retrieved the wallet from the dead man's back pocket. The man's license was for a commercial driver. "Roberto de la Cruz" had a Santa Fe address, but no information on who he worked for.

According to Johnathan Akee, Garcia was a truck driver. Maybe another part of the puzzle just fell into place. The two men, Garcia and de la Cruz, knew each other. De la Cruz stole the truck after he found Garcia dead . . . or he might have killed him.

He then picked up the girl off a street somewhere and drove her to an isolated road. He tried to rape her, then . . . what? She ripped his throat out and left him for dead. Somebody else killed him, got blood all over her, but let her go. The man was attacked by a wild animal, but it didn't touch the girl.

He was bogging himself down with all the "what ifs." Talking with Tina Morales always seemed to clarify his thoughts, but that currently wasn't an option.

When he got back to Las Palmas, he would corral Jack Rivera, his chief deputy, and the two of them would sift through the evidence. With any luck, "Jane Doe" would soon be talking, filling them in on who she was and what happened to her.

Chapter Twenty-One

Tina Morales sat in the waiting room hoping to be called soon. As ordered, she showed up 15 minutes early to complete her paperwork. It took 20 minutes to fill out all the nuisance forms and make her copay. The gynecologist was two hours behind schedule . . . a difficult delivery at the Christus St. Vincent Hospital. That's what she and the other twenty patients had been told.

The schoolteacher didn't realize how hard it was to get a doctor's appointment . . . at least in northern New Mexico. The soonest Dr. Maria Vigil could see her was 5 weeks from the time she made the appointment. All the other doctors had two month waiting lists, even in Segovia. She hated taking a sick day, but it couldn't be helped.

Tina's problems began in Nogales while visiting her grandparents. She began bleeding two weeks before her period would normally start. She cut her visit short so she could see a doctor in Phoenix. Her mother immediately got her in to see her own doctor.

Dr. Alba diagnosed her with an infection and prescribed antibiotics. When she got back to Las Palmas, he suggested having a biopsy done, just to make sure they weren't looking at cancer.

The C-word scared the hell out of her . . . but the antibiotics seemed to work. The bleeding stopped. Even so, on the long drive back to New Mexico, all she could think about was the idea that she might get really sick.

Her Tia Consuela came down with cancer. She remembered the heartache her uncle went through as his wife withered away. He seemed to suffer right along with his beloved wife.

Tina resolved she wouldn't do that to Cliff Lansing. She loved him too much. Until she knew her long-term prognosis, she thought it best to keep the sheriff at arms-length. She hated to hurt him, but a little pain for a few weeks was better for him than the agony of watching her die.

She was glad she had to drive to Santa Fe to see a physician. She wanted to keep her health issues to herself.

"Ms. Morales," the nurse said from the open door.

Tina immediately stood. "I'm here."

The nurse escorted her to a scale to get her weight, then took her to an exam room. After taking her vital signs, the nurse asked, "What exactly brought you in today?"

Tina explained the bleeding, the doctor visit in Phoenix and how the antibiotics worked for nearly a month. Unfortunately, the bleeding had started up again after she made the appointment. Plus, there was pain. She was concerned.

The nurse wrote down Tina's history in a chart. She then instructed the teacher to disrobe from the waist down and put on a hospital gown. The doctor would be in to see her in a few minutes.

A few minutes turned into a half an hour.

Dr. Vigil entered, glancing over a chart. "Miss Morales, I understand you've had some discharge?" The doctor's manner was cold and abrupt. There was no friendly greeting or apology for running late.

"Yes, doctor. I . . ."

"And they put you on antibiotics and the symptoms went away?"

"Yes, but I've started bleeding again and I have pain in the lower abdomen."

"Lie back on the table and let me raise the stirrups."

Morales did as she was told. As she placed her feet in the stirrups, Vigil put on latex gloves. She then opened a drawer and removed a stainless-steel speculum and a headlamp for the exam.

Tina had a similar examination 8 weeks earlier, along with a Pap Smear to check for cervical cancer. This one proved to be just as uncomfortable as the previous experience.

"I presume you are sexually active, Miss . . ."

"Morales," Tina completed. "Not for a couple of months."

"Have you had a lot of partners?"

"No."

After probing for nearly five minutes, Vigil gave her diagnosis. "It doesn't look like you have an STD. However, you do have inflammation." She removed the gloves and tossed them into a waste basket. "All you need is another round of antibiotics. You can get dressed." She started toward the door.

Tina sat up on the table. "Aren't you going to do a biopsy?"

"What for?"

"My doctor in Phoenix said I should have a biopsy done. Make sure I don't have ovarian cancer."

"You don't have cancer," Vigil said dismissively.

"What about my prescription?"

"You can pick it up at the front desk on your way out."

"Should I make another appointment?"

"I'd wait until you've completed the antibiotics. If you still have problems, you can make another appointment." The doctor left the exam room without a "Goodbye" or "Have a nice day."

"Yeah, I'll make another appointment," Tina said under her breath as she put her clothes back on. "It just won't be with you."

Chapter Twenty-Two

The Segovia Presbyterian Hospital boasted 80 hospital beds. They were almost always occupied. Nurses had regular assignments and positions. However, there were also floaters who filled in when necessary. It wasn't unusual for a nurse to work in the Pediatric Clinic one day, the Emergency Room the next, then on a patient floor the day after that.

No one thought anything was amiss that Wednesday morning when Miguel Cuellar, a regular ER nurse, showed up on the third floor. He walked down the corridor with purpose, and he greeted everyone with a friendly smile. Like the other RNs, he had a pocket for carrying syringes filled with saline solution for flushing IV lines.

He stopped outside the room he was looking for, glanced up and down the hallway trying not to look suspicious, then pushed the door open. As he quietly closed it, he surveyed the room.

The breakfast tray sat on the rolling meal table next to the bed, untouched. The patient was lying on her side and appeared to be sleeping.

Cuellar pulled a syringe from his pocket, then gently tried to rouse the girl. "Excuse me, miss," he said softly.

The girl woke with a start. She rolled onto her back and pulled the covers up to her chin, a look of terror on her face.

He showed her the hypodermic needle. "Don't be afraid. The doctor wanted you to get a shot of vitamin B-twelve. It will just take a second."

Cuellar ripped open a small packet containing an alcohol swab, then tried to pull down the covers to prepare an injection spot.

That's when "Jane Doe" began screaming.

"Sh-h-h," he said quickly, then looked at the door to see if anyone was coming.

The male nurse turned back to the screaming girl. "Dammit, I said shut up."

Forgetting the syringe, he grabbed her pillow and pressed it against her face to muffle the outburst. He hoped no one had heard the noise.

The teenager desperately fought the stronger man. She still screamed, kicking and clawing at her attacker's hands, trying to breathe.

Before Cuellar could do any damage, the door swung open and a female nurse yelled, "What the Hell are you doing, Miguel?" She rushed to the bed.

"I was just trying to calm her down," he said, pulling the pillow away. "I needed to administer a shot. She just started screaming."

"Jane Doe" gasped for breath and pulled her covers even tighter. The nurse helped her sit up so she could breathe easier.

"What shot?" the attending nurse demanded. "I didn't see any orders for one!"

"The order came from Dr. Garnepudi. He thought a B-twelve shot would help her recovery."

"You need to get out of here. Garnepudi is no longer her attending physician."

"I was just following orders," Cuellar said. He looked around, desperate to retrieve his hypodermic.

"What are you looking for?"

"My syringe."

"What's in it?"

"I told you . . . it's a B-twelve shot." During the struggle, the syringe had fallen to the floor. Cuellar spotted it and quickly picked it up.

"Give it to me," the female nurse ordered.

"Why?" her male counterpart demanded.

"Because I want to find out what's in it."

"You don't believe me?"

"I don't believe an ER doctor ordered anything. Not for a patient already in a ward!"

Cuellar hesitated.

"Give it to me, Miguel, or I'm calling security."

He finally handed it over, then turned toward the door.

"This isn't over," the other nurse said. "I'm talking to the floor nurse about that pillow."

Miguel stopped, but didn't turn back to the speaker.

"And you'd better hope to God we find nothing more than vitamins in this syringe."

Cuellar didn't say a thing. He stepped out of the room, then continued down the corridor, out of the hospital and into his car. No one would believe him if he claimed he grabbed the wrong hypodermic needle . . . or that he mistook a vial of potassium-chloride for B-12.

He knew his career at Segovia Presbyterian Hospital was over. His only concern now was staying ahead of the police.

Chapter Twenty-Three

"*Análí* Sarah, you cannot live at the ranch by yourself," Thomas Begaye, Jr. argued. Begaye was one of Charlie's cousins from Shiprock.

The arguments started that morning when the first of the Etsitty family arrived. Relatives planned to stay in Tuba City, but the initial gathering was at the ranch. Grandma Sarah still had chores to do. She was helped by her grandchildren . . . even great-grandchildren. Uncle Benjamin butchered a sheep while the women busied themselves in the kitchen. For the most part, the fracas was not among family members. It was between family members and the Etsitty matriarch. All the discussions were conducted in Navajo.

"I cannot give up my sheep or my cattle," Sarah argued. "If I do, I will have nothing."

"You can sell them," Aunt Deloris pointed out. "Then you can come live with us in Shiprock."

"When we don't have livestock, the Bureau of Indian Affairs will take away our grazing permit," Sarah observed. "We will not be able to raise sheep. Then we will have nothing to eat."

Many Navajo thought the federal government had become too intrusive. A court case just a few years earlier gave traditional Diné lands to the Hopi Reservation. Dozens of Navajo families were evicted from properties they had ranched on for generations. Now the BIA was pushing to limit the number of sheep a family could raise, and a family could only raise sheep if they had a grazing permit.

Permits could be handed down through the family. If it wasn't handed down, the BIA would simply rescind it, and no new permits were being handed out.

The youngest descendants sided with their grandmother. They looked forward to staying at the ranch. It was almost like camping out. After a few days, though, they looked forward to getting back to hot and cold running water, indoor bathrooms and television. Their preferences didn't matter. They had no vote.

"If I don't have my animals, how can I barter for what I need?"

"You won't have to barter for anything," Aunt Connie, Benjamin's wife said. "You will have money. Besides, you won't have to worry about anything. You'll be living with one of us." She gestured to the other women in the kitchen.

Grandmother Sarah frowned. She wasn't happy that she had lost her husband of 60 years. The prospect of leaving her animals depressed her even more. Moving from the ranch and living someplace new terrified her.

It would take a lot more to convince her to leave.

Chapter Twenty-Four

Lansing stopped by the nurses' station on the third floor. Segovia Presbyterian Hospital was only 8 miles out of his way. He wanted to get an update on the mute girl.

He seemed to get a better reception from the staff because he wore his uniform.

"Are you here already?" Floor Nurse Williams asked. "We just called two minutes ago."

"You called the Sheriff's Office?"

"No, the Segovia police. We wanted to report an attempted murder."

"An attempted murder? Who?"

"That poor girl brought into the ER Monday night. She's in room three ten."

"Who tried to kill her?"

"One of the hospital's male nurses, Miguel Cuellar."

"Where is he?"

"We don't know. He took off. Angela Tafoya caught him trying to smother the girl with a pillow. He also had a syringe that she took away from him. When she told me about what happened, I called the police."

Lansing was very worried over the news. A woman, Gloria Sanchez, tried to abduct "Jane Doe" Monday night. Now someone was trying to kill her. Who was this girl and what did she know? "What was in the syringe?"

"We don't know. It was sent to the lab for analysis."

"How is the girl?"

"Except for her refusal to speak, she's fine."

"So, she can talk."

"Well, we know she can scream. That's what alerted Angela that something was wrong."

"Can I speak with the nurse?" Lansing asked.

A few minutes later, Tafoya approached. She had been doing her rounds and was miffed that she had to break them off. While she related what she had seen, a city police officer showed up. She became even more annoyed when he not only asked her to start her story over, but to fill out a complaint against Cuellar.

Nurse Tafoya said she had to complete an incident report for the hospital. Would that suffice?

Lansing interrupted when the policeman said she needed to fill out a city form as well. He assured her all the police had to do was staple a photocopy of the hospital form onto their official report.

The officer wasn't sure about that, but he let the issue drop for the moment. After he listened to her story and was assured the girl was all right, the policeman went to Human Resources. He needed to get a photo and as much information on Miguel Cuellar as possible.

If the assailant wasn't picked up immediately, Lansing was sure an APB would be issued. For the moment, Cuellar was the Segovia Police Department's problem. The girl down the hospital corridor was his.

Lansing had to wait nearly 15 minutes for the attending physician. During the lull, he called his office. He needed Montoya to contact every Santa Fe trucking business to find out if they employed either Juan Pedro Garcia or Roberto de la Cruz.

When the doctor finally arrived, introductions were abrupt. They were busy men.

"Dr. Maceda, do you think we can move the girl?"

"Well, there really isn't anything wrong with her," Maceda admitted. "She can walk and her appetite is okay. She just doesn't seem to want to talk.

"Why do you want to move her?"

Lansing explained about the attempted abduction in the ER and the attack in her room.

"Someone's out to get her," the sheriff explained. "I don't know why. They know where she is, and I don't think this hospital is safe for her."

"Where will you take her?"

"That will have to be my secret. All I need for you to do is fill out her release forms. I'll take it from there."

"She's scared to death of men, you know."

"I do. I have a female deputy who met the girl yesterday. I'll have her handle the transfer."

"She'll need clothes."

"Yes," Lansing agreed. He pulled out his cell phone to make arrangements.

He wanted Willie Estrada to come to the hospital. On the way she had to buy the girl jeans, a top, underwear and shoes. Since they had already met, Lansing hoped his deputy could guess the young lady's sizes. It was getting cold at night. She'd require a jacket as well.

Chapter Twenty-Five

Lansing didn't wait for Deputy Estrada at the hospital. He needed to get back to Las Palmas and arrange for a place to keep the girl.

Chief Deputy Jack Rivera gave the sheriff's open door a light tap.

"Hey, Jack," Lansing said looking up. "Did you talk to Sue?"

"She's fixing up the spare room right now."

"That's great! Does she know we're not sure how long Jane Doe will need to stay?"

"I told her yesterday about the girl in the ER. She was actually excited that she could help."

"Your daughter won't be upset, will she?"

"Are you kidding? I don't know how many times Deedee's asked for an older sister. It's hard explaining to a five-year-old that's not the way the world works."

Lansing smiled and nodded. He remembered the innocent questions his son always asked. No matter how he answered, he was always peppered with an endless series of "Whys?"

Eventually, he would end the torment with, "I don't know. Go ask your mother."

That had been a long time ago. In less than a year C.J. would be off to college. His wave of nostalgia was interrupted by the phone ringing on his desk.

"Yes?"

"Sheriff, this is Marilyn," the dispatcher said. "Deputy Estrada is ready to leave Segovia. She needs to know where to take the girl."

"Have her call me on my cell. I don't want to broadcast to the world what's going on."

As he hung up his phone, he looked up at Rivera. "Do you mind calling Sue and letting her know your visitor is on the way?"

"Sure." The deputy stopped and turned back to his boss. "What are we supposed to call her?"

Lansing shrugged. "Jane, I guess . . . until she tells us her real name."

***

It was late afternoon before the sheriff finished the stack of paperwork he had been putting off. He might have finished sooner, but he had to make calls and was constantly sidetracked with calls coming in.

His biggest regret was calling the state Children, Youth and Family Department office in Segovia. Director Christina Archuleta was not the same cooperative administrator he had talked to the day before. Lansing had stepped on her office's collective toes by putting "Jane Doe" in protective custody. Taking care of the girl was her department's responsibility.

Lansing tried to explain the dire circumstances for his action. Eventually, Archuleta agreed he had made the right decision. However, she blew up all over again when he refused to allow the girl to be interviewed. He had no right to keep her sequestered. She threatened him with a visit from the State Police Special Investigations Division. (As far as the sheriff was concerned, that was an empty threat. He didn't work for the state.)

The sheriff eventually had had enough. He was able to terminate the conversation because of an incoming call.

"Sheriff Lansing, this is Sandra Williams at Presbyterian. I was the Floor Nurse on three."

"Yes, yes. Of course, Mrs. Williams. What can I do for you?"

"We got the results about what Cuellar had in the syringe. It was potassium-chloride."

"Is potassium-chloride dangerous?"

"It can be, in large doses. It's one of the three ingredients included in the cocktail of drugs used in prison executions. That's the drug used to stop the heart."

"So, Cuellar's first choice was to poison the girl?"

"The worst part is the girl would have died and we might not have found what killed her. Potassium occurs naturally in the body. I'm not sure a medical examiner would know to look for excessive potassium in a drug screen."

Late in the day, Lansing had to make one last call to Albuquerque. He had gotten a toxicology report from the MI's office. There was no explanation for the diagnosis of *pulmonary mycotoxicosis*. He recalled the conversation with Dr. Picado the afternoon before. The physician did emphasize he thought Garcia had probably been exposed to a toxic substance. The sheriff simply wanted to know what that substance was.

The lab tech had included his phone number on the report.

"It was a fungal infection," the technician explained. "Swabs were taken of the nostrils plus cross sections of the bronchioles were studied. A lot of spores were found."

"He inhaled them?"

"It appears so."

"So, drugs weren't involved?"

"No."

"Where did the spores come from?"

"Decaying organic matter."

"Could he have been exposed accidentally?"

"It's possible. Do you know what he did for a living?"

"He was a truck driver."

"Do you know what he normally hauled?"

"Not a clue," the sheriff admitted. "He appeared to have a fine coating of dust on his face. Did your people look at that?"

"Yes. There were also spores . . . mixed with bone dust?"

"Bone dust? What kind of bones?"

"It would be impossible to tell."

***

Jack Rivera came through the front door and removed his jacket. "Hello?" he called.

"I'm in the kitchen, hon," Sue answered back. "You're just in time. Supper's almost ready."

The deputy followed the sound of his wife's voice. "How's our visitor doing?"

"You were right. She doesn't talk. She spent the entire afternoon in the spare room."

Rivera looked around. His daughter usually had attacked him by this time. "Deedee, Daddy's home!"

The patter of little feet came from the back of the house. "Daddy!" she squealed, jumping into his arms. She gave him a big kiss.

"Meja, let your father go get changed. And could you ask Jane if she'd like to eat?"

"Okay," Deedee said after her father put her down.

"If the girl's not talking, how is she supposed to answer Deedee?" the deputy asked, as his daughter disappeared down the hall.

"I found out earlier that she can still nod and shake her head," Sue said.

"So, she does speak English."

"Well, she at least understands it. Go get changed," she ordered.

Chapter Twenty-Six

"I would think you're tired of taking care of those animals out there." Thomas Begaye, Sr. said, catching the tail end of another argument with Grandma Sarah. He had just come in from helping butcher the sheep. Walking over to the sink, he motioned for his wife, Deloris, to operate the hand pump so he could clean up.

Charlie had stayed out of the discussions. She was busy kneading dough for fry bread and only listened. She thought it was bad manners to have such arguments when Grandfather Nathen hadn't even been buried yet. However, she understood the need for her aunts and uncles to make their arguments now. Most would leave town right after the funeral. They wanted the issue of the ranch settled as soon as possible.

Charlie, herself, was torn. She had enjoyed the time she spent on the ranch helping her grandmother. That pleasure, though, was tempered by the thought that hers was a temporary situation. She knew she wouldn't stay after her grandfather passed.

She also knew *Análi* Sarah couldn't remain at her home by herself . . . not with the intruders that came at night. Charlie had said nothing to the rest of the family. Only she, Emily, her mother and grandmother knew about the creatures. Charlie didn't want to frighten the others. She wasn't sure they would believe her, anyway.

She really didn't think it would matter. There were plenty of other reasons why Grandmother Sarah shouldn't stay at the ranch . . . especially alone.

Charlotte, Amanda, Emily, Tina and Lizbeth represented one branch of the Etsitty family.

Aunt Rose Etsitty Tallman, Uncle David and the rest of her family drove from Farmington. The 200-mile drive took 4 hours and they didn't arrive until 2:00 p.m.

By midafternoon, 30 of the 40 descendants of Nathan and Sarah Etsitty had gathered at the ranch.

No one wanted to go to the mortuary for a viewing. For the Diné, looking on a dead body was bad luck. Such things were simply not done.

The ranch house was not big enough for the entire family. No one complained. It had been years since everyone was together. Despite the circumstances, it was a joyful reunion. Wood was gathered for a bonfire. In ages past, this was how people stayed warm during a meal. They were fortunate that there was little wind.

The feast started at 4:00. Besides mutton there was roasted corn, squash, pinto beans flavored with jalapeños, blue corn mush and fry bread. There was enough food to feed 100 people. No one would go hungry.

With bellies full, the arguments with Sarah ended. It was time for the stories everyone remembered about Grandfather Nathan. Each person wanted to share their favorite.

Charlotte thought about telling the story of how her grandfather saved her and her 3 cousins at the hunting cabin on Preston Mesa. However, after hearing their sad stories from Emily the day before, she didn't think it was appropriate. Besides, what happened that night seemed to be repeating itself.

It was nearly midnight before the last of the visitors left for their motel rooms in town. There was no hurry. The funeral wasn't until 1:00 the next afternoon.

Charlie let her daughters spend the night with her at the ranch. Everyone was tired and fell asleep once the lights were out.

Badlands

No one heard the whistling when it came from the darkness, beyond the light of the dwindling bonfire.

Chapter Twenty-Seven

The driver of the tattered, battered old Jeep slowed down as he passed the entrance to the *Southwest Antiques* shipping center. The gate was closed. It was late and nothing appeared to be happening. Light shown through only one window at the office. Beyond the perimeter chain-link fence, the rest of the compound was dark. Located south of Santa Fe, just off I-25, there was no traffic this time of night.

The medicine man counted two cars, one company van and the paneled truck. He guessed one vehicle was still on the road. He also knew one of their vans had gone missing. He was sure people were out looking for both the van and its occupants.

A quarter mile past the entrance, the Navajo turned onto a dirt road and parked. Juniper bushes hid his approach. He stepped lightly so the dried grass wouldn't crunch under his feet. At the fence, he stopped and surveyed the compound again.

Still no movement.

He quickly climbed the fence and dropped on the other side. The compound had two buildings. The office and a warehouse. The storage facility supposedly held antiques waiting to be shipped. The shaman knew better.

Since he started his surveillance, he learned *Southwest Antiques* only handled human cargo . . . young girls from south of the border or from the numerous Indian reservations in Arizona and New Mexico. At first, he tried stopping the traffickers before they reached Santa Fe. He found out that was impossible.

The compound was a distribution hub. Girls were brought in, held anywhere from a day to a month, then shipped out. The incoming delivery vehicles were innocuous . . . cars, SUVs, even RVs. It was impossible to identify them before they reached Santa Fe.

He hurried to the storage building. There was a metal garage door . . . the type used on commercial storage units. Victims were brought in, unloaded, kept, then sent out again, hidden from prying eyes.

He listened at the door. There was no activity. Stepping around to the side of the building, he tried the access door. It was locked. He had never been inside. He could only imagine the conditions. He had seen what the girls looked like after being kept in the building. They had not been treated well.

He could only hope no one was inside. It hurt his heart that he couldn't do more.

He was soon back over the fence and in his Jeep. Turning around and heading back to the Badlands, he would continue his observation of the compound when he could. He would keep disrupting their operations. He wouldn't stop his vendetta until he destroyed the people who destroyed his life.

Chapter Twenty-Eight

"Well, good morning," Halley Basa said cheerily. The school secretary knitted her brow with concern. "Are you feeling better?"

It was 7:15. Classes wouldn't start for 45 minutes. Tina Morales came in early to check her in-box in the front office, go over any notes she had and grab a cup of coffee.

"Oh, I feel fine, Halley. I just had a check-up to make sure my lady parts still worked." Tina tried to sound nonchalant.

"Hi, Tina," Marta Gomez said, heading to look into her own box. It was empty.

"Morning."

They both waved at Basa and said, "See you later!" as they left for the teacher's lounge.

"Is anything wrong?" the English teacher asked as they walked down the hallway.

"What do you mean?"

"I called to check on you after school yesterday, but you never answered your phone."

"I was tired, Marta. Down and back to Santa Fe takes three hours. Then I spent almost four hours in the doctor's office . . . plus I had to stop and eat on the way back. I just didn't feel like answering the phone after I got home. Sorry."

Marta opened the door to the lounge and held it for her friend. "That's okay. But you're all right now?"

"Yeah, I am."

The teachers each had an armful of gradebooks and papers. Their loads were deposited on an empty table, then both proceeded to the coffee counter. Other teachers in the room barely looked up from their conversations.

"Tomorrow's Friday," Gomez observed. "I thought I'd drive up to Cohino tomorrow night and check out *High Desert Restaurant*." She stirred artificial sweetener into her black coffee. "I hear it's pretty good."

"It is," Tina admitted. "I've eaten there lots of times." She loaded her own cup of coffee with sugar and whitener.

"If you don't have any plans, I thought we could go up there together."

Morales liked her new friend well enough. However, she was beginning to think inviting her to dinner Monday night was a mistake. Gomez was only there as a convenient buffer between her and Sheriff Lansing.

Tina didn't want to hurt her feelings, but she didn't want Marta or anyone else to think they had an exclusive relationship. Marta needed to meet other people. Nothing was more depressing or suspicious than seeing two single, female teachers hanging out together. Even if nothing went on, perceptions were everything . . . especially in a small school located in a small town.

The chemistry teacher shrugged. "Let me think about it . . . I'll let you know."

Chapter Twenty-Nine

"How is Miss Jane Doe doing at your place?" Lansing asked.

Deputy Rivera sat down in the chair in front of the sheriff's desk. He took a sip from his coffee mug and frowned. "Ever seen how a beaten dog will cower in a corner? That's Jane Doe."

"She hasn't said anything?"

"No to me. Not to Sue. We know she understands what we say to her. She just won't talk . . . at least, not to us."

"Is she eating?"

"Sue put some food in her room yesterday evening. About half of it was gone this morning. And we did hear her use the bathroom last night. Neither one of us approached her, though. We thought that was break-through . . . she was at least coming out of her room."

"She was still there this morning? She didn't try to escape?"

"No," Rivera admitted. "But come on, Cliff, she's not a prisoner."

"I know that." Lansing thought for a moment. "It's kind of strange. It sounds like she's more afraid of being free and out in the open than she is of staying at your place."

"Yeah," the deputy agreed. "Sue told her we would take her home. All she had to do was tell us where 'home' was."

"How did she react?"

"Sue said she just stared at her."

"Is Sue upset with your boarder?"

"I think frustrated would better describe how she feels."

Lansing nodded. He hoped he had a solution. "I'd like to bring someone over this afternoon. They might be able to help."

"What time?"

"Around four."

"I'll let Sue know." The Chief Deputy stood. "I need to hit the road. Earn my salary."

"You've more than earned it. You and Sue both."

***

Later that morning, Lansing received a FAX from the Medical Investigator's office. The preliminary autopsy of Roberto de la Cruz held few surprises. He died from loss of blood . . . the right carotid artery in the neck had been severed.

The torn, jagged skin around the wound indicated it was caused by sharp teeth or possibly a claw. It was apparent some kind of animal was involved. The MI would contact experts at the university to identify the culprit.

The other damage to the body, the face and genital area, was postmortem. Again, an animal or animals were responsible.

The sheriff had two deaths on his hands. The first man inhaled toxic spores and drowned from fluids produced from his own body. At the moment, he could only hope this was an accident. His concern was could others be exposed to the same deadly substance? He had to find out where Juan Pedro Garcia had been.

The second man had been attacked by a wild animal. It was the sheriff's responsibility to make sure no one else was killed. He just needed to find out what kind of animal he was looking for.

The state crime lab in Santa Fe confirmed de la Cruz had the same "type" of blood, O-Positive, as was found on Jane Doe's clothes. DNA results would take a few more days.

The two deaths were linked, only because Garcia's truck was found only yards away from the body of the second dead man. They both had

CDLs and probably knew each other. How they died, though, was completely different.

"Clem, I take it you had no luck with any Santa Fe trucking companies?" Lansing asked his desk sergeant when he walked to the front office.

"No. I started calling the 'big box' stores. They do deliveries. No one's heard of either Garcia or de la Cruz."

"Hm." Lansing thought for a moment. "Maybe they worked for the state. Try them."

"Wouldn't they have had some sort of state photo ID . . . a laminated card on a lanyard? Something like that?"

The sheriff sighed. "Call them anyway."

In the day room, Lansing made a call to Las Palmas Middle/Senior High School. Halley Basa assured him Tina Morales would get his message.

Chapter Thirty

The Navajo funerial chants took longer than anyone anticipated. The procession of cars only had to travel 2 miles from the Church of Christ to the cemetery. Even so, the ceremonies didn't end until 4:00. Those traveling to New Mexico decided they should eat before hitting the road.

The Etsitty family took up half of the *Hogan Family Restaurant.* Tables were pushed together. Orders were taken and it was nearly 5:30 before food was served. Before their meals arrived, *Análí* Sarah wanted to address the gathering. Everyone fell silent when she stood.

"My sons, my daughters, my grandchildren, my great-grandchildren . . . you have filled my heart with joy. Your grandfather . . . even though he is not here . . . knows the love you have given us this day.

"I have been thinking about the ranch and if I should stay. It is my fault . . . it is your grandfather's fault . . . that none of our children wanted to follow in our footsteps.

"Life at the ranch can be hard. We wanted a better life for our sons and daughters. That's why we raised you to get good educations, learn good skills, so you could have better lives . . . so you wouldn't have to follow in our footsteps.

"Benjamin has agreed to stay and help me sell my cattle and sheep. Then I will move to Lechee to live with him and Connie . . ."

"But Momma," Rose Tallman protested. "Yesterday, I told you to come to Farmington to live with David and me. We have a spare room."

Benjamin stood. "Hold on a minute, Rose. You didn't let Momma finish. She doesn't want to be a burden on any of us. I thought we could all share . . . those who can afford to help her . . .

"After we sell the animals, she will live with me for a month . . . six weeks. Then, Rose, I'll drive her to Shiprock . . ."

"And she can stay with us," Deloris Begaye chimed in. "After that, I can bring her to Farmington."

Rose nodded. "Momma, you're all right with this?"

"I know, one day, I will be too old to care for my sheep . . . my cows. I want to know they will be taken care of. Your grandfather and I had each other. We did not get lonely.

"My Charlotte has stayed with me these last few weeks. I know she has her own children to care for . . . her own life to live. I also know when she leaves, I will be alone.

"It would bring me joy to be close to my family once again. I will not be alone. So, yes, Rose, I am all right with this."

There were smiles all around. After all the pleading and cajoling the day before, Grandmother Sarah had come to accept her new reality. After the sadness of the funeral, the Etsitty family was cloaked in the mantle of happiness once more . . . just as they had been when they gathered around the bonfire at the ranch.

It was 7:30 and dark when the group finally left the restaurant.

They said their goodbyes . . . unaware of the yellow eyes that watched them from the shadows . . . unaware of the evil that stalked them in the darkness.

Chapter Thirty-One

Tina Morales was curious about the note Halley Basa handed her after classes. She was also flattered, in a way. After no communications between her and the sheriff for five weeks, he suddenly contacted her twice in four days.

Unfortunately, the reason for the distance between them hadn't changed. She was still worried about her health. Having been independent since high school, she didn't want anyone fussing over her. Also, by moving in with Lansing, she thought she had sacrificed too much freedom. (In the back of her mind she was nagged with the question, "Freedom to do what?")

If she really did get sick and couldn't take care of herself, she would go back to Phoenix. She had family to look out for her. She didn't want to burden Lansing. He was a busy man . . . Maybe more importantly, she didn't ever want him to see her sick.

She needed to see a different gynecologist. A new doctor came highly recommended by Halley Basa. Once again, she would have to travel to Santa Fe. Unfortunately, the doctor was booked until the first of December. Morales knew she could tough it out until then. In the great scheme of things, she didn't have a choice.

Lansing was waiting for her in the parking lot behind his offices. She had insisted on not meeting him inside. He was okay with that. However, he needed to give the teacher some background information about the girl. She leaned against her car while they talked.

"She's suffered a pretty big trauma," Lansing concluded. "As of this afternoon, she still hasn't talked." He had described the circumstances of how he met Jane Doe, what the doctors said she had suffered, as well as the abduction and murder attempts.

"You know that they have psychologists for this sort of thing. Child and Family Services have people trained to handle a case like hers. Why me?"

"For starters, I'm trying to keep the girl safe. I need people I can trust and the fewer who know where she is, the better off she'll be.

"Tina, you're around teenagers all day. You know how they think. You know how to talk to them . . . plus, you're one of the smartest people I know."

The teacher blushed but said nothing.

"I thought placing Jane in a family setting would help," Lansing continued. "I know Jack and Sue have tried almost everything with her. I think even Deedee has tried. I really believe you're my last, best hope to get her to talk."

***

Tina emerged from the Rivera's spare bedroom at 7:00. She had been in the room for an hour and a half. Lansing, Jack and Sue sat at the kitchen table. The sheriff stood and looked at the teacher expectantly.

"Her name is Mariah . . . Mariah Tsosie." Tina noticed the other adults were nursing cups of coffee. "Sue, I don't suppose there's any more in the pot."

"Absolutely." Sue jumped up to grab a cup from the cabinet.

Tina sat down at the table next to Lansing's seat. He sat back down and studied her face. Her eyes were red, the lids puffy.

"You look wrung out," he said. He was tempted to put his arm around her but didn't think the gesture would be welcome.

"I am," she admitted.

Sue placed the cup with coffee in front of the teacher along with a spoon. Her husband pushed the creamer and sugar toward her.

"Thanks."

"How did you get her to talk?" Lansing asked as she fixed her coffee.

"We sat on the bed together. I spoke quietly. Explained who I was and that we all wanted the best for her. I told her, whatever she needed to do, we would help her.

"When I didn't get any reaction, I started asking her what kind of things she liked . . . if she liked school, sports, animals. I think the breakthrough came when I mentioned pets. I told her about a dog I had to leave behind when I went to college. Sundown was our Golden Retriever. He weighed as much as me. He knocked me down every time I came home, he was so happy to see me.

"She looked at me and asked, 'Is he still alive?'

"I told her no. He died a long time ago. That's when she started crying. She has a dog that she misses . . . Her Blackie greets her every day when she gets home from school.

"I put my arms around her and we both started crying. She didn't want to talk about what happened to her. She needed to talk about happier times . . . before she was hurt."

"Did she say where home was?" the sheriff asked.

"Chinle, Arizona."

"So, she's Navajo," he said thoughtfully.

"Did she say how old she was?" This time it was Sue Rivera asking.

"She was going to start ninth grade so she's fourteen or fifteen."

"Did she say what happened to her?" the sheriff pressed.

"No, and I didn't ask. I didn't want her to shut down again. Give her time. I'm sure she'll fill you in on everything when she's ready."

"Does she want to go home?"

"I'm not sure," Tina shook her head. "She never mentioned it."

Chapter Thirty-Two

The four-vehicle caravan gassed up at the Shell Station where Main Street intersected with U.S. Highway 160. The Tuuvi Travel center across the road had more pumps, but that was in the town of Moenkopi on the Hopi Reservation.

Although the two nations had lived peacefully next to each other for generations, there was still rivalry and some resentment. Several Navajo families had been removed from the Hopi Reservation by order of the federal Government. Many Diné tried not to frequent Hopi establishments whenever possible.

David Tallman, wife Rose and two grandchildren in the back seat of the F-150 crew cab led the convoy. Tallman had decided since he was driving the furthest, all the way to Farmington, he should lead. He was followed immediately by his son, Mark, Mark's wife and their other three kids in an SUV

Thomas Begaye, Sr. and wife Deloris followed in his Malibu. Thomas Begaye, Jr. and his family of 5 brought up the rear.

There were some elders of the tribe that still remembered U.S. 160 when it was a dirt and gravel track. Back then horses, mules and wagons were common, and the road was called The Navajo Trail. It was still known by that name, mostly though to amuse tourists on their way to the Four Corners. Highway 160 was the only way to get there.

The late-September night was dark. Far removed from big cities, the stars shown brightly in the cloudless sky. The moon had yet to make its appearance. In the distance could be seen the twinkle of lights from ranch houses and trailers. For a weeknight, there was little traffic.

Four miles past the rock formation known as Elephant's Feet, the highway made a more easterly turn. At that point the highway paralleled the Black Mesa and Lake Powell Railroad. The all-electric rail line served one purpose . . . to haul coal from the Peabody Kayenta Mine 78 miles to the Navajo Generating Station. The power station, 3 miles east of Page, was commissioned in 1974 and produced electricity for California, Nevada and Arizona.

The Hopi Indians began using the region's coal deposits as early as 1300 A.D. for heat and to fire their pottery. Commercial exploitation of the area was considered as early as 1900. But it wasn't until 1973 that the Peabody Coal Company opened its Black Mesa and Kayenta strip mines on Navajo/Hopi joint use lands. Used primarily to generate electricity, the profits derived from mining coal provided 80% of the Hopi Nation's operating revenue.

Coal was delivered to the railcars via a 17-mile long conveyer system. Fifty-five miles from Tuba City, the enclosed conveyer transport crossed above Highway 160 to the train round-about. Up to 90 cars were loaded at a time for the two-hour trip.

Thirty minutes after passing the Black Mesa Mine, the two extended families reached the town of Kayenta. It was at Kayenta that visitors left 160 and turned north on U.S 163 toward Utah and Monument Valley. The Tallmans and Begayes continued on 160, into the darkness.

Ten miles past Kayenta was the northern tip of Baby Rocks Mesa and the series of natural sand-stone formations that gave the mesa its name. The highway then entered into a broad, flat plain. To the right loomed Red Point Mesa. Initially two miles away, the mesa and the highway would eventually converge. To the left, a thousand feet away was the usually dry Laguna Creek.

In the darkness, very near the Ford truck, a movement caught Rose Tallman's eye. She turned her head and saw the man-beast. With the head of a coyote, but running on two legs, it kept pace with the speeding truck. If she rolled her window down, she could almost touch him.

"David!" she said, trying to control her alarm.

Tallman looked only momentarily. The creature was being lit by the headlights of his son's SUV. This portion of the road was straight with an ungraded shoulder. His first instinct was to speed up. When he did, the man-beast kept pace.

A set of headlights appeared in the distance, coming fast.

The driver swerved to the right, trying to hit his pursuer. He was unsuccessful. Turning his eyes back to the road, another creature appeared in front of him, running down the middle of the highway.

Tallman was closing on the second beast. In seconds he would hit it. Swerving to the left would put him head on into the approaching car.

Slamming on his brakes he pointed his truck to the right. The ditch was masked by the vegetation. With a jarring bounce, he tried to whip the vehicle back onto the highway. He hadn't slowed enough.

Mark Tallman watched in horror as his father's truck flipped three times, coming to rest in the center of the highway.

Chapter Thirty-Three

It was well past midnight when what was left of the Etsitty family came together. Once again, it was at the Tuba City Regional Hospital. Charlie had opted to spend the night in town. Her Uncle Benjamin was staying at the ranch. Both were upset over the return of their relatives and why.

After the accident, Thomas Begaye, Jr. turned his car around and sped back to Kayenta as he was instructed. The Navajo Police had a regional office there. Cellular coverage was spotty in the area, so mobile phones were useless. Not knowing exactly where the police station was located, Begaye stopped at the first gas station he came to in town. Once emergency services were called, he immediately headed back down the highway.

It took the tribal police less than 10 minutes to get to the site of the wreck. Two ambulances arrived a minute later. Four bodies had already been removed from the truck. David Tallman, the driver, was the only one still alive.

Mark Tallman, his wife, Elise, and three remaining children clutched each other in the darkness, trying to find solace. Their family of seven was now a family of five, plus Grandma Rose was gone.

Red flares blocked traffic coming from the east. Two more ambulances were called to help transport the bodies.

David Tallman drifted in and out of consciousness. The paramedics decided his injuries were too severe to be treated at the Kayenta Clinic. Even though Tuba City was 85 miles away, he would get better treatment at the larger facility. They departed immediately with Mark accompanying his father.

The three policemen at the scene tried to piece together what happened. No one knew why David Tallman swerved into the ditch then back onto the highway. Only he knew, and he had been in no condition to make a statement. The family could only guarantee that no alcohol was involved.

The Tallman/Begaye convoy was finally able to start its journey back to Tuba City. It was minus a Ford truck, but three ambulances joined in the procession. Thomas, Jr.'s wife, Donna, volunteered to drive Mark Tallman's car. Elise rode in an ambulance with the body of her oldest daughter. She was far too distraught to drive her own car.

Once they were back in town, the rest of the family was notified about the tragedy.

An MRI indicated David Tallman had a traumatic brain injury. There was both bleeding and swelling. A team was assembled, and emergency surgery performed to relieve the pressure. Finally, at 6:00 in the morning, the family was informed the doctors had done their best. All anyone could do now was pray.

It was 4:00 a.m. before Benjamin was able to corner Mark to ask what happened.

"I really don't know," the son admitted. "My dad's truck turned to the right and hit the ditch. I think he over corrected to the left. That's when he started flipping."

Charlie stood close by, listening to the conversation. "Was he trying to avoid something in the road?"

Tallman was quiet for a moment. "In the ambulance, he kept drifting off, then waking up again. I think he tried to tell me what happened . . . but none of it made sense."

"What did he say?" Benjamin Etsitty asked. He really wanted to know why his sister was dead.

"He said he had to turn to the right because of traffic coming down the highway. The problem with that was there wasn't any other traffic. No one was coming from the other direction. Then . . ." His voice trailed off.

"Then, what?" Charlie pressed.

"Then before he passed out, he whispered one word . . . 'Skinwalkers.' "

Chapter Thirty-Four

Park Superintendent Quijano intercepted Jackson McKee at the motor pool. It was early, not long after sunrise. The Chief Ranger and one other man were headed out of the Park, still looking for Harry Miller.

"I'm not sure how much longer we can keep this up," Quijano said. "With Harry missing, we're down one ranger. With you and John out searching, we're down two more."

"What the hell are we supposed to do?" McKee complained. "Just give up?"

The superintendent avoided the question. "Where are you going today?"

"The State Police aerial patrol picked out about three dozen spots that warranted closer scrutiny. There are still ten we haven't looked at yet . . . south of the park. I'm taking five. John's going to look at the others."

"This is our fifth day of searching. If you don't find him today, I believe it's time to bring our efforts to a close."

"Listen, boss, I have some leave days saved up," the ranger offered. "I'd like to keep looking."

"I don't think you heard me, Jackson," Quijano snapped. "I need my rangers in the park. We're going to get an influx of visitors starting tonight. You know how busy the weekends get, especially with school field trips."

"All right." McKee frowned. "What are you going to tell his wife?"

"Don't worry about Jill. I'll take care of that. But I won't say anything until after the two of you get back."

Quijano turned and got back into his car. He took his time driving the quarter mile to the Visitor Center. Since reporting to his superiors that one of his rangers was missing, both the Park Service and the Department of Interior wanted updates almost hourly. He wasn't in a hurry to resume listening to their demands.

Telling Jill Miller that he was calling off the search for her husband wasn't his biggest worry. He knew telling Washington that his people would no longer be looking for their comrade would not be well received.

Only getting his butt chewed by his bosses would be a relief. After 22 years with the service, getting demoted would not be a career enhancement. He still had 8 years to go before he could draw full retirement benefits at age 55.

He didn't relish the thought of shuffling papers at a regional office in Albuquerque or, God forbid, Anchorage, Alaska.

Chapter Thirty-Five

"Navajo Police Department, Chinle Division, how can I help you?" the female voice asked.

Lansing started making calls as soon as he reached the office. He already had the number to Navajo Police Headquarters in Window Rock on file. When he called and explained the situation, they directed him to the Chinle divisional office.

"This is Sheriff Clifford Lansing, San Phillipe County, New Mexico. Could I speak to your officer in charge?"

"That would be Lieutenant Cly. Can I ask what this is about?"

"We found a Navajo girl on the highway a few days ago. It sounds like she's from Chinle."

"Oh! I'll put you through."

"Thanks."

"Lieutenant Cly," a voice said a moment later, "how can I help you, Sheriff?"

Lansing told him about Mariah Tsosie and gave a brief summary of what she had gone through. "It took three days before we could get her to speak. I'd like to get her back to her folks."

"Mariah Tsosie went missing five weeks ago," Cly said. "From what we know, she ran away . . . a pretty abusive father."

"Yeah, she didn't say anything about wanting to go home . . . but I need to get her back to the reservation as soon as I can." He had told the police lieutenant about the attempted abduction and murder. "I don't think she's safe here."

"We'll have to find a placement for her."

"Keep her away from her father?"

"No. Mariah doesn't have a home to come back to. Three weeks ago, her father got drunk and beat his wife to death. He's sitting in federal lock-up in Phoenix, awaiting trial."

"Damn," Lansing swore under his breath. "Poor kid . . . after everything else she's been through."

"Exactly where was she picked up?"

"About fifteen miles north of Segovia on Highway two eighty-five. A couple days after she showed up, we found the body of the man we think attacked her. He was murdered."

"Mariah's not responsible for this man's death, is she?"

"No, but she was present when the man was killed."

"What did she say about it?"

"Nothing yet. She isn't ready to talk about what happened to her. But we know she was there because she was covered in the man's blood."

The two officers discussed the logistics of getting Mariah from Las Palmas to Chinle. She was currently staying with the family of his Chief Deputy. Going through Farmington, it would take 5 and a half to 6 hours to drive the distance one way. With stops, round trip would take at least 12.

"Sheriff, I think I should talk to our Child Protective Services before we take her anywhere. Mariah's gone through a lot. It may be better if professional counselors worked with her first. They would know better what kind of placement she needs."

"Okay, Lieutenant, I'll wait to hear back from you." Lansing supplied both his office and cell phone numbers. Cly assured him he would call as soon as he knew something.

***

"How's Mariah doing this morning?"

Lansing could detect Sue Rivera's sigh over the phone. "I don't know how Tina got her to talk last night, but she's still hasn't said anything to me.

"I did coax her to the kitchen table."

"That sounds like a good thing," the sheriff observed.

"Yes. It got her out of her room. But she only ate a little of her breakfast."

"Listen, Sue, I've been talking with the Navajo police. They said Mariah ran away from home about a month ago. No telling how she was able to take care of herself . . . but right now, she doesn't have a place to go to."

"What about her parents?"

Lansing explained the tragedy that had taken place. "The lieutenant I was talking to thinks Mariah is going to need serious counseling."

"I don't know anything about psychology," Sue admitted. "But I believe that girl will need some long-term care. I don't know if she'll ever recover from what she's gone through."

"Don't say anything to her until I've heard from the reservation. Especially, don't tell her about her mother."

"Don't worry about that." Sue paused. "Do you think she'll leave today?"

"I don't know," Lansing admitted. "Why?"

"She needs to clean up and I'd like to wash her clothes."

"That shouldn't hurt. I'll call you when I know anything."

As Lansing hung up his office phone, his cell phone rang. The Caller ID said "Tina." This was the first unsolicited call he'd gotten from her since mid-August. "Hello?"

"Hi, Sheriff," the teacher said. "I was calling to see how Mariah was doing."

It stung that Tina didn't address him by his first name. He said nothing about it. "She's doing a little better this morning. She ate breakfast in the kitchen."

"That's great. What did she say about yesterday afternoon?"

"Nothing. You're the only person she's talked to."

"Really?" That one word dripped with concern. "You said you were going to talk to the tribal police this morning."

"I did."

"What did they say?"

Lansing didn't feel like reciting the details of his conversation with Lt. Cly again. "I'm waiting for a call back."

"Are her parents coming to get her?"

"I don't think so. I believe the police are looking for a place where she can get professional help."

"That's probably a good idea," Morales agreed. "Do you know when she's going home?"

"Like I said, I'm waiting for a call back."

"If it's possible, I'd like to say goodbye before she leaves."

"I'll see what I can do. Should I call you back?"

"I'll be in class. It would be better if I call you."

"Fine." Lansing tried to sound pleasant. "Talk to you soon."

Chapter Thirty-Six

It was 10:00 a.m. when Charlie and Uncle Benjamin reached the ranch.

Before leaving town, the paralegal called her mother to give her an update. David Tallman had survived the surgery. The medically induced coma was to help his brain heal. His son stayed at the hospital, while the rest of the family checked back into the motel.

Connie Etsitty had stayed at the ranch to keep her mother-in-law company during the long night. She had fresh coffee waiting for her husband and niece when they arrived. Neither was hungry when she offered them breakfast.

Sitting at the kitchen table, Benjamin frowned as he sipped on his coffee. "What did you think about what Mark said?"

Charlie only shrugged. She did have an opinion, but she wanted to keep it a secret . . . at least for the moment.

"I didn't want to talk about such things at the hospital . . ." Benjamin had called his wife and told her about the discussion he had with his nephew. He looked at Connie who nodded. She had guessed at what he wanted to reveal.

"We live on the south side of Lechee . . . overlooking Honey Draw. For a month, maybe two, we have seen *chaha'oh* [shadows] come up from the canyon. They come up to the house. They scratch at the door, try the handle . . ."

"They want into our house," Connie completed.

"Do these *chaha'oh* bother your neighbors?" Charlie asked.

"We don't think so," her aunt said. "They have not mentioned them."

Charlie could guess, but she wanted her uncle to say it outright. "What do you think these shadows are?"

"I know what they are." Benjamin sounded angry. "They are *yee naaldlooshii*. In the moonlight, I saw one. I thought maybe I had done something to anger a medicine man . . . or maybe one of my children did. I do not know why they threaten us.

"Now Mark says his father saw one . . . on the highway."

Charlotte Etsitty was almost relieved at the news. She no longer had to keep the secret about the night intruders. "They have been here, too!"

The revelation shocked Benjamin and Connie. Sarah was busy at the kitchen sink. Her son asked, *"T'áásh' ákóté'?"* [Is this correct?] *Yee naaldlooshii kóoní?"* [Skinwalkers here?]

Sarah turned and nodded. *"Haoh."* [Yes]

Sarah Etsitty was upset at the news of her daughter being killed in the car accident. But with age came the acceptance of death's inevitability. Benjamin was upset at how nonchalant his mother seemed over the presence of Skinwalkers on the ranch.

Sarah came and sat at the table. "I do not know why they come. They visit you . . . They killed my Rose. There is a curse on our family. I believe this now.

"Benjamin, you are my only living son. You must speak with Billy Nez. I do not fear for myself, but I do not want any more harm done to my family. While you are here . . . while you help me sell my animals . . . promise me you will speak with him."

Her son nodded. "I will, Momma."

Charlie sat in silence. Skinwalkers were medicine men who turned to evil. In the entire Etsitty family, there was only one medicine man she knew about . . . Walter Etsitty. He and his brother, William, had disappeared three years earlier. Was there a connection? Did Walter do something wrong?

If Uncle Benjamin was going to talk with a local medicine man, Charlie made up her mind that she would find out what happened to her cousins. She had an open-ended leave of absence from work. Her daughters were in school and were being looked after by her mother.

Charlie had the time and, through her law firm, the connections to investigate what happened to Walter, William and even Jennifer.

She stood.

"Grandmother, since Benjamin and Connie are staying with you now, I am going to move my things."

"Are you going back to Phoenix?" Sarah asked.

"No, not yet. For now, I'm moving into town. I'll stay with either my mother or Emily."

It took 15 minutes for her to pack her belongings and say her good-byes. She didn't get cell phone reception until she reached Highway 160. Her first call was to the law offices of Roman and Roberto Garcia.

She told Roman about her situation . . . though she didn't mention everything. She didn't think someone outside the Navajo Reservation would understand or appreciate her worries about Skinwalkers. She claimed she was looking into the disappearance of her cousins and she needed help. Was there an investigator in northern Arizona that Roman could recommend?

He said he would look at their files. Roman was sure they had someone they used before. He would have his secretary call her with the information . . . and, by the way, the law firm would be covering all expenses. Garcia appreciated the importance of family.

Before she reached her mother's trailer, the secretary called. She had the name and number of a very reliable investigator . . . Warren Yazzie, in Window Rock. He was Navajo and he was available.

Chapter Thirty-Seven

"Where the hell have you been?" Bud Baker stormed.

"Doing what you told me to do," Evan Florin said, almost timidly. The son of chameleon Wanda Florin, he had worked for *Southwest Antiques* for 5 years. He was guided by the same lack of a moral compass as his mother. The man was big and intimidating and was only afraid of two people, Bud Baker and his mother.

Baker learned early that Evan would do anything he was told to do . . . well, almost anything. Florin never became a driver because it was a struggle for him to keep his hands off the merchandise. While he was in the compound, the boss had to constantly keep an eye on him.

However, he would willingly handle any other assignment handed him.

"I expected you back yesterday afternoon."

"My mom was busy, so I had to find someone else to follow me in my truck."

"So, where is Miguel Cuellar now?" Baker asked, referring to his former contact at Segovia Presbyterian Hospital. Cuellar was on the run after the botched murder attempt at the hospital. His plan was to go to Mexico where he had family, but he needed money. Pleading for help, Bud Baker told him to hole up at a cheap motel on the west side of town. He would make sure Cuellar was taken care of.

"At the bottom of a canyon west of Bandelier. Sort of a car accident." He saw the concerned look on his boss' face. "Don't worry. I don't think anyone will find him for a long time."

"Out of curiosity, how did he die?"

"A broken neck . . . I mean what else would you expect from a car crash?"

Baker nodded. "Just checking."

"What about the missing van?"

"Still looking," Baker said, frowning. He stubbed out his ever-present cigar and took another out of the box on his desk. "Your mother is checking with local police departments to see if those three other girls were found. Nothing so far."

"Did you report the van stolen?"

"I don't want the law to ever find one of my vans. They would ask way too many questions." He snipped off the end of the new cigar, then lit it.

"I hope whoever took it headed across the Mexican border. It's safer for us if it's down there. I can always buy a new van and there's an endless supply of young girls."

Unconsciously, Florin licked his lips at the prospect of new girls coming in. The big man's response did not go unnoticed.

"I want you to make sure those vans out there are gassed up. We have orders to fill and I expect a quick turnover this weekend." He had to light his cigar a second time. The billows of smoke drifted across the room. "This person who drove your car . . . there's no chance they'll go to the authorities, is there?"

"Naw," Evan said, swatting away the smoke as if it was a mosquito. "It was my girlfriend. No way she'd go to the police. She owes me."

Baker raised a questioning eyebrow.

"I got rid of her last boyfriend for her," Florin explained.

"You killed him?"

"No, no. She killed him. I just got rid of the body."

Baker chuckled to himself. The old adage about birds of a feather came to mind. "Sounds like a real keeper."

Chapter Thirty-Eight

It was late morning before Navajo Police Lieutenant Cly called Lansing's office. The sheriff was wrapped up in a budget meeting at the courthouse. It was noon before Lansing could return the call.

After the "hellos," Lt. Cly said, "I've talked with the DPS in Window Rock and the reservation health service. They think, because of the family situation, Mariah should be brought to the Brigham and Women's Hospital in Gallup."

"Gallup's not on the reservation, is it?"

"It may as well be, but technically, no. The hospital is part of the Gallup Indian Health Center. They have complete in-patient psychiatric care. A room will come available tomorrow. Can you transport her there?"

"We'll make arrangements," Lansing assured him.

Cly paused for a moment. "When did you say Mariah was picked up by the highway patrol?"

"Monday night."

"Our headquarters at Window Rock said three girls were dropped off in Counselor sometime early Tuesday morning. Two were from the rez. The third came from Zuni. They were all abducted at different times in the past month."

"Do you think there's a connection with Mariah?"

"I think there is."

"They must have been held somewhere, if they were picked up at different times."

"They were all interviewed, but none of them knew where they were kept. They said they were blindfolded and chained up. One said she thought they were in a warehouse. Another said it smelled like a garage. They were in separate rooms."

"Did they know why they were kidnapped?"

"Evidently, not. They were ordered to do whatever they were told . . . or else they would be killed."

"So, how did they escape Tuesday morning?"

"The four of them were loaded into a van inside the building they were kept . . ."

"Four? I thought you said there were three?"

"Only three made it to Counselor. Like I said, they were blindfolded . . . and shackled to the floor of the van. After driving for maybe an hour . . . no one was sure . . . they stopped. The back doors were opened and one of the girls was unshackled and dragged out. They heard everything because the driver left the doors open. They think the name of the girl was Mary."

Lansing thought Mary . . . Mariah. The names were close, but he said nothing.

"They could hear Mary crying, pleading with the man to stop. The man shouted at her to keep quiet. After that, they only heard her whimpering. That went on for a few minutes. Then the screaming started. She sounded terrified.

"They could hear a scuffle . . . and an animal snarling . . . a dog possibly. Mary kept crying and screaming as she ran away. They said the sound of her voice trailed off the further she ran.

"Someone slammed the doors shut, started the engine and they began driving. They said it seemed like they drove all night before they finally stopped.

"The driver opened the doors and began unlocking the handcuffs and shackles. This wasn't the same driver they started out with. The voice was deeper, gruffer. As he helped them out of the van, he warned them to keep their blindfolds on until after he drove away. He also told them to stay where he dropped them off . . . the Counselor Trading Post. Someone would be there soon."

"So, they didn't get a look at this guy?"

"It sounds like one girl might have seen him. She started to say something then got quiet. The officer I talked to said she had a terrified look on her face, then shook her head. She said it was too dark to see anything."

"You keep calling them girls . . . How old were they?"

"They were all teenagers. Two were fifteen and the other was sixteen."

"What about the van? Could they describe it?"

"It was a dark paint job. That's all they could tell as it drove off. But it did have New Mexico plates."

"A dark van with New Mexico plates . . . that should be easy to find," Lansing said sarcastically. "Any logo on the van? Any lettering?"

"They didn't say." Cly paused. "Do you think Mary and Mariah are the same girl?"

"Maybe. I've been assuming this dead man we found, de la Cruz, picked her up on the highway somewhere. He tied her hands and feet so she couldn't get away, then dragged her into the backcountry so he could rape her.

"Your story puts a whole new spin on things. It would help if Mariah said something."

"Maybe after she sees a psychiatrist," the lieutenant said.

"We can only hope," Lansing sighed. "We can only hope."

Chapter Thirty-Nine

Amanda Etsitty was not happy with her daughter's announcement. "It doesn't make any sense. You just lost an aunt . . . two of her grandchildren died . . . What do you mean you're going out of town for a few days? Your family needs you here!"

Charlie sighed. She was used to being scolded by her mother.

"Your daughters asked where you were this morning when they got up. I didn't tell them about the accident. I didn't want to upset them before school . . . Besides something like that sounds better coming from a parent."

Charlie was tired after being up all night. All she wanted to do was take a nap. Maybe telling her mother about her intentions was a bad idea.

Her mother only half-believed her stories about Skinwalkers on the ranch. Just because Uncle Benjamin said they came to his place, or that David Tallman purportedly said he saw one on the highway, didn't make them real.

Amanda argued that Grandmother Sarah was an old woman steeped in old traditions. She had just lost her husband, her daughter, Rose, and two great-grandchildren. Of course, she would think her family was cursed.

Charlie knew it wasn't that simple.

"Mom, I'm not going anywhere until after I talk to Tina and Lizbeth. I'd like to spend the night here. If I do go, it won't be until tomorrow . . . or even Monday." She would decide after she talked to Warren Yazzie.

Amanda shook her head . . . resigned to Charlotte's stubbornness . . . so much like her father.

***

Before lying down, Charlie called Warren Yazzie. She had been given two numbers, one for his office, the other his cell. She opted for the cell number.

"Yes?" was his one-word response when he answered the phone.

"Is this Warren Yazzie?"

"Who's calling?"

"This is Charlotte Etsitty . . ."

"Ah, I was expecting your call. I didn't get much from the law office. They said you wanted to look for someone."

"Actually, three people . . . cousins. Jennifer went missing five years ago. Her two brothers, Walter and William disappeared three years ago."

"Just a minute. Let me write the names down." A moment later he spoke. "Okay the names were?"

"Jennifer, Walter and William. Their last name is the same as mine, Etsitty."

The other end was quiet for a moment while he wrote. "They lived here in Window Rock?"

"Walter did, for a time, I think. The other two live in Fort Defiance."

"Are the parents still around? Can I talk to them?"

"No, they were both killed in a car accident seven years ago. The two younger ones, William and Jennifer, stayed with a foster family."

"What are their ages?"

"I'll have to think . . . Jennifer was fifteen when she disappeared, so she's twenty now. That would make William twenty-two and Walter twenty-seven."

Charlie gave Yazzie the Duncans' address and phone number, in case he needed it. She then proceeded to recite her cousins' history as best as she could remember. The investigator said little, asking her to slow down a few times so he could complete his notes.

"Is that it?" he asked when she seemed finished.

"There is one more thing. I'd like to come to Window Rock and help with your investigation."

Yazzie was quiet for a moment. "Miss Etsitty, I prefer operating alone . . . I hope you understand."

"I do understand, but there is more going on than just missing family members."

"What would that be?"

"I'll fill you in when we get together."

"Just stay home. I don't need your help."

"The law office I work for is paying you. If you don't want me to tag along, they can find me an investigator who will."

"All right, all right. When do you think you're coming?"

"Tomorrow."

"You know it's a five-hour drive from Phoenix."

"I'm in Tuba City. My sister said it takes only three-and-a-half hours to get there. I'll be on the road by eight."

"It'll be lunchtime when you get here. Have you ever been to Window Rock?"

"No."

"You'll come into town on two sixty-four. At the first light, take a left. That's route twelve. There's a Mexican restaurant, *Cosina de Dominguez*, three blocks after you make the turn. It'll be on your right. I'll plan on getting there at eleven-thirty."

"Let me give you my number, in case you need to call me."

When she was finished, she ended the call with, "I'll see you tomorrow."

Chapter Forty

"Okay, Jimmy the K, where are we now?" Ron Hutton asked.

James Kritikos stopped his Yukon in the middle of the road and pulled out the topographic map. The county roads, mostly dirt and gravel, were depicted as solid, parallel lines. The jeep trails were parallel dashed lines. There were more than a few tracks that didn't show up on a map. Those were the ones that the two petroglyph hunters were looking for.

Petroglyphs were the rock graffiti left by the pre-Pueblo ancestors that lived in northwest New Mexico. Some of the carvings were estimated to be 10,000 years old. An entire Paleoindian culture was named for the projectile points found near Clovis, New Mexico. Those were estimated to be over 13,000 years of age. The 10,000-year-old Folsom points were also found in eastern New Mexico. The state had been home to ancient humans for a long time.

Chaco Canyon, Bandelier National Monument and Puye Cliff Dwellings at Santa Clara Pueblo were the more noted remnants of the Anasazi Culture. But New Mexico had hundreds of rock carvings and ancient settlements that had not been recorded . . . even discovered yet.

Kritikos found his first unrecorded ruins in San Phillipe County five years earlier. He and his wife had turned onto the road leading to Navajo Reservoir. Across a dry wash he spotted a tree covered knoll. They had recently been to Mesa Verde in Colorado and he had become fascinated with the ancient pre-Puebloan people. On a hunch, he parked and walked across the arroyo to the hill. Scattered across the ground, between the junipers, were the remnants of stone walls and broken pottery.

A recent transplant from New York State to Albuquerque, Jimmy the K didn't flatter himself that he was the first white man to find the hidden ruins. All of the San Juan Basin was scarred by dozens of roads and pumpjacks left by oil companies over the past 75 years. He was sure some geologist or surveyor had stumbled on the remnants long before he did. They were simply not reported.

Petroglyph hunting was a far cry from his vocation as a mechanical engineer at Sandia Labs. However, he was able to combine his new interest with his other passion, photography. Federal regulations prevented amateurs like himself from disturbing such sites. But nothing prevented him from taking pictures.

He was meticulous with recording the places he visited, not only in photos but in noting exact locations on maps. The information he gathered he passed on to the New Mexico Historic Preservation Division in Santa Fe. Even though they already had records of many of his "discoveries," there were also some new ones. The division always expressed appreciation for his efforts.

He found a ready partner for his backcountry treks in Ronald Hutton, a fellow engineer. Weekends were spent exploring New Mexico. Three-day holiday weekends and a few vacations were used for trips to neighboring states. They were fortunate for having patient wives.

Taking a day off from work, this Friday morning found them in southwest San Phillipe County. Within 40 miles of Chaco Canyon, Kritikos was surprised he had never scoped out the area before. The two men stood outside of the Chevy Yukon, enjoying the bright sunlight and cloudless skies.

"My guess is we're about ten miles due north of Lindsay. We've been looking in the canyons branching to the north of Rockhouse. Why don't we look at that canyon to the south?" He pointed to a dark, ominous looking cut into the mesa. The entrance was 500 feet away.

Hutton nodded. "Looks like someone's tried to drive that way before." He gestured toward faint tire tracks.

"I think we'd better hoof it from here," Jimmy the K said, reaching into the front seat to grab his 35-mm camera.

"You got enough film?"

"I have two extra rolls in my pocket." Kritikos was a purist. Despite the growing popularity of digital photography, he preferred color film. The resolution was sharper than what pixels produced. Besides, he loved the ritual of developing his own film.

"After this canyon, how about we take a lunch break?" Ron said, reaching for his wooden hiking staff in the back seat.

"Sounds like a plan," Jimmy said. Following the tire tracks into the shadows of the canyon, they walked side-by-side

They carried on their usual banter as they stepped over the broken rocks and rubble of the arroyo floor. Three hundred-foot sheer walls towered above them. Kritikos wondered out loud if he would need to increase the length of the exposure because of the shadows.

Hutton suddenly stopped. His fellow engineer stopped as well.

"What's wrong?"

Dropping the staff in his right hand, Hutton grabbed for his chest as he dropped to his knees. He let out a "Ooff," as if the wind had been knocked out of him.

"Ron!" Kritokos shouted.

That's when he heard the distant crack of a rifle shot. The sound echoed through the canyon. His first thought was Hutton was hit by a stray hunter's bullet. But that was the point of hiking that weekend. Most hunting wouldn't start until October first.

Jimmy was turned to face his friend when a second bullet slammed into his leg. He dropped to his stomach, as much to lessen himself as a target as it was out of pain. The sound of the second shot reached them.

Kritikos didn't move.

A third bullet ricocheted off the gravel a foot from his head.

He still didn't move.

The report of the third shot came as he braced himself for a fourth bullet. There wasn't one.

"Ron," Jimmy whispered, "are you all right?"

"I'm not sure," Hutton murmured.

"Don't move," Kritikos warned.

"I don't think I could if I wanted to."

The two men laid, not moving, waiting for their assailant to finish the job. There were no more shots. No one ever appeared.

They carried on the whispered conversation, off and on, for an hour. Suddenly, Hutton fell silent.

Kritikos had to check on his friend. Daring to slither closer on his belly, he reached his fingertips for Hutton's neck. He still had a pulse.

Jimmy sat up. Using his own belt as a tourniquet, he tried to stop the bleed from the shot to his thigh. He found he could stand with the help of Ron's staff. Hutton lay unconscious. Kritikos knew they both needed medical attention.

With the wooden staff in one hand for support, he latched onto his friend's collar. He had no concept of time as he dragged his friend to the Yukon. Hutton was dead-weight as Kritikos struggled to get him into the back seat.

By the time they reached Highway 550, it was dusk. The Lindsay Trading Post was 1,000-feet to the west. A café with a single gas pump and displays of Navajo rugs and jewelry, Kritikos nearly fainted from blood loss before reaching the door.

"My God!" the Navajo woman behind the counter exclaimed. "What happened?"

She rushed forward and caught Kritikos before he fell.

"Shot," he gasped. "My friend in the car . . . He needs help."

Then he too passed out.

Chapter Forty-One

"Hello?" Deputy Redwine said when he answered his phone.

"Hi, Jake. This Cliff Lansing."

"Oh, hi, boss."

"Sorry to ruin your Friday evening, but I'm going to need your help tomorrow."

"Sure. What's going on?"

"There was a shooting . . . down in the canyons north of Lindsay. I'm taking two horses down in the morning. I need for you to ride the back county with me."

Jacob Redwine grew up on a ranch, just like Lansing. All the San Phillipe deputies knew how to ride, but Redwine was by far the best horseman.

"Anyone killed?"

"Yeah . . . some hiker."

Lansing had gotten the call from the State Police after he got home for the evening. Patrol Officer Frank La Torre talked briefly with James Kritikos before he was taken to San Juan Regional Hospital in Farmington. He and his friend, Ronald Hutton, were looking for rock carvings when they were shot. He even had a topo map and could point to the location where they were shot.

La Torre agreed to meet Lansing at the Lindsay Trading post at 9:00 a.m. It was only 80 miles from Las Palmas to the trading post by the shortest route. However, it would still be a two-hour drive . . . maybe longer pulling a horse trailer.

"Damn . . . When and where do you want to meet?"

"In front of our offices. Seven o'clock. I want you to follow me in your patrol unit. We'll need it if we make an arrest. I'm taking my truck. It handles the trailer better than my Cherokee."

"Weapons?"

"Bring your sidearm. I'll get a couple carbines and ammo from the locker. Blue jeans will be fine tomorrow. I'll have trail rations for us."

"Sounds good, Sheriff. Anything else?"

"Yeah, tell your wife I'm sorry for ruining your weekend."

"Don't worry. She knows I work strange hours. See you in the morning."

After hanging up, Lansing stared at his cell phone. He needed to make one more call.

He had planned on taking Mariah Tsosie to Gallup on Saturday. He would have preferred for Deputy Estrada to take her. The two knew each other and the Navajo girl was still terrified of men. Willie, unfortunately, had prior commitments.

Lansing was unsure of how Mariah would react to being alone with him. It was a 5-hour drive one way. It would have been much more convenient for the Navajo Police to retrieve the girl, but he had already made the offer to transport her.

Depending on how late they got started, he had decided it might be wise to make it a two-day trip. That was out the window now.

He found the stored number on his phone and pressed the green "dial" button. The phone at the other end rang 3 times before it was answered.

"Yes?"

"This is Cliff. Sorry to bother you so late, Tina, but I have a problem. I was wondering if you could help."

Chapter Forty-Two

Charlotte Etsitty sat cross-legged on the end of her old bed . . . Tina and Lizbeth at the head. The younger of the two cuddled a pillow to her chest.

The girls anticipated bad news, because of how serious their mother seemed when she said, "We need to talk." After school, they knew something was wrong when she refused to tell them where she was the night before.

"There was an accident last night," Charlie began. "A car accident. Your Great-aunt Rose was killed." The girls said nothing, fighting off tears. "Rene and Terry also died."

The two Tallman cousins were older than the Etsitty girls, so they had little interaction with each other. But the thought of someone dying who you saw just the day before was overwhelming. Tears streamed down both their faces.

"Why did they have to die?" Lizbeth asked, struggling with the loss.

Charlie shook her head. Leave it to a child to ask a simple question that even the most learned adult couldn't answer.

"Where did they get killed?" Tina's question was direct, easy to answer.

"About seventy-five miles east of here," their mother explained. "They brought the bodies back here. In fact, everybody who left for New Mexico last night came back to town."

"Why?" Lizbeth asked again. "Are they going to have another funeral?"

"Probably, but I doubt if it will be here."

"Then why did they come back here?"

"Your Great-uncle David is in the hospital. He had to have surgery early this morning. That's where I was all last night."

Both girls walked on their knees, across the bed, so they could hug and be hugged by their mother. Charlie wasn't sure how long they comforted each other. When the sobbing almost stopped, she sprung her second announcement on them.

"Tina, Lizbeth, I have to go away for a few days."

Tina pulled back. "Where are you going?"

"To Window Rock. It's the Dinétah capitol."

Both girls had been attending beginner Navajo language classes. One of the first words they learned was Diné. That's what the Navajo called themselves. The Diné homeland was Dinétah and not the Navajo Reservation, though the terms were interchangeable.

"How far away is Window Rock?"

"Somewhere around two hundred miles east of here."

"Can we come?" Lizbeth begged. "Please!"

"I wish you could . . . but you've already missed enough school. I may not be back by Monday."

"Why are you going?" Tina demanded, not very nicely.

Charlotte Etsitty's oldest was nearly thirteen. She remembered her own rebellious teens and hoped (unrealistically) that her daughters would skip that phase.

Very patiently, Charlie told her daughters about the cousins she had when she grew up. They were special to her and she wanted to find out what happened to them. They were orphans now and the two youngest had to finish growing up without their parents.

"Do you blame me for wanting to know why they disappeared?"

"I guess not," Lizbeth admitted. "When are you going?"

"First thing in the morning, honey."

"When are we going back to Phoenix?" Tina snapped.

"I don't know. For now, let's take it one day at a time."

"That's what you said when we moved here!" the oldest stormed, jumping off the bed. "I hate Tuba City. I hate my school. I want to go home!" She stomped out of the room.

The rest of the evening, Tina gave her mother the silent treatment. When Lizbeth tried to placate her, she got the cold shoulder, as well.

Charlie accepted the fact that her daughter was angry. It would either fester or Tina would get over it. For the moment, she tried to not let it bother her, though she knew it would.

There were other things Charlie needed to do. She hoped one day her daughters would understand.

Chapter Forty-Three

New Mexico-122 wasn't the best kept road in San Phillipe County. It was asphalt from Highway 15 to El Vaccaro Dam. The next 20 miles were graded gravel, the first 10 on the Jicarilla Apache Reservation, before reverting to pavement again. Even so, the 62 miles from Las Palmas to U.S. 550 took an hour and a half. It was another 30 miles, through Counselor in Sandoval County, to Lindsay in southwest San Phillipe.

This wasn't unfamiliar territory for Lansing. Two years earlier he uncovered a carved Jade figurine beneath his burned ranch house. That discovery unleashed a Mayan terror across the entire county. The final confrontation took place in one of the deep canyons that straddled the San Juan/San Phillipe County boundary.

He hadn't thought about that encounter for a long time. The memory of that dark canyon was a far cry from the sunny, cloudless morning he enjoyed now.

He put on his blinker. Once the traffic passed, he turned into the paved parking lot of the Lindsay Trading Post/Café. Jake Redwine parked next to him. The two men decided to wait in the restaurant for State Patrolman La Torre.

The café had three small tables along the wall, with three bigger tables that would accommodate more than two customers. They took the larger choice.

"That dirt road portion of Route one twenty-two looks like it can get dicey," the deputy observed as the waitress filled their cups.

Lansing nodded. "If it had been snowing or raining, we would have to take the long way. That would add another hour and a half to the drive."

The sheriff had just taken his first sip as La Torre entered. Lansing stood and extended his hand as the State Policeman approached. "Cliff Lansing."

"Frank La Torre," the officer replied.

Lansing rarely met a fellow officer who didn't have a firm handshake. La Torre was no exception. "Have a seat."

All of San Phillipe County was in District 7 of the State Police. The town of Lindsay sat at the juncture of Districts 1, 7 and 10. When the State Police dispatcher got the call about the shooting, La Torre in District 10 out of Farmington was the nearest officer to the scene.

He responded to the initial call, but it would be the sheriff's responsibility to follow up with the investigation.

"Any word about the man who survived?" the sheriff asked.

"Yeah. He was lucky." La Torre signaled to the waitress for a cup of coffee. "The bullet went completely through his thigh and managed to miss any major arteries. I called the hospital this morning. The guy's awake and wants to go home."

"Where's home?"

"Albuquerque. He works at Sandia Labs. So did the man who got killed."

"Did he tell you what happened?"

La Torre produced a map from his rear pocket. As he unfolded it, the white, topographical chart appeared to be smeared with blood. He spread the map on the table.

"Here's Lindsay." He pointed at a small cluster of squared dots next to a solid, red line. "This is Highway five fifty . . . The map grid is laid out in one-mile squares."

He pointed to the western end of a long valley labelled Rockhouse Canyon. "Mr. Kritikos, the man in the hospital, said they were parked about here. They were getting ready to walk into this small canyon running to the southwest when someone started shooting."

"Did they see the shooter?"

"No, but from the description of his wound, the bullet was on a downward trajectory. My guess is the shooter was on the canyon rim."

"How far is that from here?"

La Torre spanned his fingers from Lindsay to the shooter's canyon, then compared the distance to the grid. "As the crow flies, seven miles."

"Yeah, but driving distance, what are we looking at?" Redwine asked.

"I don't have a clue," La Torre admitted.

"How high are those canyon walls?" Lansing leaned forward for a closer look, then answered his own question. "Looks like they're up to three hundred feet on either side . . ."

"Plus, the contour lines are close together," the patrolman observed. "That means they're going to be steep."

Lansing leaned back in his seat. "Before we leave here, we need to decide if we're going to the rim first or the canyon floor."

"I can understand going to the rim," his deputy said. "We're looking for the shooter . . . or at least his perch. But why do we need to go into the canyon?"

"To find out why two men were shot. There is something in that canyon they weren't supposed to see."

La Torre nodded at Lansing's evaluation.

"We could split up."

"No." The sheriff shook his head. "We stay together, just in case one of us gets in trouble."

"Do you think your shooter will still be there?" La Torre asked.

"No. But we won't know for sure until we take a look."

Chapter Forty-Four

Tina wasn't sure why it took Mariah so long to get ready. She only owned the clothes she was wearing, so she had nothing to pack. The teacher guessed the girl's procrastination wasn't that she didn't want to leave. Rather, she was reluctant to return home . . . not knowing she had no home to go to.

***

Over the phone, Lansing provided Tina with all of Mariah's history that he knew.

"How much about her parents should I tell her?" she asked.

"You'll have five hours alone with her tomorrow," the sheriff offered. "You're the only one she's spoken to . . . and you're the expert on teens. I'd say try to get her to talk some more, feel her out. If you think she can handle it, tell her."

"If it was up to me, I'd let the hospital staff spring the news."

"Speaking of springing things, I need to tell her we're going to Gallup, not Chinle. How am I going to explain that?"

"Tell her the truth. People are worried about her. Everyone knows she went through something terrible . . . but she needs to talk about what happened. The doctors and nurses at the hospital only want what's best for her."

"I'm honestly glad you asked me to help," she sighed. "But I think you're putting more faith in me than I deserve."

"I don't."

***

Mariah's "thank you" at the front door was little more than her lips moving as she stared at the floor.

Both Jack and Sue were used to her silence, so they weren't upset. Sue attempted a quick hug, but the response was stiff. Jack kept his distance.

Mariah let Deedee hold her hand as they walked to the car. The Navajo girl even gave her small friend the hint of a smile as she got in.

Driving out of Las Palmas, Tina didn't press her companion to talk. There was plenty of time for that. Instead, she ruminated about the differences between Arizona and New Mexico, Phoenix and Albuquerque.

What prompted the comparison was the raggedy yards in Las Palmas. For the most part, no private homeowner in either state had a lawn. Water was too precious. But the homes that she remembered in Phoenix at least made an attempt at landscaping . . . raked gravel with Saguaro cacti or Palo Verde trees.

Many of the houses in Las Palmas looked abandoned because of the waist-high weeds in the yards. A car or truck parked in the driveway reassured a passerby that someone lived there.

What impressed Tina most when she attended the University of New Mexico was how green the campus was. The Rio Grande was less than two miles away and always had water. The other factor that attracted her to Albuquerque was the city's population was $1/10^{th}$ of the Phoenix metropolitan area. It didn't feel so crowded.

"That's where I teach," Tina said as they passed in front of the Las Palmas Middle/High.

Mariah looked, but said nothing.

A half-mile past the school, they intercepted State Route 122. Tina turned left, toward El Vaccaro Lake and the town of Cuba. In the past two years, she had used the road twice. She would follow Route 122 to Highway 550, 550 to I-25 north of Albuquerque, I-25 to I-40, then west to Gallup and, eventually, Flagstaff. Phoenix was an hour and a half from there.

It was 10 miles longer going from Las Palmas to Albuquerque via Santa Fe, but it was faster with better roads.

Looking at the map the night before, Tina realized she could take NM 197 west from Cuba to Crownpoint. It was a short hop from there to the interstate. The new route would shave 70 miles from the trip. She reasoned that it had to be an hour faster.

After crossing El Vaccaro Dam, the pavement ended. The drive on the dirt and gravel road was picturesque but slow. Any speed over 30 miles per hour shook Tina's Chevy Cavalier mercilessly and shot small rocks into the car's undercarriage. Even at 30 mph the ride was noisy. After 10 miles they exited the Jicarilla reservation, into the Santa Fe National Forest.

The last five miles of forest road was paved. The ride became quieter and Tina was finally able to talk to her passenger.

"You doing all right, Mariah?"

The girl looked at her, pursed her lips and nodded.

"Do you feel like talking?"

Mariah gave a noncommittal shrug.

Tina watched the road ahead. "If you're nodding your head, I can't hear it. You're going to have to speak up."

"Yeah . . . We can talk."

Chapter Forty-Five

A quarter mile west of the Lindsay Trading post, Lansing turned onto a gravel, county road that headed north into canyon country. Jake Redwine had joined him in the truck. On the map, the canyon they wanted was 7 miles almost due north. The road they took had to wind its way to the top of the mesa, in spots, higher than 500 feet above the surrounding plain.

According to the topo map they got from La Torre, the canyon rim was still a mile and a half away when he finally parked the truck and trailer. It took over half an hour to drive 10 miles.

Lansing wished they'd gotten an earlier start. By the time his horses, Cement Head and Paladin, were saddled, it was 10:30. The horses had been cooped up in the trailer for over three hours. They seemed grateful for their new freedom.

"Looks like it's getting ready to rain." Redwine pointed to dark clouds building to the southwest of their position.

New Mexico's "monsoon" season lasted from the middle of June until the end of September. The northwest corner of the state, specifically San Juan County, saw no more than an inch of rain annually. Western San Phillipe County fared little better, though the southern and eastern portions saw much more precipitation, if one considered 4 inches a lot. At 15 inches, the Santa Fe National Forest attracted the most annual rain in the county.

"I wouldn't worry about it. I don't think it'll get close."

The mesa was 100 feet higher than the canyon rim. The two riders needed to find a safe place for a descent.

"Jake, let's split up. Look to the right. I'll go left."

Lansing carefully guided his horse to the mesa edge, looking for a gentle, downward route. Cement Head snorted his concern at the sheer drop in front of them.

After ten minutes of searching, Redwine shouted, "Sheriff! Over here!"

Lansing put his horse into a trot and quickly joined his deputy.

"Yeah, that looks good," the sheriff agreed, leaning from his saddle for a better look.

"You want me to take the lead?"

"It's up to you. How sure are you on that horse?"

"Paladin and I get along fine. We've been together before."

The spot Redwine found was not steep at all. It had to be a location where they could not only descend but climb back to the top of the mesa as well.

The riders descended 100 feet to reach the next plateau. The southwestern end of the canyon was a half mile west. From that vantage point, the canyon floor was 250 feet below them. An animal trail traced a path through the sparse trees, along the norther rim. They followed it, descending another 150 feet.

The lawmen stopped at the end of the ridge, one hundred feet above the broad canyon of Rockhouse Canyon. Below them was a jeep track that stopped at the mouth of the smaller canyon.

Lansing pointed. "That must be where Kritikos parked. My guess is the shooter must have been right around here." He gestured to the ground immediately beneath them.

He dismounted and held Cement Head's reins while he searched. Redwine followed suit.

"Probably a hunting rifle," the deputy observed after finding the first shell casing. He picked it up using a small stick, avoiding any contamination.

Lansing grabbed a zip-lock from Cement Head's saddle bag. He studied the shell after Jake handed it to him, then nodded in agreement. "Winchester two forty-three. Let's see if there are any more around here."

Eventually they found an additional two.

"I don't see any tracks. Do you?"

Jake shook his head.

"What do we do now?" Redwine asked, climbing back into his saddle.

Lansing swung himself into his own saddle. He first looked in the direction they came from, then toward the canyon below.

"It took us at least thirty minutes to get here. It will take us at least that long to get back to the truck. I want to see what's in that canyon that's so important, but it will take us another hour to drive around.

"Looks like the deer trail continues into the canyon. Let's follow it down. I'll wager we'll save ourselves at least a couple of hours."

"The shooter might be down there."

"I hope he is . . . That'll save us a whole lotta looking." Lansing took the lead.

"You realize we could get shot," Redwine said, pointing out the obvious as he fell in behind his boss.

"Wouldn't be the first time."

Chapter Forty-Six

"Do you have a lot of friends back home?" Tina remembered their first encounter two nights earlier. Mariah opened up when Tina got her to talk about things other than her recent trauma.

"A few . . . mostly from school."

"Is it a small school, like mine?"

"Oh, no. It's bigger."

"Las Palmas has two hundred students, but that's both Middle and High School."

"Chinle High is ninth through twelfth grade and we have over a thousand students." There was a hint of pride in her statement.

"I've never been to Chinle. It must be pretty big with all those students."

"Not really. Some of the kids have to ride a bus for over an hour to get to school. Probably half the school comes by bus."

"Do you?"

"No, I walk."

Tina paused. She wasn't sure how far she should push the questions. "What does your dad do?"

"My father's dead," Mariah snapped.

Tina was truly surprised at the answer. "But I thought . . ."

"I live with my mom and her husband." The Navajo girl was getting angry.

"You don't like him?"

"He's a drunk."

"Is he the reason you ran away?"

"I didn't run away," the girl choked. Tears started streaming down her face. "They took me!"

Tina pulled her car to the side of the road and stopped. The revelation deserved all her attention. "Who took you?"

"The men . . . on the road." She started sobbing uncontrollably.

The teacher realized her young companion was finally releasing a lot of pent up emotion. The center console of her two-door coupe prevented her from wrapping her arms around the girl. Tina released her seatbelt, then reached behind her for a tissue box. She quickly pulled out three tissues and handed them to Mariah.

The teenager nodded, grateful for the gift, then blew her nose.

After a few moments, once the sobbing subsided, Tina turned off her engine and opened her door. "Why don't we get out and walk around?"

She stepped to the passenger door and opened it. Mariah hesitated, then got out. Grazing pasture lined either side of the highway. The fence lines were 20 feet from the road, so the two would not be crowded by the sparse traffic as it passed.

Tina dared to put her arm around Mariah's shoulder. The girl didn't resist the comforting touch. They walked in silence for five minutes before Tina finally asked. "What can you tell me about those men?"

After a deep breath Mariah began talking.

"I had gone to the filling station to get a coke. I was walking home when an RV pulled up. I thought they were going to ask direction to the Canyon."

"Canyon?"

"Canyon de Chelly . . . We get a lot of tourists . . . Anyway, they stopped and before I knew what was happening, a man jumped out and grabbed me. I started screaming and tried to get away.

"He dragged me into the RV." She started trembling. Tina held her tighter.

"They put tape over my mouth . . . wrapped it around my wrists and ankles . . ."

"These men . . . what did they look like?"

"I thought the man who grabbed me was Navajo. The man that helped him, the driver . . . I think he was Mexican. He had an accent. But I didn't get a real good look, because after they tied me up, they blindfolded me."

"Did they do anything to you?" the teacher asked, careful not to upset her any more than she was.

"No. They threw me on a bed in the back of the RV. I thought they were going to rape me . . . but they didn't."

"What did happen?"

"We just drove . . . for a long time. They pulled over . . . three times, I think. I know they picked up someone else . . . another girl. I heard her screaming when they put her in the RV. It sounded like they hit her to keep her quiet.

"I don't know where we finally stopped. It was at night. They cut the tape off my ankles so I could walk, but I could barely stand. They dragged me into a building and shoved me into a little room. They cut off the tape and made me wear a shackle on my ankle. I was chained to the floor. Then they shut and locked the door."

"What was the room like?"

"The walls didn't go up to the ceiling. They were open on top, like fitting rooms. And it was noisy. It sounded like we were in a warehouse."

"We?"

"There were other girls there. I don't know how many, though."

"How long were you there before you got away?"

"It was the fifteenth of August when they took me."

"Today's September twenty-fifth. You must have been there for five weeks." She stopped and looked back at the car. They had walked half a mile.

"Are you ready to start driving again?"

Mariah nodded.

Chapter Forty-Seven

As Charlotte Etsitty drove out of Tuba City, she couldn't help but think how intertwined the Navajo and Hopi cultures had become. Tuba City, itself, was named after Tuuvi, a Hopi Indian who, after his conversion, illegally invited white, Morman settlers to the area in the 1870s.

The Hopi had been in the immediate vicinity for over 700 years, drawn there by the numerous natural springs. Moenkopi village and the associated "wash" were part of the Hopi Reservation. After 10 miles, Highway 264 crossed back into Navajo territory, then reverted to Hopi lands again 8 miles later. All of the 2,500 square-mile Hopi reserve was surrounded by the Navajo Reservation.

Taking State Highway 264, it was 157 miles from Tuba City to the Diné capitol of Window Rock. Half of the drive was on the Hopi Reservation.

The debate raged inside her about remaining on the reservation with her daughters or returning to Phoenix. The one thing she knew for sure was that she could never leave Arizona. There were too many hidden gems she had yet to explore.

Arizona had bragging rights for spectacular features such as the Grand Canyon, Sedona, and the Superstition Mountains. However, much of the state was comprised of flat, featureless, desert scrub lands. Even those were deceptive, though.

Thirty miles east of Flagstaff and 8 miles south of Interstate 40, what appears to be a hill from a distance was, in reality, the rim of Meteor Crater.

A half-mile from Highway 264, 20 miles east of Tuba City, was the 400-foot deep Coalmine Canyon. The series of steep cliff and sandstone columns called hoodoos covered 40 square miles. The runoff from the rare rains flow past Tuba City, eventually reaching the Little Colorado River at Cameron. Looking north from the road, however, the flat landscape seemed to stretch for miles.

These were the hidden sites that always intrigued and beckoned to her.

The heart of the Hopi Reservation was three mesas. Traveling east, Third Mesa came first. Jutting 400 feet above the surrounding plain, it was visible from 8 miles away after passing Howell Mesa. Deceptively, the winding highway brought you to the mesa top before you knew it. The flat countryside was visible for miles.

The descent on the east side of the mesa was more impressive. Cut into the side of the rock face, 264 wound its way to the flood plain of Oraibi Wash and Kykotsmovi Village. Three miles past the wash, the highway climbed to the top of Second Mesa.

Charlie drove past the Hopi Cultural Center and Museum, a roadside souvenir stand, and dozens of isolated homes. She could occasionally catch glimpses of the desert prairie stretching to the horizon. The descent was even more dramatic than the one from Third Mesa.

This was Charlie's first excursion across Hopi lands. She could understand why their people occupied the mesas. They must have been easy to defend, and enemies could be seen approaching from miles away.

First Mesa towered above her and the road as she continued east. It was another 45 miles further down the highway before she reached Navajo territory. At the town of Ganado, she stopped at *Mora's Gas and Grocery* for a cup of coffee and the chance to relieve herself.

"How far is it to Window Rock?" Charlie asked the clerk when she paid for her drink.

"Thirty miles," the girl behind the counter said, smiling.

"Oh, so half an hour from here?"

"Closer to forty-five minutes . . . Where you coming from?"

"Tuba City."

"Well, then, you're almost there."

There was a subtle change to the surrounding countryside. The road gradually ascended to higher terrain. As it did, scrub grass was replaced by more and more juniper trees. Soon, the junipers gave way to tall pines. Three miles short of Window Rock the pines surrendered once again to sparse junipers and dry desert.

When Charlie reached the first traffic light in Window Rock, she turned left.

It was exactly 11:30 when she parked in front of *Cocina De Dominguez.*

Chapter Forty-Eight

If Lansing had studied the topo map contours more closely, he would have found the floor of Rockhouse Canyon was only 150 feet below the end of the ridge line. Even so, the descent stretched out to a third of a mile. Getting back to the top would be tough on the horses, but not impossible.

The spot where Kritikos parked was 1,000 feet to the south. They crossed a dry creek bed where water flowed intermittently. Lansing dismounted again and studied the ground. He could see where the Sandia Labs engineer had dragged his friend.

He led Cement Head by the reins, following the faint trail, finally reaching the spot where the men fell. The parched ground was stained with human blood. Redwine had followed, still seated on his horse.

Both men looked to the canyon rim. There was no expectation that the shooter had returned. Still, there was the nagging thought that he might have.

Lansing climbed back on his saddle and pointed the horse to the far end of the canyon. The fissure was engulfed in shadows even though it was near noon. The far end of the box canyon was a half mile from the entrance. As the walls closed in, they became nearly vertical.

"What do you think is in here?" the deputy asked.

"I don't have a clue," Lansing admitted. "We'll see soon enough."

They followed what appeared to be faint tire tracks as the canyon bed ascended 60 feet from the mouth. They didn't discover what they were looking for until their quarry was 30 feet in front of them.

"Are those camouflage tarps?" Redwine asked as he dismounted.

"I believe so," his boss agreed, dismounting as well.

Lansing handed his reins to his deputy, then walked up to the first tarp and pulled. He had to step backward as he dragged the heavy, green and brown splotched canvas mesh from whatever it concealed.

A moment later, the lawmen were staring at a dark blue, paneled van. The commercial plates identified it as being registered in New Mexico. Lansing walked toward the front of the vehicle. Big, golden letters along the side read *Southwest Antiques*. Commercial vans and trucks usually advertised where they hailed from. The van was silent on that subject.

Opening the driver's door, he discovered the keys were in the ignition.

"Sheriff, you'd better come look at this."

The deputy had opened the rear double doors. When Lansing looked inside, he found metal benches facing each other along the walls, bolted to the floor. Also bolted to the floor were steel loops. Of the eight loops, four had metal chains threaded through them. The chains had shackles attached. Also strewn on the floor were four sets of handcuffs.

The set up reminded Lansing of a prisoner transport . . . the kind used by police. The van, obviously, did not belong to a police department.

"What do you think?"

"Human trafficking." Lansing was 100% sure of his conclusion. "I told you about my conversation with the Navajo police . . . the three girls that were dropped off in Counselor Tuesday morning."

"Yeah."

"I think we found the van they rode in."

"Damn."

Pulling away the tarp covering the vehicle parked next to the van, the two men were again shocked by the discovery. They were staring at a white, national park service, pickup truck. Not surprisingly, the keys were inside.

Lansing looked at his deputy. "Didn't we get a BOLO out of San Juan about a missing ranger from Chaco Canyon?"

"Yeah, I think we did . . . Monday."

"Wrap the reins around that bumper. Let's see what else is hiding here."

Two more vehicles were found in front of the truck and van. One was an old, beat up Ford F-150 from Arizona. The other was a rusty, Chevy coupe from the seventies, New Mexico plates.

"Check the glove compartments for registrations. Maybe we can figure out what's going on here."

Chapter Forty-Nine

The sign above the two windows facing the parking lot read *Cocina De Dominguez Mexican and American Family Restaurant*. As Charlie walked in the front door, a Navajo girl in her early 20s greeted her, as did wonderful aromas from the kitchen,

"Welcome to Cocina De Dominguez. I'm Tara. Would you like to be seated?"

"Actually, I'm meeting someone here," Charlie said, looking over the hostess' shoulder.

The L-shaped interior had windows on 3 walls along one extension. The other seating area was illuminated by ceiling lights. A man seated at a table on the windowed side stood and waved at her.

"I think that's him."

"Oh, you're meeting Warren?"

"You know him?"

"Everyone in Window Rock knows Warren Yazzie." Tara smiled and led her guest to Yazzie's table.

"Charlotte Etsitty?" Yazzie asked.

"Yes." Charlotte extended her hand.

The investigator shook hands with the new arrival, then pulled out a chair. "Please, sit."

"Thanks."

As they sat, Tara handed Charlie a menu and asked, "Can your waitress get you something to drink?"

"Unsweetened iced tea, please." She turned to her companion. "I didn't know you were famous, Mr. Yazzie."

"What do you mean?"

"The hostess said everyone in Window Rock knows you."

"There's a fine line between famous and infamous." Yazzie neither smiled nor frowned at his own remark. "And you can call me Warren."

"All right . . . Warren. Please call me Charlie."

Yazzie nodded, seemingly uninterested in how a woman came to be called by a man's name.

Charlie was trying to get a read on the man. The first thing she noticed was his large hands and his height. He was tall. Probably 6 foot. His hair was close cropped, not long as in the style of many Navajo men. He didn't look like he had missed many meals, but he wasn't fat either. She guessed he was in his 40s.

His black cattleman's hat rested on the corner of the table. The brim was flat. It had an Indian-bead band around the crown. He wore a cream colored, long-sleeve shirt with a braided leather, bolo tie. The slide was intricately crafted silver with a turquoise stone in the center. A tan, fringed leather coat hung on the back of his chair. He came across as ALL Navajo.

"You did a good job of getting here on time," Yazzie observed. He took a sip of coffee.

"Are you surprised?"

Yazzie shrugged noncommittally. "I did some digging this morning." He pushed a manila envelope toward her. "Your three cousins were well known by the police . . . for a while, anyway."

"What does that mean . . . for a while?" she asked, picking up the envelope and removing the contents.

"The brothers were a pain in the butt for two years after their sister disappeared," he said. "Then they quit being a pain in the butt."

Charlie did a scan of the photocopied paperwork. There was a "missing person's" report regarding a fifteen-year-old Jennifer Etsitty. There were 8 different "incident reports" involving either Walter, William, or both. They involved confrontations with Navajo police or private citizens from Window Rock, Shiprock and as far west as Page, Arizona.

"Those are just the complaints on the rez the police in Window Rock know about. There could be more."

"These are all dated from ninety-five and ninety-six."

"Yeah," Yazzie said. "No one's heard from either one in three years."

Charlie nodded, slipping the papers back into the envelope. "That's what the Duncans told my sister."

Their waitress returned with the tea. "I'm your server, Kitty. Have you decided what you'd like?"

Charlie looked at Yazzie. "What would you recommend?"

"I'm partial to the chicken enchiladas."

"I'll take the chicken enchiladas then." She handed Kitty her menu.

Yazzie held up two fingers, indicating he wanted the same.

Chapter Fifty

Warren Yazzie had no problem finishing his 3 enchiladas and most of the refried beans and rice. Charlie was full after one and a half enchiladas. She didn't bother with the sides. She tore off small pieces of her fry bread and used them to sop up enchilada sauce.

"Why am I doing this investigation?" Yazzie finally asked after the nearly silent meal.

"What do you mean?"

"Your cousins all disappeared three years ago. Why are you looking for them now?"

"Do I need a reason?"

"I'm curious why you weren't interested in finding them when they went missing."

Charlie leaned back in her chair, thinking. She was honestly ashamed. Three years ago, she was working full time and raising 2 daughters on her own. She was too busy to worry about cousins she hadn't seen in 10 years.

"I've lived in Phoenix for the past seven years . . . in fact, I grew up in Phoenix."

Yazzie appeared to study her while she talked but said nothing. His silence told her she needed to continue.

"Of course, growing up we would visit relatives in Tuba City, but I never felt being Navajo was important. We had to move to the reservation after my father died . . . my senior year. But I was always treated like an outsider . . . and it didn't help that I was raped."

"When was this?"

"Half-way through twelfth grade."

"Did you keep it?"

"The baby?" she asked, shaken by the question. "Of course, I kept her . . . she's twelve now. I love her and her sister with all my heart. They're the reason I get up every day."

"You still haven't answered my question."

"My grandfather was diagnosed with cancer this past summer. I took an extended leave of absence from the law firm so I could help my grandmother on the ranch. I brought my daughters and enrolled them in school.

"He passed away on Tuesday . . ."

"Sorry to hear that."

Charlie nodded, then continued. "In the last five weeks, family has become important to me . . . and I don't just mean my daughters. I've been giving serious thought to staying in Tuba City permanently."

Yazzie still said nothing.

"Thursday night, after we buried my grandfather, there was a car accident. My aunt and two of her grandchildren were killed."

"Your cousins?"

"I guess you'd call them second cousins . . . but they were just kids."

"So, you're thinking by looking for long lost cousins, you'll help your family heal?"

"No, that's not it at all." Charlie hesitated, not sure how her next statements would be received. "The Etsitty family is cursed. My grandmother believes it. My uncle believes it, and I believe it."

"Cursed?" the private investigator sounded doubtful.

Charlie calmly explained the nightly visitations on her grandparents' ranch by the *yee naaldlooshii*. Her Uncle Benjamin was being bothered by Skinwalkers in Lechee. They now suspected the accident two nights earlier was caused by one, maybe two Skinwalkers on the highway.

"How does this all tie into missing cousins?"

"Woman's intuition . . ." Charlie supplied a weak smile. "I think cops call it a gut feeling. But ever since my sister, Emily, told me about my cousins, I knew something was wrong.

"Their parents were killed in a car accident seven years ago. No one ever came up with a plausible explanation on how the crash happened."

Yazzie raised a questioning eyebrow.

"It was a cloudless night. No bad weather. Evidently no other traffic on the highway. They were driving back from Gallup. My uncle somehow crossed the median, missed a guardrail, and flipped over in a dry arroyo. No one found them till the next morning."

Her companion reached into his coat and pulled out a notepad and pen.

"What were their names?"

"Isaac and Julia Etsitty."

"And this was in ninety-two?"

"Ninety-three."

"What did your uncle do for a living?"

"He worked for the Navajo Historic Preservation Department."

Yazzie frowned at the news. "Your cousins, were they still in school?"

"William was in high school. Walter was in his twenties. He was apprenticing to become a medicine man." Charlie could see Yazzie seemed disturbed over her story. "Warren, you don't think I'm crazy, do you?"

"No, Miss Etsitty, I don't." He signaled for Kitty to bring their ticket.

Chapter Fifty-One

The jeep track where the truck and trailer were parked left little maneuvering room. Cement Head and Paladin weren't loaded into the trailer until Lansing managed to turn it around.

Once the horses were situated and the lawmen were back in the truck, Lansing had his deputy retrieve road maps from the glove compartment.

"According to the Chevy's registration, this Joe Hernandez was from Red Valley, Arizona. How far is that from here?"

Jake had to find the map's legend to figure the distance. "It's a hundred miles, but that's going in a straight line. To get there by road you have to pass through Farmington. I'd say driving distance would be closer to one hundred and fifty miles. Maybe further."

"How about White Horse? That's where Keyanna's truck is from."

The deputy studied the map. "That's fifty miles south of us."

"Counselor is about twelve," Lansing said, thinking out loud. "Santa Fe is what, a hundred and fifty miles from here?" Santa Fe was where the van operated out of.

"At least."

"And Ojo Caliente has to be over a hundred miles east of here."

"Ojo Caliente?"

"That's close to where the State Police picked up Mariah Tsosie."

"How do you figure she's related to all this?"

"There were four sets of handcuffs and shackles in the back of that van. Three girls were dropped off in Counselor Tuesday morning. Dollars to doughnuts, that's the van that brought them there . . . so, where's the fourth girl?"

"That would be Mariah? Is that what you're saying?"

"It's just a guess . . . but it makes sense. She was found the night before. The van back there had commercial plates. The DB we found, De La Cruz . . . he had a CDL. He might have been driving that van."

Lansing connected two more dots. Juan Pedro Garcia's truck was found near De La Cruz's body. Garcia also had a commercial driver's license. The men must have known each other. What was more, they both probably drove for *Southwest Antiques*.

His self-satisfaction over putting together a larger picture was short lived. If everything going on only happened in San Phillipe County, he was confident his office could handle it. However, he realized other departments had to get involved.

Southwest Antiques operated out of Santa Fe County. The three Native American girls were dropped off in Sandoval County. White Horse was in McKinley. Chaco Canyon was in San Juan. Red Valley was in Arizona on the Navajo Reservation.

The New Mexico State Police needed to be consulted. They may even want to take over the investigation. He shuddered at the thought of the Special Investigations Division getting involved. At the very least, they were heavy-handed and bullies to other law enforcement agencies. At the most, they were incompetent.

Then there were the Feds. The FBI had jurisdiction over major crimes on the Navajo Reservation. Child abduction would definitely qualify as a major crime. Kidnapping and transporting the victims across state lines would interest them, as well.

There was also the issue of the stolen National Parks pickup and the missing ranger. He knew the Park service operated their own law enforcement. As far as he knew, though, that enforcement was confined to park boundaries.

Whatever the case, these were all issues way out of his jurisdiction.

It was after 1:00 p.m. before Lansing and Redwine got back to the Lindsay Trading Post. Contacting anyone by mobile phone was impossible. The cell phone carriers were slowly spreading their networks throughout the nation. Western New Mexico was a low priority. There weren't enough customers to make it profitable.

"Get in your unit and see if you can raise dispatch," Lansing ordered.

"What should I tell them?"

"Tell them what we found in the canyon. Also, get the number for Chaco Canyon. I need to let them know we found their truck." He started walking toward the trading post.

"Do you want me to wait till you get back?"

"No," Lansing said over his shoulder. "Make the call. I'm going inside to contact the State Police."

Chapter Fifty-Two

It was past noon when Tina Morales and Mariah reached the village of Cuba.

"Are you hungry?" the teacher asked.

"I think I could eat something."

Tina had never paid much attention to the restaurants in the small town. She was never hungry on her previous trips, so finding a place to eat wasn't important.

Presciliano's was the first café they came to.

"That must be a good place to eat," Tina observed, as she slowed down. "I don't see any place to park."

A quarter mile later, just after crossing the *Rio Puerco,* they found *El Bruno's Restauranté y Cantina.* The place appeared a bit more upscale. It was a larger building with a larger parking area. The many cars in the lot indicated *Bruno's* must be a good place to eat as well.

"This place look okay to you?" Tina asked as she pulled in.

"Sure."

They were not on a schedule. Tina estimated by taking New Mexico Route 197 to Crownpoint, she would save an hour of driving. She was sure they only had another 2 ½ hours to Gallup. She had already made the decision to spend the night and drive back to Las Palmas on Sunday.

The inside of the restaurant was dark, but pleasantly warm. There was already a chill in the air, even though Autumn was only a few days old.

Mariah selected the luncheon taco platter. Tina had a salad.

There had been no more discussion about Mariah's experiences. Morales figured they had plenty of time to talk after they ate. She hoped a full stomach would induce further conversation.

Tina decided to talk about herself and her experiences growing up. She knew that would take the pressure off her friend.

Mariah was mostly quiet. The teacher answered the few questions with little effort. That is, until Mariah asked, "Do you have a boyfriend?"

"I'm not . . ." Tina hesitated. "No, I don't."

"You must have had one."

"I did." She shrugged, then admitted, "I've had a few. I just don't have one currently."

Tina was grateful Mariah didn't pursue the issue anymore.

Everything was going fine until they finished their meal and stepped out of the restaurant.

"Damn," Tina swore under her breath.

"What's wrong?"

"My front, right tire . . . it's almost flat." She knelt to inspect. "Ah, Midnight, don't do this to me."

"Who's Midnight?" Mariah asked, looking around.

"My car."

"You named your car?"

"Doesn't everyone?" Tina saw her companion's confused look. "I take long drives from Las Palmas to Phoenix and Nogales. I talk to my car to keep me company. Giving her a name makes conversation more personal."

"Does Midnight answer back?"

"No," the teacher admitted. "But she is a good listener."

"Do you have a spare?" Mariah asked, getting back to the current problem.

"It's one of those donut tires. I can't go very far on one of those."

Mariah looked around to see if there was someone who could help. "Miss Morales, there's a tire place across the street."

Tina stood and looked where the girl pointed. The free-standing, metal canopy indicated *Freddy's Tire Shop* used to be a filling station. There was still enough air in the tire that she could make it across the street without doing damage.

She carefully crossed the highway and parked in front of the former convenience store. White, painted lettering across three glass window panels advertised the business phone number. A fourth panel next to the open door had AIR in white letters with $1.00 painted underneath. A coin operated air dispenser hung on the brick wall on the other side of the door.

Tina went inside.

"Can I help you, miss?" the owner asked from behind the counter. A man in his fifties with a thick Hispanic accent jumped to his feet when she entered, obviously eager for the patronage.

"I was wondering . . . do you fix flats?"

"Oh, no. I'm sorry, we don't . . . but let me look at your tire. Sometimes they can't be fixed."

Freddy followed her outside, then got on one knee to study the problem. He ran his hand along the tread, then looked at the front, left tire. "Miss, both these tires look worn." He wiped his hand on his jeans as he stood. "I know I've got your size. I wouldn't feel right letting you drive off unless you let me help you."

Tina knew better. He wouldn't feel right about her driving off unless he sold her something she didn't need. She had replaced all four tires at the end of the last school year. Even with her trip to Mexico and Phoenix over the summer, they still had less than 7,000 miles on them. Her guess was that she picked up a nail, probably when she pulled over to talk with Mariah.

"My tires are fine. All I need from you is some air and directions to a tire repair shop."

Freddy was no longer friendly. He waved his hand dismissively and said something crude in Spanish. Before continuing inside, he gestured to the far end of town, "Down the road a mile."

Tina found four quarters, then filled her tire, grateful she didn't have to deal with Freddy again. It was exactly a mile to *Larry's Tire and Power Saw Shop.* There was no pressure to buy anything and a $5.00 repair job was much more reasonable than $250 for new tires.

It was 2:00 p.m. before they got on the road again.

Chapter Fifty-Three

The Bureau of Indian affairs established Window Rock as the Navajo Central Agency in 1936. It was initially called *Ní Alníigi* (Center of the World), after it's ceremonial name. The Navajo were not impressed with the choice and renamed its capitol *Tséghádhoodzání* (the rock-with-a-hole-in-it). "Window Rock" was a more convenient translation for the English speakers.

Not more than a village with 2,500 permanent residents, it ballooned to 20,000 with government employees during the week. The nearby towns of Fort Defiance and St. Michaels, and the hamlets of Hunter's Point, the Summit, and Tse Bonito in New Mexico supplied the workers.

Charlotte Etsitty was used to the broad streets and the clean, modern buildings of downtown Phoenix. The two-year-old Navajo Nation Museum on Highway 264 could not help but impress visitors. However, her first opinions of Window Rock were skewed by the newness of the Navajo Shopping Center and strip mall. When she finally got to tour the Navajo "capitol" she discovered the government buildings reflected the poverty of the rest of the reservation. Nearly all the structures were single stories of native stone . . . none of which looked new.

The highways, owned by the state and the feds, were mostly new and well maintained. By comparison, the asphalt streets of Window Rock were cracked, poorly patched, and plagued with the potholes . . . that is, if they were paved at all.

"Are you staying with relatives in the area?" Warren Yazzie asked as they stepped out of the restaurant.

"I don't know anyone around here," Charlie admitted. "I was going to stay at the Quality Inn."

"Good thing you're checking in on a Saturday. It fills up on week-days." He walked toward his truck with a slight, though noticeable, limp. To Charlie, he looked taller wearing his broadbrimmed cattleman's hat. "Follow me over there."

Charlie did as she was instructed, falling behind his truck, both stop-ping often for the pedestrians in the parking lot. They drove past a strip mall, housing Navajo Government offices, insurance agencies, a Chinese restaurant and an Ace Hardware.

At the far end of the lot, they reached Main Street. A block and a half block down, Yazzie turned into the Quality Inn parking lot. All 56 rooms had outside access. The office and restaurant were in a separate building.

As they walked to the entrance, Charlie noticed a sign indicating check-in didn't start until 3:00 p.m. She gestured toward the sign. "I guess I have to wait to get a room."

"We'll see." Warren continued toward the double-doors, which opened automatically as he got close.

The rumors regarding Warren Yazzie's notoriety were reinforced when he approached the Inn's front desk. Two female clerks in her early 30s waved at him and smiled. One said, "Hi, Warren. What are you doing here?"

"Annie," Warren nodded to the speaker. "My friend needs a room."

"No problem. We have plenty available," she said, manning her computer.

Charlie stepped up to the counter to fill out her registration and an-swer a barrage of questions: Smoking or Non-smoking; number of people; any pets; preference – first or second floor. She had to look to Yazzie when asked how long she would need the room.

Warren held up four fingers. "There won't be a problem if she needs to stay longer, is there?"

"I don't think so."

Annie ran a copy of Charlie's credit card, then handed her the key to a bottom floor room. "Lunch is served till two thirty."

"Thanks," Charlie said. "We ate already."

As they stepped back outside, she asked, "Do you think this investigation will take longer than four days?"

"Depends on what turns up."

"When will we get started?"

"As soon as you put your bags in your room."

***

Charlie left her small SUV at the motel. She was impressed at the investigator's eagerness, though she expected a little down time after her drive.

The interior of Yazzie's Dodge Ram looked like a mobile office. He had to remove a stack of folders and miscellaneous papers from the rider's side of the crew cab to make room for her.

"Where are we going?"

"Gallup."

"What's in Gallup?"

"McKinley County seat. Coroner's office. Headquarters for State Police District Six. Indian Medical Center. Lots of places where we can ask questions."

"On a weekend? Aren't most offices closed till Monday?"

"Yes, but if you ask nicely and coordinate ahead of time, it's possible to make things happen . . . even on a weekend."

"What questions are we asking?"

"The New Mexico State Police will have a record of your aunt and uncle's crash. I'd like to see where that was. We'll also ask about law enforcement records on William and Walter. Everything's getting computerized . . . even the archives. Maybe they were as much a pain in the butt in New Mexico as they were on the rez.

"The county morgue and coroner's office will have records of local deaths. We'll check to see if your cousins' names show up."

"Will people actually be in their offices?"

"I was told they would meet us. Is there a problem?"

"No. I just thought I would have a chance to catch my breath before we jumped into things."

"Miss Etsitty . . ."

"Charlie," she corrected.

"Charlie . . . you insisted on getting involved. I'm doing my job, just like I'm getting paid to do. I can take you back to the motel if you want."

"No, no . . ."

"What had you planned on doing when you got here?"

"I wanted to talk to Cecil and Marsha Duncan."

"The foster parents your sister spoke with?"

"Yes."

"Why?"

"I was hoping they remembered something else after they talked to Emily."

"Like what? Maybe your cousins didn't disappear after all?"

Charlie shrugged. "No . . . I don't know. Maybe they'll come up with a name they forgot . . . or they remembered something else that happened."

Yazzie tried not to sound condescending. "Why don't we stick with my schedule? We can always circle back and talk to the Duncans if we have to."

Charlie thought for a moment, then nodded. "Sure."

Chapter Fifty-Four

The parking lot of Whitehorse Lake Chapter House was empty except for Wes Daisy's Chevy pickup truck. He sat on the tailgate and watched the rainstorm drift from the northwest. It was moving slowly, drenching everything in its path.

Daisy cursed his luck. Of all days to have a monsoon rain drift across the high desert of McKinley County, this had to be the worst. It was bad enough he had rounded up three amateurs for the robbery. Indian Route 9 was paved but still a poor excuse for a highway. Now they would have to make their escape on wet roads. The only consolation was, if they were chased, the Navajo Police would have to use the same roads.

Kevin Silversmith finally pulled up in an old, two-door Toyota. Kevin and Germaine Billie opened their doors and slid from the bucket seats. Junior Kee awkwardly climbed out from the back. When he did, he dropped his gun on the asphalt. He quickly retrieved it, but not before getting an ugly scowl from Daisy.

"It's about time you boys showed up," Wes growled.

"We're here on time," Silversmith growled back. Just because Daisy had organized the foray didn't mean he had any more authority than the next man.

"All right, all right," Daisy said quickly to defuse a confrontation. "Everybody bring a gun?"

"I've got a twenty-two with seven shots," Billie said, thumbing in the direction of the Toyota.

Silversmith pulled a small automatic from his jacket's pocket. "Twenty-five caliber Beretta."

Junior held up his .45 caliber Colt Automatic Pistol. Except for Junior Kee, all the participants were in their early 20s. Kee was bigger than the other three, almost 30, slow at understanding anything, and quick to anger.

"Have you ever shot that thing?" Daisy asked.

"Of course," Kee said defensively.

"Whose is it?"

"My uncle's."

Daisy stopped with the questions. It didn't matter whether Junior had borrowed the gun or stole it. The important thing was he brought one.

"Okay, we're going for two things . . . the liquor behind the checkout counter and the money in the register," Daisy said. The other three nodded. "When we walk in the door, the counter is just to the left. We grab what we can, then head out.

"Kevin, you and Germaine go in your car. When we're done, you head directly back to Whitehorse. Junior, you ride with me. We'll head for Torreon. Cops won't know who to follow.

"I'll circle back to Whitehorse. We'll all meet back at my cousin's garage in Crownpoint." He looked at his companions. "Any questions?"

"Yeah. What about beer?" Junior asked. "Can we grab beer?"

"If you have to, yes," Daisy agreed. "It's in a cooler along the wall to the right. Don't grab too many. We want to be in-and-out quick."

"Don't worry," Kee snapped. "I know what I'm doing."

"Sure, you do," Daisy said under his breath. Then, out loud "If any-thing goes wrong, I'm leaving you behind. You understand that, right?"

"Yeah, I understand."

"All of you, remember. Nobody gets hurt. Nobody shoots nobody. Understand?"

His companions all nodded.

When Daisy turned to get in his truck, Junior pointed the gun at him and pretended to fire a shot. He smiled and looked at Silversmith and

Billie to see if they saw his gesture of defiance. Both men just shook their heads as they got back into the Toyota.

The Pueblo Pintado store was only 15 minutes away.

Chapter Fifty-Five

The medicine man slowed his Jeep as he got close to the Lindsay Trading Post. Besides a truck and horse trailer, the lot was crowded with a county sheriff's Tahoe, two State Police units and a white Ford Explorer with a National Park Service emblem on the door. A knot of men were gathered at the front of a State Police cruiser. They appeared to be studying a map spread on the hood.

The Navajo parked as far away from the congregation as he could. As he got out of his beat-up Wrangler, he pulled his flat-brimmed hat down to mask his face.

"Hey, Jeep Man," Ida, the waitress, said, acknowledging her new customer when he came inside. She didn't know his first or last name, but Jeep Man had been visiting the post regularly for 4 months. The man was aloof . . . neither friendly nor unfriendly . . . and seldom spoke. After his fifth visit, Ida gave him the moniker, Jeep Man. He didn't protest, so the name stuck. He seldom stopped long enough to eat. "What can I get you?"

"Coffee, to go," he said. He gestured toward the parking lot with his head.

Ida understood the question. "The cowboys out there are the county sheriff and a deputy. A man came in here yesterday. Somebody shot him up in the canyons . . . him and a friend. The friend died. The sheriff went up there this morning looking for where it happened.

"I heard him talking to the State Patrol on the phone in here. He found a bunch of trucks up where the men were shot. I guess he needs help."

Jeep Man nodded but said nothing.

"I have no idea why those park rangers are out there." Her customer gave a slight shrug. "I'll get your coffee."

Ida returned with a large paper cup with a plastic lid. She knew Jeep Man drank his brew black, so she didn't worry about offering him cream or sweetener. She handed him the cup. He handed her a dollar bill.

After ringing up the purchase, she handed him a nickel in change.

Jeep Man pocketed the coin, turned and left without a thank you or goodbye. Ida wasn't offended. That was typical Jeep Man behavior.

The Navajo frowned as he got back into his Jeep. To the southwest, a storm was drifting across the barren land. His destination was being pounded with rain. To be safe, he put up the tarp for his Jeep. He worried about flash floods through the many dry creek beds.

Having been in the area for over three years, he knew the most treacherous stretches.

He took a sip from his cup. As expected, the black liquid was bitter. The coffee in the pot had to have been at least two hours old. He poured the rest of the contents onto the ground.

Starting his engine, he pulled onto the highway, turning toward the east. Five hundred feet from the trading post, he turned right again onto a gravel road, and headed deep into the Badlands.

Chapter Fifty-Six

As soon as Tina pulled out from *Larry's Tire and Power Saw Shop*, she saw a green highway sign. A white arrow pointing to the right, announced the way to Crownpoint, Grants and Gallup. Fifty feet further down, a white road sign with black numbering indicated the turn would put drivers on New Mexico Route 197.

After the turn, a mileage sign indicated Crownpoint 96, Grants 124, and Gallup 156. One hundred feet later, another sign said Speed Limit 45.

Tina quickly understood the reason for the low speed limit. The road was anything but smooth. A quick calculation told her Gallup was at least 3 hours away . . . about the same time as driving to Albuquerque before hitting the interstate. It was still 70 miles shorter using Route 197. If nothing else, she would at least save on gas.

In the distance, far to the west, an ominous storm was building. At first it appeared they would be heading into it. The highway made an abrupt turn to the south and it looked like they would miss it completely.

"Mariah," the teacher asked cautiously, "do you feel like talking about what happened?"

The Navajo girl turned her head to look at the distant rain. She was quiet for a long moment. Tina assumed she had posed the question too soon, but Mariah, though she refused to look at her companion, began to talk.

"They let us out of our rooms once a day to use the restroom and clean up. The rest of the time my ankle was chained to the floor. I had a filthy mattress for sleeping.

"I heard other girls yelling to get out. That usually didn't last long. Someone would open their door and slap them around. You could hear them getting hit. After that you could hear them crying . . . but not very loud.

"I just kept quiet. Every day I expected someone to come in and rape me. When I used the bathroom, a couple of the guards said they were going to take care of me. Show me what real men could do. They never did."

"You said they let you go to the bathroom once a day. What happened if you needed to go before then?"

"I had a bucket . . . a metal bucket. I guess the other girls did too. They gave us water in bottles, but I learned don't drink too much. And the food was awful.

"The night I got away, they put cloth sacks over our heads and handcuffed us. They led us into the big part of the warehouse and lifted us into a van, then chained us to the floor.

"One girl asked what was happening. Someone laughed and said we were finally going to earn our keep.

"After they closed the door to the van, you could hear a garage door opening. Pretty soon, we were on the road.

"The benches we sat on were hard. We whispered to each other but not too loud. There were four of us in the back there. Me and two other girls were from the rez. The other girl was from Zuni.

"I don't know how long we drove, but it was uncomfortable. We made a turn and the road got really rough. You could tell we went up a hill. Then we stopped.

"The driver opened the back door and unlocked the chains on my ankles and my handcuffs. He pulled the bag from my head and dragged me out by my hair."

"Why you?"

"I was the closest to the door. I guess I was the easiest to get to."

Mariah paused. When she resumed her story, her voice cracked. "He threw me on the ground and pulled my jeans down. I tried to kick and hit him, but he was a lot bigger. I was screaming for him to stop. He just laughed and got on top of me."

She stopped talking. Tina looked over. The poor girl, still looking out the window, was shaking. "He was trying to get inside me. I was hitting his face with my fists. It was dark. I thought I heard tires on gravel and a car come to a stop. I screamed for help.

"The next thing I know, I see a shadow. It grabs the driver by the throat . . . then I feel hot blood on my face. I know it was blood because it got in my mouth. I could taste it.

"Then the . . ." She fumbled for the right word. "The monster . . . dragged him off me."

"Monster?"

Mariah turned to the driver. Her eyes were wide with terror. "I don't know what else to call it," she said in a whisper. "It was dark. I couldn't see it . . . but I heard it. It sounded like a wild animal.

"I pulled up my pants and started running. I don't know where I was or how long I ran.

"Some man picked me up on the highway. I think he took me to a hospital . . ." Her voice trailed off.

Tina knew the rest of the story from there.

Chapter Fifty-Seven

Ranger Jackson McKee picked up the topographical map and looked closer. He was more familiar with deciphering topo chart tracks and elevation lines than the lawmen gathered in the parking lot. After a full minute, he handed the map to his fellow ranger, Ranse Herrera.

"I can't find a shorter route. I agree with the sheriff," McKee concluded. "We'll need to follow county road three eighty-eight to the end of Blue Mesa. Then we can take the jeep track through Rockhouse Canyon to where they found the trucks."

"How far is that?" State Police officer La Torre asked. The patrolman had returned to the trading post after Lansing called the State Police in Segovia.

"It looks like eleven, twelve miles to the turnoff," Herrera estimated. "Another five miles back to that canyon the sheriff found. Best guess, around thirty minutes to get there."

"All four vehicles had keys in the ignitions," Lansing said. "I don't know if they'll start, though."

"It might be a good idea to bring a couple of gas cans," Deputy Redwine suggested.

"That and jumper cables," La Torre added.

Lansing nodded, but said nothing further. Lindsay and Rockhouse Canyon were in San Phillipe County. Trooper Will Aguilar had been dispatched by State Police District 7 in Segovia to join the meeting. The sheriff's greatest fear quickly materialized. The state officials began undermining his authority as soon as they arrived.

The State Police Special Investigation Division announced they would lead the investigation. The FBI was getting involved as well. A federal employee was still missing. Stolen federal property had been found.

Lansing wasn't sure if his office could even afford to be involved. As always, his biggest issue was manpower . . . and distances. Las Palmas was 2 hours away. He normally had 10 deputies for patrol, but his office was one man down. Former deputy Leroy Ramirez was sitting in county lockup, waiting for his trial for accessory to murder. His position hadn't been filled.

Besides Ron Hutton, the murdered hiker, the sheriff had two deaths on the other side of the county to investigate. His suspicion was that those dead men were associated with *Southwest Antiques*, but he had no proof . . . not yet, anyway.

The van in the canyon was being used for transporting prisoners of some type. It wasn't a leap to connect the Mariah Tsosie with the van, especially after hearing about the three girls released in Counselor. It was only five miles from Counselor to Lindsay.

"You are going with us to that canyon, aren't you?" Patrolman Aguilar addressed Lansing.

The sheriff was lost in his own thoughts. "I'm sorry, what?"

"Rockhouse Canyon . . . you're taking us up there?"

"Yeah. I need to make arrangements for my horses."

He signaled Redwine to follow him as he walked toward the trailer. "I don't think we'll need the horses anymore."

Not sure how long they would have to wait for the State Police, Lansing had unloaded the horses from the trailer. He didn't want them cooped up any longer than necessary. The saddles were already secure in the trailer's tackle compartment. The horses' reins were tied to a gate behind the trading post.

Lansing and Redwine led their horses to the trailer, then loaded them.

"We're switching vehicles," the sheriff said as he latched the rear doors.

"What do you mean?"

"I'm taking the Tahoe. I may need the radio. I need for you to take the horses back to my ranch. Oscar will make sure they're fed and bedded down."

"How am I going to get home from your ranch?"

"Just keep my truck till I get back."

"When will that be?"

"Tonight. If it's too late, we'll switch back tomorrow."

As Redwine pulled away with the truck and trailer, Lansing walked back to the others.

"I'm ready to head up to the canyon," he announced.

"We can't . . ." La Torre said. "Not yet, anyway. We have to wait on the SID."

"You're kidding me!" Lansing grunted.

"That's what Santa Fe said. They just notified me over my radio. Also, the FBI is sending an agent from Farmington."

Lansing wasn't sure if the State Police had surrendered their jurisdiction to the FBI or were sharing the load. Both had access to more resources than his office. He would bide his time and keep his mouth shut. Let them presume he was too ignorant to play with the "big boys." It wouldn't be the first time.

Chapter Fifty-Eight

The town of Gallup, New Mexico stretched for 12 miles, east to west, along I-40. It was barely 2 miles, north to south, at its widest point. State Police District 6 offices were on the old Route 66 on the east side of town.

"Can I help you?" the female receptionist asked when Charlie and Warren entered the visitor entrance.

"I'm here to meet with Trooper Gaspar," Yazzie said. "He said he would be here till four."

"One moment, please. I'll ring the back office." She pushed a single button on her phone console. "Yes, Sergeant Gaspar, there's a man in the lobby to see you . . ." She looked at the Navajo. "Your name?"

"Warren Yazzie."

"It's a Mr. Yazzie." She hung up the phone. "He'll be right out."

The two investigators waited less than a minute. A door opened to the back offices and a man dressed in a black uniform with grey pockets and lapels motioned them back. When they got close, he extended his hand. "Good to see you, Warren."

The Navajo shook the extended hand. "When did you make sergeant, Larry?"

"It's been at least six months," Gaspar said.

"This is my client, Charlotte Etsitty," Warren said by way of introduction.

"Ma'am," the patrolman said, "Larry Gaspar."

Charlie shook the offered hand. She tried to hide her astonishment that not only did the two men know each other, they came across as long-time friends. She couldn't help but think, "Is there anyone who doesn't know Warren Yazzie?"

Yazzie noticed her expression. "We worked on a few cases together, back when I was still with the Navajo Rangers." They followed the trooper down a short hallway.

"Navajo Rangers?" Charlie asked. She had never heard of them.

"They handle natural resources," was all he said. They had reached Gaspar's office.

"Please sit down." The trooper indicated two chairs in front of his desk. He pushed a file toward Yazzie, then sat. "Warren, I hope you realize I'm stretching the rules by doing this."

Warren picked up the file and thumbed through the two-dozen pages.

"We're not breaking the law here, are we?" Charlie was honestly concerned. She had learned a lot about Arizona law in the past seven years. She knew her lawyer bosses were always careful to stay within prescribed legal boundaries.

"State law says arrest records can't be released to civilians," Warren said. "Is that what you're getting at?"

Gaspar nodded. "They say once a Marine, always a Marine. The same goes with lawmen. That's the way I see it, anyway. So, Warren, I'm extending you that courtesy . . . lawman to lawman."

"I appreciate that." He held up the file. "The State Police had quite a dossier on the Etsitty brothers."

"No, we didn't. Our records office only gets actual reports when a suspect is sentenced to more than six months in jail. Walter got a twelve-month sentence for assault in Albuquerque in ninety-six."

Yazzie looked at the file page. "It says here that sentence was suspended."

"The arresting officers were a bit too zealous in the execution of their duties . . . plus they falsified evidence. That never came out until after Etsitty was found guilty."

"So, why didn't they throw out the charges?" Charlie asked.

"You'd have to ask the judge."

"What about these other reports?" Yazzie interrupted. "How did you get those?"

"I went directly to Santa Fe and Bernalillo County records. They're mostly harassment complaints."

"By who?"

"Massage Parlors . . . a few low-end motels. They claimed they were looking for their sister."

"They thought Jennifer was a prostitute?" Charlie sounded doubtful. She knew from Phoenix cases she worked that massage parlors were popular fronts for prostitution. She had a hard time believing her younger cousin would sink to that level.

"I get the impression they thought she was forced into the trade after she was abducted." Gaspar noticed the questioning looks from his visitors. "It happens more than you'd think. Earlier this week we got a report from Sandoval County. Three Indian girls were dropped off in Counselor. They had been abducted and held as prisoners.

"Somebody rescued them before they started their new professions."

"How old are we talking?"

"Fifteen, sixteen years old."

Charlie looked at Warren. "Jennifer was fifteen when she went missing."

Warren gave a short nod. "One more thing, Larry. The parents of the three cousins were killed in a car accident in ninety-three. Would you have any information on that?"

"Where did it take place?"

"Between here and Window Rock."

Gaspar shook his head. "The State Police only gather accident information for statistical purposes. Individual accident reports are kept by the local sheriff or police departments. If the incident was here in McKinley County, you probably need go to Sheriff Madrid's office."

Yazzie stood. "Thanks a lot, Larry."

Charlie stood as well. "Yes, thank you Sergeant Gaspar."

"Glad I could help."

Chapter Fifty-Nine

"I need a cup of coffee," Yazzie said as he pulled into the *Route 66 Railroad Café.*

The café was barely three miles from the District 6 office. Charlie hadn't had a chance, yet, to read the stack of papers in the file.

"Should I bring these?"

"Yes," was Warren's short answer.

Inside the café they both ordered coffee.

"Split the files so we can both review the material," Yazzie said.

Charlie did as requested. Warren Yazzie had such a calm and pleasant manner about him, she didn't view his suggestion as an order. She handed him the Bernalillo County reports which were basically Albuquerque Police records. The Santa Fe County reports also came from the local police department.

Their coffee was soon delivered, and they sat in silence for several minutes, engrossed with the reading material. They swapped their stacks. Instead of reading, though, Yazzie pulled out his cell phone and scrolled through the address book. He pressed the call button, then put the phone next to his ear.

"Hello . . . yes, sir, this is Warren Yazzie. Is Deputy Tarrio available?"

He waited for the answer, then said. "Could you tell him I'll be there in thirty minutes. Thanks."

Across the highway, a locomotive pulling a string of cattle cars blasted its horn. The Burlington Northern Santa Fe Railroad snaked its way for 400 miles from Gallup to El Paso, Texas. At one time the lifeblood of commerce for the Southwest United States, it still remained one of the most economical forms of transport for large cargos such as a herd of cattle.

Charlie waited for the horn to stop, then asked, "How many places will we really visit this afternoon?"

Warren flipped open his phone to display the time. "It's two thirty. It'll be three thirty before we finish at the sheriff's office. You've already had a long day, so, let's head back to Window Rock after that."

Charlie nodded. "Sounds good. This coffee will keep me going for just so long."

"After looking at those reports, what do you think?"

"I think my two boy cousins really wanted to save their sister. It looks like they put their lives on hold while they looked for her."

Yazzie pulled his note pad from his jacket. "You said Walter was studying to become a medicine man?"

"Yes."

"Do you know who he apprenticed under?"

"Not in Window Rock. In Tuba City he studied under Billie Nez."

The investigator jotted down the name. "You seem pretty sure about that."

"He's the same medicine man who tried to cure my grandfather," she said bitterly. "For all the good it did."

"Don't knock traditional medicine," he gently scolded. "I've seen sick men try everything modern doctors had to offer. They stayed sick until a medicine man intervened. One day the man is on his death bed. The next he's up walking around, as healthy as they come.

"But back to Walter . . . how long had he been studying traditional medicine?"

"Since he was twelve."

Charlie told about the encounter with Skinwalkers at the Preston Mesa hunting cabin when she was fifteen. After seeing the fear on his siblings' faces, Walter swore he would dedicate his life to fighting that kind of Evil.

"From what I heard, his parents were proud of his chosen avocation."

"In this day-and-age, it is very unusual for young people to pursue our ancient customs. I can understand their pride." He paused for a moment. "You're not going to like what I'm about to say, but it needs to be said."

"What?"

"Walter and William are probably dead."

Charlie wasn't surprised or upset by the statement. The police records were clear. The Etsitty brothers hadn't had run-ins with the law in three years. The Duncans had no word from William in that time. Deep inside her, she had come to the same conclusion.

"I can't argue with you about that." She stared at her cup of coffee. "Who do you think killed them?"

"They were probably killed by the people they upset the most. Top of the list are the people responsible for abducting Jennifer. Your cousins might have gotten too close to finding her."

" 'Top of the list?' Who else would it be?"

"You said Walter wanted to become a medicine man to fight the evil of Skinwalkers. He might have crossed paths with them . . . In fact, I believe he must have. I think the curse on your family is a result of something Walter must have done."

Warren's statement made complete sense. "So, Skinwalkers killed my cousins?"

"I'd put them on the list."

Charlie found herself rocking forward and backwards as she pondered the possibilities. Finally, she stopped rocking and asked, "Do you think Jennifer is still alive?"

All Yazzie could do was shrug.

Chapter Sixty

"Do you want me to pull over?" Tina asked.

Mariah shook her head and cleared her throat. "I'll be all right."

The schoolteacher was disturbed by the girl's story. Her description of her captivity was frightening. Just as unnerving, though, was what ultimately saved her. Tina couldn't imagine what kind of "monster" Mariah had encountered . . . but something had happened to her. It was bad enough it put her into a near catatonic state.

Lansing had provided only a brief description of Mariah's attacker. The man looked like he had been killed by a wild animal . . . his body further mutilated by scavengers. Finding out what kind of animal/monster the poor girl had seen was beyond Tina's capabilities. There were professionals in Gallup better equipped to deal with Mariah's trauma.

The important thing was the girl was finally willing to talk about what happened to her. Tina knew that would be a huge step toward healing a very damaged psyche.

At the Torreon Day School, Route 197 made a near 180° turn to the northwest then turned west. They passed the Torreon Store and gas station.

There were not many towns in western New Mexico. That meant there were few grocery stores. Small operations like the Torreon Store had to service the ranches and farms close by. In addition to gas, they carried eggs, milk, bread, some vegetables, some fresh meats, anything a family might need on a daily basis. Maybe once a month, ranchers would make the hour-long drives to the grocery stores in Cuba or Crownpoint.

Highway 197 made a turn to the north, then to the northwest, which put Tina and her passenger on a collision course with the storm. Droplets began to pepper the windshield, promising the arrival of more rain.

Two things happened. There was no sign to announce New Mexico Route 197 was now Indian Route 9. The road became suddenly narrower and rougher. At the same time, Tina's car began pulling to the right. She slowed down to maintain control.

"What's wrong?" Mariah asked.

"I think we're losing air in that tire they supposedly fixed."

"What are you going to do?"

"Next gas station we come to I'll get some air. It's still fifty miles to Crownpoint. Maybe we can get a new tire there. If I have to, I'll put on the donut spare."

***

The rain had picked up by the time Wes Daisy parked in front of the Pueblo Pintado Store. Kevin Silversmith pulled in next to him. There were three other trucks parked in the lot. None at the gas pumps. For Daisy, that was a good sign. There would be few customers.

The ringleader didn't think they needed masks. Crownpoint was nearly an hour away and he was sure no one would recognize them.

A small, enclosed overhang guarded the front door, blocking the wind and rain. The four robbers crowded into the space. Daisy looked from one man to the next, making sure one last time that they were ready. Each one nodded.

Daisy led the way, pushing the door open. All four menacingly waved their guns.

"Everyone knows what this is," the leader said, confident the customers didn't need an explanation. "No one needs to get shot. Let us grab what we want, and we're gone."

All the patrons were men in their 50s. Three of them. Two were near the checkout. The third was toward the back looking for milk. The man behind the counter looked to be 60.

Silversmith and Germaine Billie rushed behind the counter. Billie tapped on the register with his gun indicating he wanted the owner to open the till. Silversmith double sacked some plastic bags, then began filling them with bottles of liquor.

Junior Kee had disappeared down an aisle, heading for the coolers. He hesitated at the glass doors, not sure which brand of beer to get. When he found what he wanted, he started grabbing six-packs. Awkward as always, he held the gun in his left hand as he grabbed for the beers with his right. It didn't dawn on him to grab a case neatly packaged in cardboard with a handle. Instead, he cradled three six-packs in his left arm.

Silversmith and Billie were finished in under a minute and were heading for the exit.

Daisy looked in the direction of the coolers. "Junior, get your butt moving!"

"I'm coming. I'm coming."

Kee was so focused on his objective, he never noticed the man holding a gallon of milk just a few feet away. Loaded down with three six-packs and his gun, he didn't notice the foot the older man stuck out. Junior, the beer and the gun went sprawling. Two cans burst open, making the floor slippery.

"Son-of-a-bitch!" he swore.

At the sound of the commotion, all Daisy said was, "Crap!" He pulled the door open and ran for his truck.

The man with the milk tried to grab the gun. Junior scrambled to his knees and reached for the .45 as well. The man slammed the plastic gallon jug against the side of Junior's head.

Already angry at being tripped, Kee was infuriated at being struck. He wrested the gun away from his opponent, pointed it at the man, and fired three quick shots.

Chapter Sixty-One

When Tina parked next to the air pump, the rain was getting heavier. She knew she was about to get soaked, but she didn't have much choice. There was still 1/3 of a tank of gas. If it hadn't been for the rain, she would have considered filling the tank. There was still enough fuel to reach Crownpoint, so, air for her tire was her only concern.

As she removed the cap from the stem, she heard car doors slamming behind her. A moment later, engines started, and she looked up to see a car and a truck speed out of the parking area. The car turned right, the truck left.

From inside the store she heard three distinct gunshots. While she filled her tire . . . perhaps 20 seconds later . . . a man with a gun limped out of the enclosed covering at the front door. He stood in the rain, looking confused.

***

Junior Kee's assailant fell backwards. The plastic container of milk fell to the floor. The lid popped off and its contents began to gurgle out. Milk, beer and blood mixed, creating a sloppy, slippery mess.

Junior tried to stand. On the fall to the floor, he twisted his right knee, aggravating an old football injury. He had to grab a grocery shelf to steady himself as he tried to find footing.

The two men near the checkout didn't hesitate. They ran to the man Kee had just shot, unmindful of the danger.

Kee tried to wave them back with his gun, but he was in too much pain to pose a threat.

He was hurting. He had just tried to rob a store. On top of everything else, he had just shot a man. All he could think about was getting away.

He pointed his pistol at the man behind the counter. The man dropped the phone he was using to call the police. As soon as Junior hobbled out the door, the owner picked up the phone again to report the robbery.

Standing in the rain, Kee's first thought was he'd forgotten where the truck was parked. It took a few seconds for him to realize he had been deserted. With that realization came anger.

Anger and fear. How was he going to get away?

He had the fleeting idea of stealing one of the trucks in the lot. He didn't want to go back inside to confront the angry customers. That's when he saw the woman kneeling next to a two-door Chevy Cavalier.

With his damaged knee, he knew he couldn't operate the pedals. The woman would have to drive. He limped toward her, moving as fast as he could.

"Ma'am, I need you and your car," he said, pointing his .45 at her head.

Tina raised her hands. "Whatever you want, mister."

She hurried around to the driver's side while Junior opened the passenger door. The gunman was surprised to find Mariah in the seat. The girl was even more surprised at being discovered.

"Get out!" he ordered.

Mariah first looked at the gun, then to Tina as she slid into the driver's seat. "Do what he said, Mariah. Get out."

The girl hesitated, then said defiantly, "No!"

She gave the teacher a determined look. The frightened young lady Tina first met had disappeared.

Kee was in no mood to argue. His knee was throbbing, and he desperately needed to sit.

"Little girl, get out!" he ordered again. His voice strained with a mixture of desperation, anger and pain.

"I'm not leaving Miss Morales." She saw the worried look on Tina's face. "I'll get in the back."

The rain was coming down hard now. Mariah stepped outside the car just long enough to push the bucket seat forward. She slipped into the back, moving schoolbooks, paperwork and an overnight bag to make room.

Junior Kee shoved the seat upright again, then tried to get in. There wasn't enough leg room. He put his gun in his left hand as he fumbled to find the correct lever to adjust the seat.

As second later, he scooted the seat as far back as it would go. There was no space between his seat and the back sitting area.

Mariah had already moved, so she was now directly behind the driver.

Junior pulled his door shut. "Let's go!"

Tina started the car and backed up. She turned the wheel toward the highway when Kee stopped her. "No." He pointed to a dirt road. "We're going that way."

"Why?"

"Police," was all he said.

Tina could only assume the man was a local and knew where to go. Her windshield wipers were on the highest setting and slammed back and forth. The sheets of rain covered the glass immediately after a blade wiped it away. Visibility was terrible.

The teacher cautiously pulled onto the dirt road, unsure of where she was going, unsure of how much air she had put into her tire.

Junior turned to look at the store. One of the men emerged from inside. It looked like he carried a long gun. A moment later came the sound of a shotgun being fired.

With the pounding rain, it was impossible to tell if pellets had hit the Cavalier or not.

"Step on it!" Kee ordered.

Tina sped up as much as she dared . . . into the storm . . . into the Badlands.

Chapter Sixty-Two

Lansing led the convoy to Rockhouse Canyon. One of the two FBI agents rode with him in the Chevy Tahoe. The other agent rode with the two Special Investigations Division officers in their Explorer. The National Park Rangers brought up the rear in the F-150.

After they were on the gravel road, heading into the canyons, Special Agent Vic Hempstead began asking questions. Experience told Lansing to keep his answers short and only address the question asked. Locals were notorious for bragging about everything they knew, usually offering up too much information.

"What do you know about the two men who were shot up in this canyon?"

"Not much. I never talked to the man in the hospital."

"What were they doing up there?"

"I was told they were taking pictures."

"Pictures? Of what?" Hempstead had a pocket notebook out to record Lansing's answers.

"Petroglyphs."

"Why?"

"You'd have to ask the survivor."

"Has the Medical Investigator completed the autopsy?"

"I haven't heard."

"So, you don't know what kind of weapon was used?"

"I would guess a long rifle." He considered offering up the fact that he and Redwine had found three .243 shells on the canyon rim. That, however, was proof of nothing. They were not necessarily from the shooter's rifle. Anyone could have left them there. Besides, they were in a zip-lock bag headed to Las Palmas.

The agent was quiet for a moment. "You found what . . . four vehicles up there?"

"Yes."

"Men are going missing on the Navajo reservation . . . mostly older men. My office has been looking into those reports. The names on the registrations you found matched the names of two of the missing men. That's one reason why we're interested in this investigation."

"We were told those two hikers were shot because they got too close to that canyon . . . probably to keep them from finding those trucks."

"That opinion came from the State Police. I just started my own investigation this morning." Lansing looked sideways at the agent. "Who are these missing Navajos?"

Hempstead ignored the question. "My office was also told about three Indian girls that were abducted, then released not far from here. What do you know about that?"

"As much as you do."

"We're trying to track the girls down. If they were taken from reservations or transported across state lines, the FBI definitely needs to be involved in that as well."

"So, why am I driving you to a canyon? Why aren't you looking for those girls?"

"There are other agents doing exactly that." He stared out his side window for a moment, then turned toward Lansing. "What can you tell me about this stolen van you reported?"

"What did the State Police tell you?"

"Just that you found a suspicious van. You thought it was used to transport those three girls. Why would you say that?"

"In the back of the van, I found four sets of shackles and handcuffs. The shackles were anchored to the floor with chains. The girls were released only five miles from here. You don't need to be Sherlock Holmes to figure out the van is probably linked to the girls."

Hempstead mulled over the answer. "You said four sets of shackles. Only three girls were released. Is there a fourth somewhere?"

This is where Lansing wanted to be cautious. He and the FBI were on the same team . . . supposedly. He didn't want to provide more information than he had to.

"The State Police picked up a Navajo girl on the highway near Ojo Caliente. She could be the fourth victim."

"I see. Where is she now?"

"On her way to the Indian Medical Center in Gallup. She may be there already."

"Was she hurt?"

"No," Lansing shook his head. "Not physically."

Chapter Sixty-Three

It was a half-mile hike from where the convoy parked to the abandoned vehicles. Lansing stood back as the four other lawmen and two park rangers swarmed over the "stolen" property. The SID agents were busy recording plate numbers and registration information . . . a duplication of what Lansing and Redwine had done earlier.

The two FBI agents were in a heated discussion with Chief Ranger McKee. Chaco Canyon wanted its truck back. The FBI wanted to hold it for forensic analysis. The truck could hold vital clues. After several minutes, McKee agreed to Hempstead's demands. He conceded that finding out what happened to his missing ranger outweighed all other considerations.

Everyone conducting examinations wore latex gloves. After winning their argument with the park service, Hempstead and his partner began a detailed study of the van. They both agreed with Lansing's conclusion that it had been used to transport captives. Thorough analysis would be needed to determine if it once held the three girls dropped off in Counselor.

After the initial examination of the vehicles, the state and federal officers discussed their next steps. Should the van, the two truck and the auto remain in place for forensic studies or be moved to a more accommodating location? Everyone knew it would be impossible for tow trucks to back into the smaller canyon for retrieval. At a minimum the four vehicles needed to be driven to the Rockhouse Canyon floor a half-mile away.

Both the SID agents and the FBI agreed their mobile Crime Scene vans were too cumbersome to venture very far into canyon country. It was finally decided all four vehicles would be moved to another site. The agents needed to coordinate with their superiors in Santa Fe and Albuquerque.

Lansing made two observations that he kept to himself. Getting things done in San Phillipe County were a lot simpler and less unwieldly when one person was in charge . . . mainly himself. The second thing he perceived was his opinion was neither asked for nor wanted.

The Ron Hutton murder investigation was supposedly his office's responsibility. If the other agencies intended taking it over, he had no problem stepping aside. His dance card was already full. However, he wanted the courtesy of being asked to relinquish control of the murder inquiry as well as assurance he would be kept informed.

While the SID and FBI plotted their approach to the investigation and established boundaries, McKee walked over to Lansing. "The park service has been looking for Ranger Miller since Monday."

Lansing nodded. "I heard."

"For three nights in a row, the canyon was getting intruders at night." It seemed McKee needed to explain the park service's position.

"Intruders?"

"The park is closed from dusk till six a.m. We found evidence of nighttime visitors in the ruins. Specifically, activities in one of the kivas. Those are ceremonial rooms . . ."

"I know what a kiva is," the sheriff said, cutting him off.

"Sorry. Anyway, we found someone was using a kiva for their own purposes. Completely unauthorized purposes. Harry Miller went missing Sunday night when he tried to catch the culprits."

"Do you know who they are?"

"We have our suspicions." He studied Lansing for a moment. "I presume you know about the Navajo Badlands."

"I've heard stories."

"We're certain Navajo witches are involved."

"Why witches?"

"The Navajos always considered Anasazi ruins as sacred. The witches think conducting rituals in the kivas imbues them with special powers. What was left behind pointed us in their direction."

"What was that?"

"Human bones."

The answer disturbed Lansing. He had seen a desecrated grave on Monday. The casket had been opened and bones had been taken from the corpse. He pushed the thought aside. Why would a Navajo witch dig up a grave a hundred miles away?

"Chaco Canyon has always been a favorite target . . ." the ranger continued. "Particularly Pueblo Bonito."

"That's the large ruin in the center of the park."

"Right. You've been there, then?"

"I have."

"The complex has over thirty kivas. The four largest ones were probably used for major religious ceremonies. Those are the ones intruders like to use."

"Does this happen often?"

"Actually, two, three times a year. But they will only use it one night and try to cover up the fact that they've been there. Like I said, this time they hit the ruins two nights in a row . . . let's make that three nights in a row. They must have been there Sunday night when Harry went missing."

"And his truck turned up here."

McKee nodded. "We were sure Harry chased the intruders out of the canyon. When we started looking for him, we expected to find him or the truck in the Badlands. The State Police conducted aerial searches in San Juan and McKinley Counties. They marked suspicious sites and we followed up with ground inspections. We got help from the sheriffs' offices.

"We didn't think to expand our search into San Phillipe. We'll have to now."

"You'll continue looking for Harry?"

"Yes, but I don't think this is a rescue any longer. It's probably a recovery now."

"I don't know where you would start looking. Between here and Colorado, there are a thousand little canyons like this. I've had to do investigations out here before. Finding anything is pure luck.

"Two hikers stumbled onto this place by accident. You would have never seen your truck with an aerial search. It was covered with a camouflage tarp."

"So, you don't think we should even try?" The ranger sounded crestfallen.

"It's up to you . . . but I don't have the manpower to support that kind of search." Lansing thought for a moment, then, "You said these intruders showed up three nights in a row. Do you know why?"

McKee shook his head. "You'd have to ask them."

Chapter Sixty-Four

A block from the McKinley County Sheriff's office, Warren Yazzie turned north on New Mexico Route 602. After crossing I-40 the road suddenly became the infamous US Highway 666. He and his passenger road in silence for several minutes.

"I'm sorry about your cousins," the investigator finally said.

"Thanks, but you did brace me for the idea that they were dead."

***

Deputy Michael Tarrio had prepared a dossier on William and Walter Etsitty before they arrived. The brothers had been arrested several times in the county. Tarrio made copies of their mug shots and charge sheets. He also had copies of the crime scene photos taken when William's body had been found.

"We were able to identify him by the fingerprints we had on file. He was dumped on China Springs Loop a few miles east of Yah-Ta-Hey," the deputy explained.

People heading west to Window Rock turned at Yah-Ta-Hey village onto Route 264, the same road where Charlie's Uncle Isaac and Aunt Julia were killed. Tarrio had marked the exact spot on a map.

"How do you know the body was dumped?" Yazzie asked.

"The MI's office said the body had been moved. They determined that by the way the blood had pooled."

"So, you don't know where he was killed?"

"No. It could have been anywhere. China Springs Loop doesn't get a lot of traffic. The killer probably figured he could get rid of the body there without being seen."

"There are ten thousand square miles of wilderness out there. Why wasn't he dumped in the desert?"

Tarrio shrugged. "Maybe they wanted the body found." He saw the quizzical looks on his visitors' faces. "As a warning. Don't get too close."

"Too close to who?" Yazzie pressed.

The deputy could only shake his head. He had no idea.

"I don't understand why you think Walter's dead, too." Charlie held up a finger as a point of order.

"Because he disappeared after William was found. Our office never ran into him again. I was talking with the Navajo Police on a different matter and Walter's name came up. They hadn't heard from him either. My guess is he's a pile of bones out in the Badlands somewhere."

"The Badlands?" The name unnerved the paralegal. "I've never heard of a place called the Badlands, before. Where's that?"

"It's most of northwest New Mexico," Warren explained. "Basically, from here north to Shiprock, then all the territory east for sixty miles. It's about six thousand square miles."

"Damn," Etsitty swore softly. "I guess it would be stupid to ask why it's called the Badlands?"

"The name's self-explanatory," Yazzie said, nodding.

***

Three miles outside of Gallup, Warren slowed his truck and pointed to a side road. "That's China Springs Loop. Would you like to see if we can find where William was dumped?"

Charlie shook her head. "What would be the point?"

Yazzie turned west on Route 264. Six miles further down the road he slowed when he reached a set of guardrails. When traffic was clear, he turned across the twenty-foot wide, asphalt-topped median, then parked on the shoulder.

"Why are we stopping?" Charlie asked. She sounded tired, even defeated.

"This is where your aunt and uncle were killed."

"So?"

"I want to get a feel for how the accident happened." He got out of the truck, then looked up and down the highway. The road was straight. Yazzie had a hard time imagining how Isaac Etsitty crossed a 20-foot wide median, another 40 feet of road and shoulder, then plowed through a barbed wire fence and flipped into the dry arroyo below.

Charlie got tired of waiting and joined him on the shoulder. "What are you pondering so seriously?"

He explained his concerns. "The traffic report said the weather was clear . . . no other vehicles on the road, evidently." He turned and looked at his companion. "Tell me again about the accident from the other evening . . . the one where your aunt and cousins were killed."

Chapter Sixty-Five

It was a 15-minute drive from the accident site to Charlie's motel. She had known Warren Yazzie for only 5 hours and decided she liked the man. As they pulled into the Quality Inn parking area, she asked him, "Are you hungry?"

It was 5:30 p.m. already, so it had been six hours since lunch.

He thought for a moment, then nodded. "I could eat."

"Is the restaurant here at the motel any good?"

"It's not bad. It's a buffet, but they have a lot of local foods."

"I'm willing to try it."

The restaurant was more crowded than Charlie expected.

"It's Saturday night," Warren explained. "A lot of people go out to eat on the weekends. This is a popular spot."

After being seated, the hostess asked if they wanted the buffet or a menu. They both agreed the buffet would be fine. As the couple picked their way through the selections, Charlie realized she wasn't very hungry. When they returned to their table, she did little more than poke at her food. All she could think about was the crime scene photo of William's dead body.

For her own sanity's sake, she decided to concentrate on something else.

"What are the Navajo Rangers?"

"They're a small division within Department of Natural Resources," Yazzie began, after swallowing a mouthful of food. "There are only sixteen rangers for the entire reservation. They're responsible for managing archeological sites, search and rescue operations, even livestock inspections.

"I started off with the tribal police. Trained at the state police academy and eventually attended the twenty-week FBI course at Quantico. The Rangers opened an office of Special Investigation about ten years ago. That's when I joined them."

"What kind of special investigations?"

Warren considered his answer for a long moment. "There are around two hundred and ten officers on the entire Navajo police force. Only a hundred and forty are on patrol duty. That's not a lot of officers for twenty-seven thousand square miles.

"The other seventy sworn officers handle administration, training, gang control and criminal investigations. The police respond to two hundred and fifty thousand calls a year. But they can't respond to everything.

"One of the things the Special Investigation unit was created to handle was . . ."

He hesitated. Charlie couldn't tell if he was looking for the right words or if his pause was for dramatic effect.

". . . paranormal activity."

Etsitty was honestly surprised at Yazzie's revelation. "What kind of paranormal activity?"

"Hauntings . . . like poltergeist activity. UFO sightings . . . Skinwalkers."

"You know about Skinwalkers?"

The former ranger nodded. "Probably more than most . . . not enough to stop them.

"In eighteen seventy-eight, about ten years after the long walk from Bosque Redondo, there was a great purge. The Navajo people tried to eradicate all the evil medicine men from the reservation. These medicine men followed the Witchery Way. They became witches and some learned to take the forms of wild animals. They were the ones called Skinwalkers.

"The witches that survived the purge fled east into the desert of western New Mexico. For forty years God fearing Diné hated venturing into large portions of what's called the Navajo Badlands. There are still some places no one goes."

"But the Skinwalkers . . . they're not just in the Badlands now."

"No, they're not."

"I thought medicine men only did good things."

"That's the way they start off. I guess after so many years of good works, they seek more power by turning to evil. Believe me, these witches are truly evil."

Charlie leaned forward and whispered. "How do they become witches?"

Yazzie spoke in low tones, so he wouldn't alarm the other diners. "I'm told they go through specific ceremonies to acquire their powers. Of course, they need to have a firm foundation. They study for years to become a medicine man first. But before they can begin the Witchery Way, they have to do something truly evil to demonstrate their commitment."

"Like what?" Charlie still whispered.

"Kill someone they know."

Yazzie wasn't completely honest in his answer. Charlie wouldn't find that out for another day.

Chapter Sixty-Six

The grey/black storm clouds stretched to the edge of the horizon. The daytime darkness was disrupted by a sizzling welder's arc. A second later the Chevy Cavalier was nearly knocked from the road by the deafening blast.

The pounding rain was nerve racking.

Tina strained to see the gravel road. Her hands ached from holding the steering wheel too tightly. She cringed every time she hit a bump because the man in the front seat screamed in pain.

"Where are we going?" Tina kept asking.

"Just keep driving!" the man with the gun snapped.

After 10 minutes of poorly maintained gravel and mud, they reached a road that appeared more heavily trafficked. Tina stopped the car. Their choice was left, right, or straight ahead on the same muddy track. "Which way should I go?"

The gunman looked up and down the new road, confused. "This isn't the highway," he complained. "I want the highway. Keep going straight!"

Tina hesitated. Her little car couldn't handle the road if it got more rugged. "Are you sure?"

"I have the gun. That means I know where I'm going. That way!" He pointed the gun toward the road ahead.

Tina pressed the accelerator, and they crossed the wider road. Twenty feet later, they heard the grinding of tires on gravel and the swoosh of a car passing behind them. The idiot driver had not turned on his lights. In the driving rain, Tina never saw the car coming.

If they had paused 10 seconds longer, all three would have been dead. Tina began to shiver at the thought.

"Miss Morales, are you all right?" Mariah leaned forward and touched the driver's shoulder.

The schoolteacher involuntarily jumped at the human contact. She was a spring wound too tight by the stress of the gunman, the storm and the wretched road she was trying to follow.

She cleared her throat. "I'm all right . . . just sit back."

A mile further down . . . or maybe only 100 yards . . . Tina couldn't tell . . . their road dipped as it crossed a usually dry creek bed. It was quickly filling with water.

The driver gave the gunman a nervous glance. He saw her concern. "Keep driving," he ordered.

Tina sped up, hoping the momentum would counteract the rushing stream. The effort worked and they were quickly on the other side.

The rain and the questionable road conditions kept the Cavalier's speed at 20 miles per hour. Junior Kee gently rubbed his knee. The pain was getting worse. The car's interior was much too cramped. He needed to stretch out his leg, but there wasn't room. He considered laying the seat back as far as it would go, but that wouldn't work. He needed to keep the gun pointed at the driver. He needed to watch where they were going.

Tina felt the car pulling to the right again, just like it had on the highway. She prayed that it was just the poor excuse for a road that gave the impression the tire was going flat again.

"Not now, Midnight," she said under her breath. "Not now."

The rain was beginning to let up. Morales was able to see the road and the surrounding landscape better. It looked like they were 1,000 miles from civilization. The only indication men had ever been there was the single lane trail they were following.

Two miles after the first creek, they came to another arroyo. It was deeper and wider than the first. There was more water, as well. Tina stopped the car at the top of the bank.

"I don't think we can get across."

"I don't care what you think. We're not stopping out here in the middle of . . ." Kee couldn't find the word he was looking for. "We can't stop here," he said, finishing the thought. "You have to keep going!"

"I think I'm getting a flat."

"I don't care."

"What if we get stuck?"

Kee almost said, "Then we'll walk." That would have been an idle threat. He knew he couldn't walk. Instead, he fell back on wishful thinking. "We're not going to get stuck. Just keep driving. We need to find the highway." He thought for a moment. "We need to go west."

"I don't know where west is," the driver admitted. "I don't know what direction we've been going."

The high desert was getting chilly. The rain had dropped the temperature into the 40s. However, Junior Kee was sweating . . . from the pain, from the stress, from the fear of being arrested. He had a greater fear building inside him now. The fear of being stranded in the Badlands.

"Get across the creek! We'll take the next left we find. That will get us to the highway." There was no real conviction in his words.

Tina edged her Chevy down the bank. The current pushed against the car. She fought to keep it headed straight. The deflating tire added to her struggle. The car was being dragged from right to left.

She gunned the engine. The back tires dug into the arroyo's sand before they finally got traction. "Come on, girl. Come on, come on," Tina whispered desperately.

Slowly the car crept its way across the stream as the tires slipped, then pushed them forward. At the far bank, the dark blue Chevy, never designed for off-road excursions, climbed out of the water.

"I knew you could do it, Midnight," Tina said proudly, patting the dashboard.

"Wow," Mariah said from the backseat. "I didn't think we were going to make it."

"Shut up!" Junior barked. He pointed his gun straight ahead. "Keep going."

Chapter Sixty-Seven

Bud Baker impatiently strode across the parking area from the *Southern Antiques* warehouse to his office. Evan Florin matched his boss step for step. Wanda Florin followed as best as she could on her fat, stubby legs.

The police were notorious for maintaining confidential informants to keep track of law breakers. Operations like Baker's needed their own informers to keep one step ahead of the law. These ranged from nurses in hospitals like Miguel Cuellar to sheriff's deputies and police sergeants.

Baker's van went missing Monday night. For five days he had men searching for his property and its contents. He had also put out the word about what he was looking for.

Wanda Florin failed at recovering the Navajo girl in Segovia. After Cuellar couldn't finish the job, the sheriff's department helped the girl disappear. Baker had no informants on the payroll in the San Phillipe sheriff's office. For the time being, the missing girl would have to remain a loose thread.

Bits of information came in a sliver here, a shard there. The pieces began to take the form of a shattered pane of glass, a mosaic of what must have happened. Roberto de la Cruz was found dead near Highway two eighty-five. Someone killed him and stole the van. The Navajo girl escaped, probably when de la Cruz raped her.

The murderer took the van and dropped the three remaining Indian girls at the Counselor Trading Post. That was Tuesday morning. None of Baker's contacts had heard anything about what happened to the van.

He was still trying to fit two spare pieces of information into the larger puzzle. A truck had been found near de la Cruz's body. The truck probably belonged to the man's killer. If he could find the owner, he would learn who was messing with his business.

The other spare piece was more a lack of information. Juan Pedro Garcia, one of his most reliable drivers, had gone missing. He never answered his cell phone. He never responded to notes left on his door. Baker could find no record of an arrest anywhere. The Segovia police claimed they had not heard a thing.

"We need to fill those orders we missed last week," Baker growled.

"Do you think it's safe?" Wanda usually asked the questions. She was the brains of the mother/son team.

"If the cops had found the van, they would have been crawling all over us by now. How many girls do you have at the motel?"

Baker always had a contingency plan for everything. Until the van was found, he didn't want any kidnap victims kept at the warehouse. A local dive of a motel was kept on a retainer for back-up operations.

"Only three . . . and they're Honduran."

"I can find places for them. No problem. But I have very unhappy clients in Denver. See if you can reach the Navajo. Tell him to fire up his Winnebego. At a minimum, we need three Indian maidens, like, a week ago."

"He said he has some prospects south of Farmington," Wanda said. "I'll tell him to round them up."

"What about that van?" Evan asked, feeling left out.

"Don't worry about it. That van is probably deep in the Navajo Reservation . . . getting stunk up with sheep. Whoever stole it isn't going to advertise the fact that they have it. I'm sure they'll say an uncle sold it to them. Some hogwash like that.

"We'll never hear about that van again."

Chapter Sixty-Eight

It was already late afternoon. The last of the summer monsoon rains was dying out just 5 miles south of Lindsay. Cooler air wafted over the assembly of lawmen gathered again in the trading post parking lot. Lansing slipped on his fleece-lined jacket, then stood with his hands shoved deep into the pockets . . . waiting.

The two park rangers needed to find out where their truck would be taken. They sat in the café, drinking coffee.

The SID and FBI agents were getting their instructions from Santa Fe and Albuquerque. The State Police District 10 office in Farmington would be the temporary headquarters for the task force. It was across the road from the Four Corners Regional Airport and the New Mexico National Guard. The vehicles in the canyon would be transported to a Guard hangar for thorough analysis.

The FBI hierarchy had already decided the van was probably involved in interstate crimes. The Mann Act was first passed in 1907. It was intended to protect immigrant women brought to America and forced into prostitution. Over the years, the act became a catch-all for many immoral offenses. The 1986 revision made it illegal to transport a woman across state lines for any sexual activity where a person can be charged with a criminal offense, i.e., prostitution.

The feds also suspected they were looking at child abduction, kidnapping and violation of tribal sovereignty. They needed to track down the three Indian girls dropped off in Counselor for statements. A joint team of FBI and SID agents would be assembled to begin surveillance of the *Southwest Antiques'* property in Santa Fe. It might take more than a few days of observation before enough evidence was gathered for a search warrant.

The State Police agreed not to stop any *Southwest Antiques* vehicles on the open highways. The shackles and handcuffs in the van provided them with all the probable cause they needed, but the FBI didn't want interference with their operations.

As the SID/FBI meeting began to break up, Lansing approached.

"I know you folks consider county business a low priority, but I have a shooting and a murder on my hands. Am I free to investigate or are you going to handle them?"

The state and federal agents were so engrossed in establishing their own boundaries and responsibilities, they had forgotten about the killing that initiated the operation.

Special Agent Hempstead cleared his throat. "I would think this should fall to the state. The FBI doesn't get involved in local investigations."

SID officer Adam Dale looked at Lansing. "Are you even equipped to handle a murder investigation?"

Lansing wasn't surprised at the condescending question. He was expecting it. "All I wanted to do was make sure there wasn't a duplication of effort. I can step back and let the state handle it. I only request that my office is kept informed. I'll even assign a deputy as a liaison, if you want."

Dale turned to his fellow officer. The two stepped aside and whispered back and forth for a full minute. Dale finally came back to Lansing.

"This is San Phillipe County, isn't it?"

"Yes." The sheriff was a bit miffed at the question.

"I think it's the wise thing for the state to roll both investigations together."

"Exactly what are those investigations?"

"Grand theft, auto. The probability there were murders in other counties besides yours. There's still the missing ranger. We have plenty to keep us busy."

"Just asking."

"And, Sheriff, please, don't bother sending a deputy to help us. They'll just get in the way."

"But you will keep my office informed, right?"

"Of course, we will, Sheriff. Your county will still be responsible for any prosecutions."

Lansing walked back to the Tahoe, chaffing at how readily he had been dismissed. Any other time he would have fought to keep a murder investigation in his office, mostly because his department would ultimately be responsible for any state screw-ups.

"Dispatch, Patrol One," the sheriff said into his mic.

"Roger, Patrol One," Sid Barns responded. "This is dispatch, go ahead."

"Sid, I'm still in Lindsay. Probably be heading back to town shortly. I'm getting no cell phone coverage out here. I need for you to check on a couple of things for me.

"Call Jake Redwine and see if he dropped the horses off at my ranch. Then find out if Tina Morales made it to Gallup with the Navajo girl."

"Give me a few minutes. I'll call you right back."

Chapter Sixty-Nine

The rain finally stopped. A breeze from the northwest brought even colder temperatures. The only consolation was the clouds were being swept away. Tina's Cavalier barely made it to the top of the next hill. The occupants could see for miles. The only visible living things were the sage and grasses that soaked up the nourishing rain.

There were no cattle. No sheep. There weren't even power lines to be seen, let alone buildings of any type. In the distance was another ribbon of road similar to the one they were on.

Driving down to the barren plain nearly 50 feet below, something loud started beating against the front wheel-well. Tina immediately stopped the car at the flat bottom of the hill.

"What are you doing?" Junior Kee demanded.

"I've shredded my tire!" she snapped. "It's going to tear up my car." She threw open her door and rushed to the front, right of the car. Inspecting the damage with folded arms, all she could do was shake her head.

Mariah joined her from the back seat. "What are you going to do?"

"Change it." Tina walked back to her driver's side to pop the trunk latch.

"You have a spare, don't you?" Junior Kee asked.

"It's a donut spare, but yes, I do."

"Well, you better put it on."

"I don't suppose you could help, could you?"

The gunman considered the question. Any other time changing a tire wouldn't be a problem. At the moment, he wasn't sure he could walk. There was also the issue of his gun. He wasn't about to just set it down.

He didn't answer the driver. He opened his own door and attempted to get out. When he tried to stand, he screamed in pain and crumpled to the ground. He dropped the gun and clutched his right knee.

Tina's first instinct was to rush to help the suffering man. She was too angry for that. She simply stood next to her open door.

"Miss Morales, I can help you with the tire."

They walked to the now open trunk. As the two women surveyed the tire and tools they would need, Junior yelled, "Hey, I need help!"

Tina frowned. "Yeah, so do we."

Kee realized he had dropped his gun. He looked around and reached for it while still trying to hold his knee. He gave an involuntary yelp.

Mariah looked at her mentor. Their abductor was obviously hurting. Her expression asked if they should help. The response was a subtle shake of the head.

Tina handed her helper the lug wrench/pry bar and scissor jack while she pulled out the tire. They walked to the front of the car with their gear.

The front, right tire was indeed shredded. There was a dent in the fender where a flap of loose tire had slapped against it. The car was resting on the rim.

Junior waved his gun at the women. "I need help. I need to get back in the car!"

Tina looked at her car, the open door, and the gunman sitting on the ground. "We need to get him out of the way. Grab him under his arm pit. I'll take the other side."

They unceremoniously latched onto either side of the man and began pulling.

"What the hell are you doing?" Kee demanded.

"Making room," Tina grunted. The man was dead weight. His only contribution was constant screaming. They leaned him against a small mound of sculptured sand 5 feet away, then returned to their task.

While the car rested on the rim, Tina attempted to loosen the five lug nuts. She had changed tires before, but she always had access to a 4-way lug wrench. The plus pattern gave her much more leverage. The Cavalier's lug wrench/pry bar was constructed at an angle. Even with both her and Mariah pushing on the bar, they couldn't budge three of the nuts.

Tina sat on the ground and leaned against her car. "Midnight, why are you doing this?"

Mariah sat next to her. "What if we jack up the car? That might give us more room for pushing the rod down."

"It's worth a shot."

The scissor jack was useless. It took 20 minutes to find a spot where they could get the jack under the frame. Once they started winding on the mechanism, the jack dug itself into the sand. They needed a piece of wood or flat rock for a base, neither of which was available. Tina attempted to use a schoolbook from the rear seat. All she managed to do was tear up the book.

By the time Tina realized they would not be changing her tire, the sun was beginning to set. Both women were thankful for having jackets to wear.

"You women are worthless!" Junior Kee shouted.

Tina didn't say a thing. She simply walked over to her abductor, grabbed his knee and squeezed.

"What the hell!" Kee screamed. He dropped the gun and grabbed his excruciatingly painful leg.

Tina picked up the gun and threw it as far as she could, then walked back to her car. Grabbing her cell phone, she opened it, then held it high over her head, looking for a signal. She never found one.

"What now?" Mariah asked.

"We walk."

"Shouldn't we stay with the car . . . just in case somebody is looking for us."

"Who? Nobody knows where we are. No one even knows we're missing." She opened the passenger door and retrieved a flashlight from the glove compartment. "Come on."

"Which way?"

Tina looked up the hill, then in the direction they had been headed. "Let's keep going."

"Hey, you two. What are you doing?"

"We're going to walk out of here."

"What about me? You can't leave me here!"

"We're not. You can come along, if you want."

"I can't even stand!"

Tina shrugged, turned, and started walking. Mariah hesitated for a moment. "What's your name?"

The former gunman was jolted by the question. "Junior . . . Junior Kee. Why?"

"In case anybody asks who dragged us out here." The Navajo girl hurried to catch up with her companion.

"Don't leave me out here!" Junior Kee screamed. The terror in his voice crescendoed. "You can't leave me out here. Not in the dark. Please! Don't leave me!"

Chapter Seventy

Cliff Lansing sat in the Chevy Tahoe contemplating his next move. He was still in the Lindsay Trading Post parking lot. The other agencies had left to begin their assigned tasks.

Jake Redwine had delivered the horses to his ranch, but that was the only thing that had gone right. Tina Morales and Mariah Tsosie had not made it to Gallup. Through a series of phone calls, Dispatcher Sid Barnes attempted to track them down. Deputy Jack Rivera said the women left his house at 9:30. The Gallup Indian Medical Center confirmed they had not checked in. They had been on the road for 9 hours and could be anywhere between Las Palmas and Gallup. Checking with the State Police, there were no reports that the women had been in an accident.

Late in the afternoon, Barnes contacted Lansing. There had been a robbery at the Pueblo Pintado convenience store. A customer had been shot and was in critical condition. The McKinley Sheriff's Department had issued an APB on a dark blue or black Toyota Tercel . . . or possibly a Chevy Cavalier . . . used in the getaway. The shooter and his accomplice had escaped onto the back roads. The occupants should be considered armed and dangerous.

Lansing pulled out a highway map. Pueblo Pintado was 20 miles south of Lindsay. Chaco Canyon National Historical Park was 25 miles to the southwest. Faint lines traced the several "Indian Service Routes" and oil company roads through the Badlands, none of which were paved. If Tina Morales had been forced by gunpoint to assist an armed robber, they could escape into that semi-wilderness and never be found.

The sun was dragging itself below the distant horizon. It would be a two-hour drive back to Las Palmas. Lansing was reluctant to make the trip. He wasn't concerned about getting to the ranch late. That was normal.

He was worried about Tina Morales . . . and the Navajo girl. But mostly Tina. (Despite her aloofness in the past six weeks, he still cared for her. Maybe more than he was willing to admit.) Going home would put too much distance between himself and the two women. It was possible they were only 10 or 15 miles from Lindsay. If he left, he may not make it back to search for them.

As always, jurisdiction was an issue. He was in San Phillipe County, only a couple miles from Sandoval. Pueblo Pintado was in McKinley County, but just a few miles north the gunman and his hostages would have crossed into San Juan County.

He could look for Tina's Cavalier as a private citizen, but he should at least give his fellow sheriffs a courtesy call. He looked at the map again. It would be insane for him to begin a solo search. He wouldn't know where to begin.

Starting his engine, the sheriff had not made a final decision. He pulled onto Highway 550 and headed east. In the back of his mind the thought lingered that he needed to do something. He just didn't know what.

Five miles down the road he reached Counselor. That morning he had a murder and the canyon search on his mind. He slowed as he approached the trading post. It was the spot the three Indian girls had been released.

Instinct told him he needed to stop there. Besides, his gas gauge indicated he needed a fill-up. He stopped at the single gas pump, then walked inside. He was the only customer.

"Can I help you?" the man behind the counter asked. He was obviously Navaho and wore his hair long. His name tag said "Art."

"I need to gas up. Can you turn the pump on?"

"Sure, no problem."

"Do you have any coffee?"

"Nothing fresh. If you care to wait, I can start a new pot."

"I'm in no hurry," Lansing admitted. "I'll fill up while you take care of the coffee."

Five minutes later, he was back inside.

"It will be a few more minutes," Art said. "I noticed your patrol unit out there. Are you a Sandoval deputy?"

"No, I'm from San Phillipe County," he admitted. "Art, I heard three girls were dropped off here the other morning." He tried to sound casual. "Were you the one who found them?"

"Yes. They were huddled outside . . . scared to death. I brought them inside, gave them blankets to wrap up in. Got them something warm to drink."

"Did you call the sheriff's department or State Police?"

"No," Art shook his head. "I called the Chapter President. Asked him what I should do."

"Chapter President?"

"Stephen Clah. He's the Counselor Chapter House President. He's like a county judge. He told me to call the Navajo Police in Crownpoint. They're the ones who picked up the girls and made sure they got home. Why are you so interested?" Art asked suspiciously

"The night before those girls were dropped off, the State Police found a Navajo girl on the highway not far from Segovia. I think she might have been one of that group."

"Why do you think that?"

"Because of some evidence that's recently come to light."

Art the manager thought for a moment. "I need to make a phone call. Can I ask you your name?"

"It's Lansing. Sheriff Cliff Lansing."

Art's eyes widened. He had never met an actual sheriff before. "Would you mind waiting, Sheriff?"

"Not a problem. I still need some coffee."

Art disappeared into a back office. A few minutes he returned. "President Clah asked if he could talk to you."

"Sure. Where's your phone?"

"Not on the phone. At his place."

The sheriff frowned. "Is it far?"

"No . . . and it's easy to get there."

Lansing agreed, provided he could get his coffee first.

Chapter Seventy-One

It was dark when Lansing left the trading post.

The Clah ranch was indeed easy to find. Across the highway was a road that climbed a hill past two-story apartment buildings. The gravel road continued for another mile, ending at a collection of outbuildings and a sturdy house. A low corral contained two-dozen sheep.

Stephen Clah greeted the sheriff at the door. The Chapter House president was a solid man of about fifty. He had the weathered look of a man who spent a lifetime outdoors.

The household held three generations. Grandparents and grandchildren sat in the living room watching television. They barely noticed the visitor.

Clah led the sheriff to a large kitchen where his wife and daughter were finishing dishes. They excused themselves so that the men could discuss business. The president gestured to a seat at the kitchen table.

"I was going to offer you coffee," Clah began, "but I see you brought your own."

"It's been a long day." Lansing removed his jacket and hung it on the back of his chair, then sat. "You have a nice family."

"Thanks." Clah took a seat across the table. "I hope you didn't mind coming out here."

"Not at all." Lansing didn't want to beat around the bush. "Mr. Clah, I take it you wanted to talk about the Navajo girl picked up earlier this week."

"Please, call me Stephen . . . but yes. I do want to ask about her and why you think she might be involved with the girls dropped off at the post."

Since the state and the feds had decided they were in charge, Lansing saw no point in withholding information from a Navajo tribal official. He told Clah everything he knew about Mariah Tsosie, her abduction, her discovery on the highway, the attempt on her life. He described the van he found in the canyon and evidence four people were shackled in the back.

Clah specifically asked for more details about Mariah's escape from the van.

The sheriff admitted all he had was his own guesses. As far as he knew, Mariah still refused to talk about what happened to her. He described how the girl was found covered with blood. Someone had attempted to rape her. Two days after she was rescued, the body of a man was found not far off the highway. He had been brutally murdered. To Lansing and to the Medical Investigator's office it appeared the man was killed by a wild animal.

Clah stared at the tabletop and drummed his fingers lightly. "Who do you think tried to kill her in the hospital?" he finally asked.

"Whoever held her captive. They didn't want her to talk."

"You don't think it could have been the same person who rescued her from the van?"

Lansing gave Clah a bewildered look. "Why would they do that?"

"When the three girls were released, the man who dropped them off told them not to remove their blindfolds. He didn't want to be seen . . . The Zuni girl, her name was Lolisha Quam, peeked anyway. What she saw scared the hell out of her."

"What did she see?"

Clah hesitated. "From her description . . . I think she saw a Skin-walker. In Navajo they're called *yee naaldlooshii*. Translated, it means 'with it, he goes on all fours.' "

"I've heard about Skinwalkers since I was a kid," Lansing admitted. "I know I've never seen one. What exactly is a Skinwalker?"

"They are medicine men who have turned to evil. Some don the skins of a wild beast . . . a coyote or a cougar or a bear. They follow what's called the Witchery Way. It's thought there is a hierarchy within their ranks, and they have to follow specific rules."

"Pardon my Star Wars reference, but you're saying a medicine man wakes up one day and decides he's going to turn to the Dark Side?"

"In a way," Clah admitted. "But before he can follow the Witchery Way, a man must commit a most foul deed. He must kill a close family member, usually a sibling.

"Once they are inducted, many choose to wear the mantle of a wild animal. Through their rituals, they take on the characteristics of the animal they've assumed. They become Skinwalkers. They have extraordinary abilities. Some say they can run faster than a car.

"During the day they appear normal. No one would know what they truly are. It's at night when they change. The Skinwalker Lolisha saw . . . the wild animal that killed the man you found . . . I think they are the same person. It could be the Skinwalker came back to the hospital to kill Mariah so she couldn't identify him."

Lansing assured him they knew who tried to kill the girl and it was no Skinwalker. "Are there a lot of these 'witches' on the Navajo Reservation?"

"Maybe, too many," the Chapter House president admitted.

"Do they live in the Badlands?"

"Not just the Badlands, but yes. The Badlands cover a large area. In fact, we're in the Badlands here on the ranch."

Lansing suddenly became even more worried about Tina and Mariah. "Pueblo Pintado, everything south of Counselor, that's all part of the Badlands, isn't it?"

Clah nodded.

The sheriff filled him in on the robbery and his fear Tina was car-jacked by a shooter. "She could be lost out there right now!"

"There's nothing you can do tonight."

Lansing stood. "I probably need to get an early start tomorrow, then. Is there a motel anywhere close?"

"Cuba, about thirty-five miles from here," Clah said. "But I wouldn't advise going outside."

"Why?"

"The Badlands aren't very safe at night . . . at least not recently."

"If you're referring to Skinwalkers, I'm not afraid."

"You should be," Clah said grimly.

Chapter Seventy-Two

After 10 minutes of walking, the two women couldn't hear Junior Kee's yelling any longer. He was either too far away . . . too worn out to continue . . . or something worse. Whatever that "something worse" might have been was never discussed.

Once the sun was down, Tina tried to limit her use of the flashlight. She had no idea how much battery life she still had. Even with just a quarter moon low on the horizon, there seemed to be plenty of light.

The teacher had always heard about light pollution from human civilization but didn't appreciate the concept until that night. Each star contributed a tiny bit. A million stars contributed a lot. The broad swath of a hazy ribbon known as the Milky Way added its share. With no towns nearby, the heavenly light had no competition.

The total result was, when their eyes adjusted, there was enough light for the two women to walk safely. That is as long as they stayed on the dirt road. There were occasional puddles from the earlier rain. Fortunately, the ground was more sandy than muddy.

When they talked, it was in whispers. Subconsciously, they understood they were intruders. They needed to keep their presence as inconspicuous as possible. The smallest shadow seemed ominous. They both stopped and listened intently if they heard a sound.

"Is someone following us?" Mariah asked nervously.

The bravery Tina had seen the girl exhibit earlier against their abductor had diminished somewhat.

"I don't think so," Tina whispered reassuringly. "Our imaginations are working in overdrive. That's all."

When the stars came out, Tina and Mariah both spotted the Big Dipper, then Polaris. They realized they had been walking north. They soon found a crossing road. Junior Kee insisted a highway was to the west, so they turned left, toward the west.

After two miles, the road split at a deep arroyo. For no particular reason they turned north again. Their road descended into another arroyo, then suddenly disappeared . . . washed away by the storm.

"What is this place?" Mariah asked.

The small canyon they found themselves in was populated by bizarre sandstone mushrooms with flat rocks for their caps. Some pedestals were only a few feet tall and were missing their cap rocks. Others stood as much as 8-feet high, looming, silent sentinels over the sandy wash.

"I have no idea," Tina admitted. "I'll bet this is impressive in the daylight."

"It's impressive in the dark," the Navajo said. "And spooky."

They wandered down the wash for a short way, marveling at Nature's handiwork, momentarily forgetting about their plight.

Finally, Tina said, "We need to find where that road picks up."

They attempted to backtrack to the point they entered the arroyo. They discovered they had left no tracks in the hard-packed sand.

"No need to panic," the teacher said softly. "We know we were heading north. Let's find a path up the bank and follow the North Star again."

When they did get to the flat ground above, there was no road to be seen. They picked their way through the barren sage and dried grass, looking for a path to follow. At the bottom of a hill, they found a two-track road they could use. It too led north. Though neither knew it, they were moving deeper into the Navajo Badlands.

"Miss Morales, how much longer are we going to walk?" They both had slowed their pace considerably.

"Getting tired?"

"And thirsty."

Before Tina could suggest they continue just little further, she saw the glow of a fire on the other side of a hill just ahead. She pointed at the light, then raised her finger to her lips. They had no idea what awaited them. They needed to assess the situation before they barged in.

When they neared the top of the hill, they began crawling on all fours for a peek. At the bottom was another arroyo, not unlike the wash with the sandstone sculptures. A small campfire lit the area, the flickering flames causing shadowy images that danced on the steep banks.

A lone figure wearing a board-brimmed hat sat in front of the fire, wrapped in a Navajo blanket. The head was bowed. The person seemed asleep.

Indicating they needed to keep silent, Tina stood and began walking down the bank. Mariah tiptoed behind her. Almost to the bottom of the wash, Tina saw the figure stir.

"You two must be thirsty," the man said, turning to his visitors.

Chapter Seventy-Three

In the semi-darkness, it was impossible to tell the Navajo man's age. His long hair hung straight. His blanket was red and black, the colors separated by a white zigzag motif. He stood and produced a canteen from beneath his blanket. He removed the cap which remained attached by a short chain, then offered the container to Tina.

She hesitated, looking at her companion first. Mariah stared at the canteen, unconsciously licking her dry lips. Tina stepped forward, accepting the container. She smelled the contents first, then took a sip. Realizing they had nothing to fear, Tina took a large swig, then handed the container to Mariah.

The girl took a long drink, choking on the water when she tried to swallow too much. Tina firmly patted her back.

"Careful, little one," the man said.

Mariah caught her breath. "I'm okay."

"Come sit by the fire. It is only going to get colder." The man turned and resumed his seat.

Tina and Mariah positioned themselves on the opposite side of the fire.

"You are hungry." It was a statement, not a question. He tossed a small, cloth bag across the fire that landed at Tina's knee.

Tina opened the draw string and found several strips of dried meat. She took a piece, then handed the bag to her friend. Mariah removed a piece as well.

The venison jerky was as tasty as it was tough to chew, but neither complained. After eating the dried meat and soaking up several more swallows of water, the women visibly relaxed.

"My name's Tina Morales. This is my friend Mariah."

The man under the hat nodded. "I am called *Nizéé'*."

Mariah leaned close to Tina and whispered. "That's Navajo for 'the quiet one.' "

If *Nizéé'* heard the remark, he ignored it. Instead, he stared at the girl. Tina couldn't help but notice.

"Is something wrong?"

"No," he shook his head and looked away. "She just reminds me of someone."

Tina looked around. "We sure are lucky you happened to be here."

"Not so much luck . . . I live in this place."

The teacher could see no buildings, no trailer or truck. She couldn't fathom what kind of existence he lived.

"Didn't you get soaked in that storm?"

"Not so much."

"You live in this canyon?" It was Mariah's turn.

"I didn't just mean this canyon." *Nizéé'* stuck a finger in the air and made a wide circle. " 'This place' is very big."

"But you sleep here?"

"Sometimes, yes. Sometimes, no. I waited for you."

"You knew we were coming?" Tina pursued the questions now.

"I have been watching . . . since you left your car."

"You saw us trying to change our tire?" She was indignant.

All the man did was give a noncommittal shrug. "I needed to keep guard."

"Why? Were we in danger? From what?"

"There are many things out here that can harm you."

"What about the man we left at the car?" Mariah seemed alarmed. "Is he all right?"

"It is late." *Nizéé'* stood and walked over to the two women. He removed the blanket from his shoulders and draped it over them. "Try to get some rest."

It wasn't long before both Tina Morales and Mariah Tsosie were asleep.

Nizéé' threw a few more dried sticks on the small fire. He then climbed to the top of the arroyo and crouched. He spent the rest of the night making sure his new friends were safe.

Chapter Seventy-Four

It was 4:00 in the morning when the whistling woke Charlotte Etsitty. The sound came from just beyond her motel room door. It was a sound she had heard too many times before.

Her first thought was to call the front desk. She dismissed the idea just as quickly. She had seen the night security. He was an old man armed with a set of keys and a flashlight. Hardly a match for a *yee naaldlooshii.*

She resisted the temptation to turn on the lamp next to the bed. She felt around and found her cell phone, then retreated to the bathroom. When she opened the clam shell, there was enough light for her to find Warren Yazzie's number.

After three rings, a sleepy voice said, "This is Warren."

"Warren!" Charlie whispered as loudly as she dared. "This is Charlie . . . Charlie Etsitty. I need your help."

"What's wrong?"

"Someone's whistling outside my room. It's a Skinwalker."

"Are you sure?"

"I've heard them before, on the ranch."

"I'll be there in five minutes." There was a sense of urgency in his voice. "Pack your things. You will need to check out . . . and whatever you do, don't open your door. When I get there, we'll use a password . . . Shiprock. Understand?"

"Yes. Shiprock." She understood the instructions. She just didn't understand why they needed a special word.

Warren Yazzie lived in a stone house on Circle Hill Drive, less than a mile from the Quality Inn. Despite Yazzie's instructions, Charlie stayed in the bathroom until Warren pounded on her door. She didn't open the door until he supplied the password.

"Why did we need a password?" she asked as she began filling her suitcase.

"*Adiłgąshii* don't just appear as animals." He used the Navajo word for witch. "They are shape-shifters and can assume the identity of other humans. An impersonator, however, would not have known our secret word."

Charlie was satisfied with his answer. She looked at her assembled clothes. "What should I wear?"

"Dress warmly . . . Jeans will be fine."

"Are we going somewhere?"

"Lake Valley, about thirty miles north of Crownpoint."

"What's there?"

"Hopefully, answers."

***

The coffee they grabbed at the Food Mart 24-hour Convenience Store did nothing to keep Etsitty awake. She dozed off before she could ask the dozen questions she wanted to pose about the sudden trip.

Charlie woke when she sensed they had stopped moving. She stretched and yawned. "Where are we?"

"Grandma's Restaurant, Crownpoint."

"What time is it?"

"It's six. The place will open in a few minutes."

"Good," Charlie said, yawning a second time. "I think I'm hungry."

They both welcomed the fresh-brewed coffee. After ordering, Charlie started in on her questions.

"We're going to . . . Lake City, you said?"

"Lake Valley," Yazzie clarified. "I was up till almost midnight making phone calls."

"What about?"

"Your cousins."

"Do you think this is even worth the effort? They're both dead."

"Don't you want to know why they died?"

Charlie nodded as she sipped her coffee. "I suppose."

"And don't you want to find out about why the Etsitty family has been cursed by Skinwalkers?"

"That, for sure."

"From what I learned last night, your cousins' deaths and the curse might be related."

"Really? How so?"

"Your Uncle Isaac worked for the Navajo Nation Historic Preservation Department. He wanted to survey an area north of Chaco Canyon called *Kimbeto Wash*. It allegedly had significant Diné structures that could be dated to before the time of the long walk." Yazzie paused. "Isaac was evidently told to back off. Drop the whole idea."

"By his department?"

"No."

"Who then?"

"No one knows for sure. He and your aunt were killed in that car accident before the matter was settled. His superiors knew about the threats. Evidently, they decided the alleged ruins were not important enough to pursue."

"Who did you talk to?"

"One of my Ranger friends. The Rangers are tasked to manage archeological districts. They knew about this potential site, but no one in charge was interested in researching it."

"How does this involve my cousins?"

"Maybe they found out who threatened their father. Maybe there weren't just threats. What if someone followed through and eliminated your uncle. Your aunt would have been collateral damage."

"You're saying my cousins were killed because they discovered who killed their parents."

"Makes sense, doesn't it."

Charlie thought for a moment. "You think it's the *adiłgąshii*?"

"Your cousins probably pissed off some very powerful people. That's why they were killed. I think that's why the Etsitty family has been cursed."

When the food came, Charlie said little. She was trying to get her mind around the new information Yazzie had handed her.

Chapter Seventy-Five

The star-lit night gave way to a dark blue. As the sky lightened Mariah Tsosie became aware of two things . . . she was cold and the woman lying on the ground next to her was moaning. She sat up, realizing she had hogged the blanket given to them the night before.

"Miss Morales," the teenager said softly, "are you all right?" She gently laid the blanket over her friend, thinking the chill was causing her discomfort.

"What?" Tina asked groggily.

"Are you okay? I'm sorry I took the blanket. You must be cold."

The teacher had been on her right side. She slowly rolled onto her back and blinked. Raising her head slightly she tried to survey the surroundings and grasp where they were. When she tried to sit up, she was struck by a stabbing pain to her lower abdomen.

"A-a-i-i-i," she screamed. She fell backwards, curling into a fetal position and hugging her stomach.

"Miss Morales . . . Tina," the girl yelled. "What's wrong?" When she looked closer, she realized all the color had drained from the teacher's face.

"The pain," she blurted. "The pain . . . I can't take it."

"What do you want me to do?"

"I don't know," Tina whimpered. "Find that man . . . last night . . . Oh, my God it hurts!" She rocked back-and-forth, squeezing harder, trying to lessen the pain."

"What hurts? Tell me," Mariah pleaded.

"My guts . . . It's cramps . . . They're the worst cramps I've ever had," she whimpered. "Find that man! He has to have a truck . . . I need a doctor!"

Mariah stood and looked around. She and Tina were the only occupants of the arroyo.

"*Nizéé'*!" she yelled. "*Nizéé'*!" She listened for a response. When none came, she called again. The only sound in the wash was Tina's groaning and whimpering.

Desperate, she had to find their benefactor from the night before. She knelt next to Tina. "Miss Morales, I'll be right back!"

Mariah jumped to her feet and ran up the bank. From the top she could easily see a quarter mile in every direction. There was no *Nizéé'* . . . no truck . . . no other person in sight. Though she knew it was a waste of time she yelled, "Help! Help! Anyone, can you hear me! Please! We need help!"

She was only greeted with silence.

Disheartened, she hurried back down the steep slope and ran back to Morales.

"What can I do?"

"You need to find help," Tina choked.

"No!" Mariah grabbed her arm. "You need to get up. We'll walk out of here together."

When she pulled, Tina let out another scream. "Don't! Stop. I can't stand up. Please, let go!"

Mariah did as she was requested. "Miss Morales, I can't just leave you here!"

"You have to! Either that or we'll both die here."

The Navajo looked around. If she was going to abandon her friend, even for a short while, she wanted to make her comfortable first.

Near the now-defunct fire was the canteen and the jerky bag. When she retrieved them, she realized they were both full. She had no idea when *Nizéé'* filled them or where the resupply came from.

She knelt next to Tina. "Would you like a drink?"

Tina nodded. Mariah helped her to sit up, but the experience was obviously painful. After two short sips, the teacher needed to lie back down.

"I'm going to leave the water with you," the teenager said after taking three long swigs. "There's jerky here, too." She had emptied half of the jerky into her pocket, the rest of the bag she set next to the canteen.

She picked up the blanket to shake it out. When she turned back, she noticed Tina's pants were soaked with a dark liquid. She was positive it wasn't urine. She had no idea why the older woman was bleeding, but she had bled a lot.

Mariah was scared to leave her, but she had no choice. She tucked the blanket around Tina, then stood. "Can I get you anything?"

Tina shook her head. "Just go!"

"I'll be back as soon as I can."

Mariah decided it was stupid to continue looking for Junior Kee's mythical highway. She would head back in the direction she had come. She knew there was civilization that way, she just had no idea how far.

Chapter Seventy-Six

Twenty miles north of Crownpoint, Yazzie slowed, then turned onto a dirt road. Charlie looked around. She had seen no sign announcing the turn-off to Lake Valley.

"How did you know that's where we need to turn?"

Yazzie shrugged. "My outstanding tracking skills." He wanted to keep his true abilities a mystery. That he knew to take the first road past mile marker 43 would be his secret.

Charlotte Etsitty was a smart woman who knew her limitations. Map reading and understanding geographic orientation was not one of her talents. She saw the sign for the *Kim-me-ni-oli Ruins* but couldn't appreciate the fact that it was an outlier for Chaco Canyon . . . or that the main park was less than 10 miles to the east.

They parked on the north side of the Lake Valley Chapter House . . . a single-story, stone building with a red, metal roof.

"What now?" Charlie asked, looking around the empty parking lot.

"We wait. Simon Hatale said she would meet us here at eight."

"He's the medicine man you were talking about?"

Yazzie made one short nod. "You know, it's easy to tell you were not raised on the rez."

"How?"

"You keep referring to them as 'medicine men.' They are *hataałii* . . . singers. Their 'medicine' is the chants and ceremonies they conduct. Their prayers are intended to bring balance to the individual who is sick."

"I know what they're called," Charlie said, frowning. "I just haven't been impressed with their results."

"You had a relative an *hataałii* couldn't heal?"

"I told you. My grandfather . . . cancer."

"My only observation is modern medicine isn't infallible, either."

Their conversation was interrupted by the arrival of a beat-up, green pick-up truck. It stopped in the handicapped parking spot next to them. A man of 70 with long, white hair emerged from the cab. He wore an old, round crown fedora with a single eagle feather and carried a gnarled, walking stick.

Warren opened his door and got out. Charlie joined him.

After their introductions, Hatale led the way to the chapter house. Unlocking the door, he ushered his visitors into large meeting room. When they were seated, Simon spoke to Charlie.

"You want to know about your cousin."

She was surprised at the direct statement. "Actually, I was trying to find out about both of my cousins, Walter and William."

"I only knew Walter. He's the one who stayed with me."

"When was this?"

"Five years ago . . . maybe six. These days, the years flow together as one, long river."

"Did he come to learn a new ceremony?" Yazzie asked.

"Oh, no. It takes years to learn a new song. He only stayed for a week."

"Why was he here?"

"He wanted to learn about *adiłgąshii* . . .witches . . . and the Badlands."

"You're not an *adiłgąshii*, are you?" Charlie asked warily.

"No," Hatale shook his head. "But we are close to the Anasazi ruins of Chaco. The *adiłgąshii* go there often to replenish their powers. The *hataałii* of Lake Valley and Nageezi Chapter Houses have had to learn their ways . . . as much as is possible . . . to combat the evil they bring."

"Why did Walter want to learn about the witches?"

"It was his belief that *adiłgąshii* killed his parents. He wanted revenge. I think he believed I would help."

"Did you?"

"I gave him all the knowledge I had. There is a ceremony . . . The Enemy Way . . . that is used often to battle illness. Sometimes illness brought on by witches can be cured this way."

"What about the revenge you talked about? Did you help him with that?"

"Unless you join their ranks to follow the Witchery Way, the only way I know to stop a witch is to kill them."

"Warren told me what shaman must do to follow the Witchery Way. I can't believe Walter would kill a close friend so he could become a witch."

"No," Hatale corrected. "Not kill a friend. They must kill a very close relative . . . like a sibling . . . to show their commitment to evil."

Charlie gave Yazzie a stern look. He had given her misleading information.

"That would be worse," she agreed. "And I know Walter could never do something like that. He and William were very close. They loved each other."

"Both brothers went missing three years ago. Only William's body was found," Warren explained. "We presume Walter's dead as well. His body just hasn't been found, yet."

"Where was William killed?"

"No one knows," Charlie admitted. "His body was found just outside Yah-Ta-Hey."

Hatale raised an inquiring eyebrow.

"The authorities think he was killed on the reservation," Yazzie said. "Whoever dumped the body beyond the rez boundaries did it to make sure the FBI wasn't brought in to investigate."

"I have another question," Charlie interrupted. "My family . . . the Etsitty family . . . has been plagued by *yee naaldlooshii* since early summer. My aunt and two cousins were killed Thursday in an accident caused by a Skinwalker. Why are these creatures attacking us?

"Warren thinks this curse is because of something my cousins did. If they've been dead for three years, why is it happening now?"

Hatale thought for a long moment. "I know of a place . . ." he finally said. "A killing place . . . a profane place used by the *adiłgąshii* . . . that is not on the reservation."

"This place . . . could Walter's body be there?" Charlie asked anxiously.

"If it is there, after three years, would you even be able to identify it?" Warren sounded doubtful.

"I do not have an answer for you. I can only take you there for you to see for yourself."

"Is it far?"

"Twenty miles, maybe. It is called *Kimbeto Wash*. But there are few roads for us to take."

Charlie and Warren looked at each other. *Kimbeto Wash* was the archeological site Isaac Etsitty wanted to survey . . . the site that got him killed.

"What exactly will we find at this *Kimbeto Wash*?" Yazzie tried to sound casual.

"There are ruins there. Not Anasazi ruins. Ancient hogans. Ancient Diné burial places. Evil places."

"Would it even be safe for us to go there?" It was hard for Charlie to contain her excitement.

"I think it would be safe in daylight," Hatale said. "My truck will not make it there, though."

"We'll take mine," Warren said, "as long as you can be our guide."

Hatale stood. "I have a map. Because of the rains yesterday, we cannot just drive across Chaco River. But there is a bridge in Chaco Canyon. That will take us north to where we want to go."

Chapter Seventy-Seven

Lansing and Stephen Clah sat talking till past midnight. Being ranchers, they had a lot in common. The sheriff was grateful the household started stirring before 6:00. He was given a blanket, a pillow and the sofa for his bed . . . a bed that was beyond uncomfortable. One of the lumps made him feel like he was sleeping on a bowling ball.

Like any other ranch, some chores were started before the coffee finished brewing. Stephen and his two oldest were out the door before the rest of the family were even up. Lansing offered to help, but he was told to stay inside and enjoy the peace and quiet. He managed to snag the third turn in the bathroom and had to be satisfied with using a finger for a toothbrush.

Ellen Clah was fixing breakfast for the three other adults and five children in the family. Lansing suggested he should find a meal elsewhere, but she would not hear it. He was a guest. He had to stay and eat.

The traditional Sunday breakfast for the Clah's was bacon, eggs, and pancakes. As with every Sunday, activities started with chores, then food, then church.

"We attend the Lindsay Community Church," Ellen explained, while Lansing sipped on coffee at the table. "For a long time, we went to the Baptist church in Cuba. They got a new preacher we didn't like, so we switched. Besides, Lindsay's a lot closer."

By the time breakfast was served, Lansing felt like a member of the family.

With a total of 10 people to feed, not everyone could sit at the table. The three youngest kids got to eat in the living room. They didn't complain.

The phone call came at 8:00. Lansing listened to Stephen Clah's side of the conversation.

"Hey, George . . . Uh, huh . . . Uh, huh . . . 'Bout how far south? . . .Okay . . . Who have you called so far? . . . I see. Yeah . . ."

Clah looked up at the clock. "I would say half hour at the most . . . All right, I'll see you then."

He turned to Lansing. "That was George Abasta over at the Nageezi Chapter House. We have a situation, Cliff."

"What's going on?"

"An oilfield worker was out checking tanks this morning south of *Red Mesa Express*. He found an abandoned Winnebago RV."

"So, what's the situation?"

"The interior was splattered with blood. Someone was hurt . . . maybe killed."

"Who's been notified?"

"The Navajo Police and the San Juan Sheriff's office."

Lansing nodded. That made sense to him.

"I'm going over there . . . see if I can help."

"What's your interest in an abandoned RV?"

"The two Navajo girls dropped off at the trading post . . . when I talked to them, they both said they were abducted by men in a Winnebago."

Now, Lansing was interested in the "situation." It was possible Mariah Tsosie suffered a ride in the same vehicle.

"Maybe this is the same RV they talked about. Would you like to come along?"

"I should get back to Las Palmas. This is not my jurisdiction."

"There's something else. The worker took out his binoculars to see if he could spot the RV's owners . . . maybe they wandered off after getting hurt. About a mile away he saw a dark blue car . . . a little coupe.

"That could be your friend's highjacked car."

"How far would that be from Pueblo Pintado?"

"Ten, twelve miles, maybe."

Lansing stood. "I would very much like to come along. I'll follow you in my patrol unit, if you don't mind."

Chapter Seventy-Eight

The washes and arroyos of southeastern San Juan County flowed to the southwest, dumping their meager run-off into the Chaco River. The Chaco River then meandered to the west, then north, eventually merging with the San Juan River at Shiprock.

The dozen, named washes were laced with smaller, unnamed ditches. The flat landscape, usually covered with sage brush and seasonal grasses, was irregularly interrupted by 100-foot drops into the arroyos. Some drops were sudden. Others gradual. There was no consistent sameness and every 2 to 4 miles was something different.

There were also vegetation free moonscapes like *Bisti/De-Na-Zin Wilderness Area.* Nature's sense of humor was on full display. Sculpted by eons of erosion, there were solitary, 20-foot high chimneys and broad, flat rocks supported by dozens of gnome-like pedestals. There were cathedral organ pipes and mushrooms, all painted with a grey-white hue that eventually blended with the surrounding buff-tan sand. Located fifteen miles northwest of Chaco Canyon, a dozen people got lost there every year . . . some never to be found.

Oil companies, both large and small, began exploiting the vast petroleum reserves of the San Juan Basin in the 1920's. Pump jacks, pipelines and storage tanks invaded the Badlands. Despite the modern incursions, the region kept its ominous reputation. For 80 years oilfield workers filed reports involving strange sounds, stranger creatures, and unexplained fatalities. Those workers who knew better never ventured into the area at night.

Leaving the Clah ranch, Lansing contacted his department to let dispatch know of his location. He told Sid Barnes to refer all major issues to Chief Deputy Jack Rivera while he was out of pocket.

Four miles west of the San Phillipe County line and 600 feet past the *Red Mesa Express/Sinclair Gas Station* was the turnoff Stephen Clah was looking for. Lansing followed 50 feet behind. The Indian Service Route took them 6 miles into the oil fields where they joined George Abasta and Don Pickles, the oilfield worker. They were parked next to a 24-foot long, Class-C Winnebago RV. All three doors to the vehicle were open.

Pickles saw Lansing emerge from the patrol unit and hurried over.

"Are you the sheriff?" he asked impatiently. "I need to get back to work."

"Sorry, I'm not the sheriff you want."

The man turned away, angry.

"Just a minute, Mister...?"

"Pickles . . ." he said, stopping. "Don Pickles."

"I'm Cliff Lansing from San Phillipe County. I'm here about that blue car you spotted."

"Oh, yeah . . . sure," he nodded, unable to mask his disappointment.

He walked over to his service truck and retrieved a set of binoculars. He motioned Lansing to follow him to the front of the RV. From their vantage point on the high ground they could see for miles.

Pickles raised the binoculars and began a slow scan of the land to the south. A moment later, he handed the binoculars to Lansing.

"There," he said, pointing. "The bottom of that hill."

Lansing looked in the direction Pickles pointed. He adjusted the focus, then looked again. There was indeed a small, dark blue car parked a mile away.

It very well could be Tina Morales' car.

He handed Pickles the binoculars. "Is there a road to get down there?"

The oilfield worker looked around. "It doesn't look like it. You may have to do some off-roading."

Lansing told Clah his intention to inspect the distant car.

"Would you mind looking at the RV, first?"

Lansing didn't think his observations would matter much, but he said, "Yeah, sure."

There were blood stains on the driver's seat and door. There was another area where a bloody struggle took place just inside the side door. Flies made brief stops on the now dried blood, looking for a fresh treat. A handgun laid on the floor in the middle of the cramped living area. It was impossible to tell if it had been discharged.

Lansing only surveyed the scene. He didn't touch anything. The San Juan authorities were responsible for the investigation.

"I can see why Pickles contacted someone," Lansing said. "It looks pretty bad in there."

"Where do you think they took the bodies?" Clah asked.

"I wouldn't have a clue." Lansing walked back to his patrol unit.

Once inside the Tahoe, he tried calling his dispatch. All he got was static. He was just beyond the reach of his remote relay towers. It was reminiscent of only a few years earlier when the entire county radio system was dodgy. The excuse he consoled himself with was that he was no longer in San Phillipe.

The sheriff started his engine, then edged past the four other assembled vehicles. The sage brush was sparse and only 18 inches tall at the most. He looked for a path of least resistance, soon realizing one route was as good as another.

Chapter Seventy-Nine

Mariah constantly studied the ground in front of her, looking for assurances that she was retracing her steps. She couldn't depend on landmarks because she had seen none in the dark.

She had no guesses as to how long she and Morales had walked the night before . . . or how far.

As the sun crept above the horizon, she came across a semi-familiar sight. It was the wash containing the mushroom people. She remembered walking through it. Walking, sliding down the steep bank, she looked for their footprints when she reached the bottom. The hardpacked sand refused to reveal many tracks, but there were a few.

After fifteen minutes of looking, she found where they first entered the wash.

The climb to higher ground was tougher than she expected. At the top, she had to sit and rest. The sun had done little to warm the morning air. There was still a chill that she hadn't noticed while she kept moving.

The cold seeped through her clothes. She also realized her legs were sore. She was young, so there was no good reason for them to hurt.

No, she thought. There was a reason. She had been cooped up in a small room for five weeks with no exercise. Then yesterday, she and Tina had taken a long walk. She was just a little out of shape.

She pulled a strip of jerky from her pocket, then tore off a bite with her teeth. She was quick to realize her jaw was sore from all the chewing the night before. She would let the meat soften in her mouth first, then chew.

The venison also made her thirsty. She halfway wished she could have brought the canteen with her, but Tina Morales needed the water more than her.

Instead of sitting and making wishes, she had to get moving again. She stood and started walking.

She found the parallel tire-tracks they had followed twelve hours earlier. Boosted by her brief rest, she felt a surge of confidence. She knew she would find help.

***

Tina Morales slept fitfully. She was exhausted from the pain. The cramps came in waves. When they hit, her whole body tensed into one, huge knot. When the pain subsided, she began shivering from the chill.

As the sunlight gradually reached the bottom of the arroyo, she began to warm slightly. She wished she had something to drink. With her eyes still closed, she tried to remember where she was and how she got there.

Mariah . . . The car broke down . . . No, the car had a flat. She and Mariah tried to fix it.

Why did the car have a flat? She remembered they fixed the flat before leaving Cuba.

Wait . . . The tire was going flat again . . . They stopped to put air in it . . . and a man with a gun ran out of the store. He made her drive him into the backcountry . . . that's where they got the flat.

They left the car just when it got dark. They kept walking until they found a man sitting next to a fire. He gave them food . . . food and water.

The canteen! Mariah left. Mariah left her there alone! But the canteen! Mariah said she would leave the canteen.

Tina could barely open her eyes. The sun shone directly into them. She felt around with her hand . . . sure that Mariah would have left the canteen close.

She heard a sound. Someone scooted the canteen closer to her.

She squinted into the sun. All she could make out was the form of a person close to her.

"*Nizéé*?" she choked.

The figure said nothing. It turned and began walking away.

Through the pain, Tina managed to unscrew the canteen's cap, then take a few sips. She spilled as much as she swallowed.

After closing the container, she looked around as best she could, looking for the person who helped her.

"Hello?" She paused, hoping for a response. "Is anybody there?"

If anyone answered, she didn't notice. She was suddenly wracked with another wave of debilitating cramps.

Chapter Eighty

The 3-mile long jeep trail from Lake Valley to the *Kin Klizhin* road was slow and bumpy. The *Kin Klizhin Ruins* were at the western edge of the main Chaco Canyon National Park and the road leading to them from the canyon was much better maintained. Four miles further east, they intercepted Indian Service Route 7030, which took them another 4 miles north between West and South Mesas.

Warren Yazzie turned left onto State Highway 57, which ran through the floor of the canyon. Yazzie slowed as they crossed the bridge. He and Charlie could appreciate Hatale's insistence on not trying to drive through the river. The water might not have been deep, but it was swift and looked dangerous.

"I've never been to Chaco Canyon before," Charlie admitted, looking wide-eyed at the cliffs. The surrounding mesas were 400 feet above the usually dry riverbed.

"In the main canyon there are fifteen major ruins," Warren explained. "But throughout the immediate area there are over one hundred known archeological sites.

"Anasazi ruins can be found as far south as old Mexico, all the way up to Utah and Colorado. There are probably thousands of them."

Charlie promised herself, one day she would come back to Chaco Canyon. Today, though, there were other things to worry about.

The paved highway looped, then, just before the *Casa Chiquita Ruins*, it made an abrupt turn to the right. It was now a gravel road that gradually climbed through Clys Canyon to higher ground. Once outside the canyon, Highway 57 turned north.

After a mile, another bridge took them across *Escavada Wash*. Traces of the previous day's rains were still visible.

"In two miles there will be a jeep trail to the right," Hatale said from the back seat. "That will take us to *Kimbeto Wash*."

"That's where the ruins are?" Charlie asked.

"No. We will turn to the left when we reach the wash. There are no roads. We will follow the bed of the arroyo. That will take us to the ruins."

"How far is it to the ruins once we reach the wash?"

Hatale stared out the side window. "Not far, I don't think."

Warren glanced at Charlie, a slight frown on his face. They had driven for an hour and a half and traveled a total of 15 miles.

"This brings back memories of driving the backroads on the rez," he admitted.

Charlie knew what he meant. On a good day, the 20-mile trip from Tuba City to the Etsitty ranch took the lion's share of an hour.

When they reached the jeep trail, the terrain began to gradually slope toward the arroyo. By the time they reached *Kimbeto Wash*, Yazzie only had to negotiate a 20-foot drop to the creek bed. He was relieved to find the sandy bottom was firm enough to grant him plenty of traction.

The bed of the arroyo varied between 100 and 200 feet in width with little vegetation. The banks alternated between shallow and steep and sometime towered over the bottom by 100 feet. There were occasional puddles, concentrated in rock pools dug out by flowing water.

They were heading northeast now. For three miles, Yazzie found the driving relatively easy. They suddenly came across a soft patch in the sand. The truck slowed.

Warren stopped the truck, and quickly put it in reverse.

"What's wrong?" Charlie asked.

"I need to put us on more solid footing. If we get stuck, I don't know how we'd ever get out of here."

Warren backed up the truck fifty feet, making sure they were well clear of the soft ground.

"What now?" Yazzie asked, looking at their guide in the back seat.

"If you want to continue, we will walk."

"Then we walk," Charlie said, opening her door.

Chapter Eighty-One

As Lansing got closer, he was positive the dark blue car he'd seen at a distance was Tina's Chevy Cavalier. At the same moment he saw the shredded front tire, he spotted a body on the ground a few feet away.

He parked the Tahoe on the same road as the Chevy, then rushed to the man on the ground. He knelt and felt the carotid artery for a pulse.

The man was dead.

The sheriff studied the features. He was looking at a Navajo man in his late twenties. There were no apparent wounds, but as he looked closer, the face was covered in a fine, grey powder. It was concentrated around the nostrils.

Lansing had seen that powder before. The dead man Johnathan Akee found outside Segovia, Juan Pedro Garcia, had identical powder on his face. Forensics would have to confirm if it was the same substance.

If it turned out to be the same, Lansing could guess the cause of death . . . the man drowned. He also guessed this was the robber who carjacked Tina and Mariah, though he saw no gun.

He turned his attention to the car.

The front, right tire was shredded. A donut spare lay a few feet away. Two of the five lug nuts had been removed. The combo lug wrench and prybar laid on the ground. The scissor-jack was under the frame at the front of the car.

It was obvious Tina had abandoned her attempt to fix her tire. He didn't understand why she simply left the spare and her tools laying out. She must have been in a hurry to get away.

He checked the registration in the glove box. He wanted to make absolutely sure this was Tina's car. Satisfied that it was, he started checking the ground, looking for signs as to what direction the two females had taken.

It made sense they went back the way they came. He inspected the dirt road in both directions. Coming down the hill, the car had obviously disturbed the surface gravel. It was impossible to tell if that was the direction they took.

Twenty yards in the opposite direction he found a footprint leading away from the car. That had to be the direction they had taken.

His personal instinct was to start looking for Tina and Mariah. His sheriff instinct told him to drive back to the RV and report the dead body. The preset frequencies on the Tahoe's radio kept him from communicating directly with either the Navajo Police or the San Juan Sheriff's department. If they hadn't arrived yet, he would make sure Stephen Clah would relay them the information.

The trip back up the hill delayed the beginning of his search by nearly 15 minutes. Before he started, he made sure he had water for the two women. Don Pickles carried a gallon of water in his service truck for emergencies. After hearing the circumstances, he handed it over with no complaints.

Once he was back down the hill, Lansing pointed the Tahoe in the direction he assumed Tina had taken. In the distance, a half-mile away, he saw a lone figure walking toward him.

He anxiously sped up the SUV, hoping he had just found Tina Morales.

As he got closer, he was slapped with disappointment. It wasn't Tina. But it wasn't a total bust, either.

Mariah Tsosie was frantically waving both arms in the air, as if afraid the approaching vehicle was not going to see her.

Chapter Eighty-Two

It was an easy walk up *Kimbeto Wash*. Even Hatale didn't have problems.

Charlie suspected his walking stick was more of a prop than a necessity. For herself, after all the driving the day before, it felt good to stretch her legs.

The sun was to their right, warming the arroyo nicely. The jacket she began the day with was almost too warm now.

Both Charlie and Warren expected the ruins to appear at any moment. They had walked for 20 minutes already. By Charlie's estimate, they must have traveled at least a mile.

The bottom of the wash narrowed and started to bend to the right. Whatever was ahead was masked by the steep wall of the arroyo.

"Are they around this bend?" Yazzie asked. Charlie was about to pose the same question.

"It has been a long time," Hatale admitted. "I am not sure."

As the arroyo straightened out, it became broader. There was nothing resembling a ruin of any kind. There was, however, a figure wrapped in a black and red Navajo blanket 1000 feet further up the wash.

"What do you think it is?" Charlie asked.

Warren looked around, cautiously. "I don't know. I don't see anyone else around."

They didn't alter their pace. They apparently still had some distance to go . . . plus, there was the walk back to the truck. Besides, as anxious as Charlie was to find a clue as to what happened to her cousin they could only travel as fast as Hatale could walk, and he seemed to be slowing down.

As they got closer, they saw the ashes from a small fire a few feet from the person in the blanket. There was a canteen on the ground.

The figure in the blanket started shaking and let out a stream of painful "oh, oh, ohs!"

"Hello?" Charlie called out as they got closer.

The person in the blanket was obviously a woman. She stopped her shaking and tried to look in the direction of the voice. "What? Is somebody there? Help me, please!"

Charlie and Warren rushed to the woman. Charlie knelt next to her, "Yes, we can help you. What's wrong? Are you hurt? Were you in an accident?"

The woman on the ground was a Latina of about thirty. Her long, black hair was wet and matted from sweat. Her complexion was ashen, as if the blood had drained from her body.

"No . . . not an accident . . . Oh! Oh!" she nearly screamed. Then, "It feels like my guts exploded! I can't take the pain."

Yazzie looked around. "Are you here alone?"

"Mariah went for help . . . Did she send you?"

"No," Charlie confessed. "We don't know a Mariah . . . What's your name?"

"Tina," the woman whimpered. "Tina Morales."

"What?" Charlie took a closer look. She could hardly believe it, but the suffering woman was definitely her childhood friend. So wracked with pain, she was nearly unrecognizable. "Tina!" she squealed. "It's me! Charlie Etsitty!"

"What? Charlie? What are you doing here?"

"No, girl . . . what are you doing here?"

"You know this woman?" Yazzie asked incredulously.

"We grew up together . . . She's my best friend in the world!" She turned back to Tina. "How'd you get all the way out here?"

"My car . . . a man with a gun . . . he shot someone then made us drive out here."

"Where's your car?"

"It's . . . I don't know." She doubled over in pain. "Oh! I need a doctor. Please get me out of here!"

Yazzie knelt next to her. "We're going to have to carry you. It's about a mile to my truck."

"I don't care! Do whatever you have to do!"

Three feet away, the sand exploded when the bullet slammed into the arroyo's floor. The rifle report followed a second later.

"What the hell!" Charlie exclaimed.

"Get down!" Warren barked, pulling her flat. He looked back at Hatale. "Simon!" he motioned with his hand. "Lay down. Quick!"

Simon Hatale wasn't quick enough. The next bullet caught him in his thigh, knocking him to the ground.

"Son of a bitch!" Yazzie growled. "Simon, where are you hit?"

"My leg!"

Warren crawled on his belly. "We've got to stop that bleeding! Charlie is there any place we can take cover?"

Etsitty cautiously raised her head. "The riverbank . . . I think we can hide next to that rock wall."

Two more shots rang out, followed by a pause.

"He's reloading," Warren said. "Help your friend get to the bank! I'll grab Simon!"

"Tina, can you walk?"

"I – I don't know."

"You have to try . . . I'm not going to leave you here!" She pulled the blanket off her friend. That's when she saw the blood-soaked jeans. "Oh, my God, Tina! What happened?"

"I don't know . . . I don't know!"

They heard the sound of another rifle shot, but they were too busy to notice where the bullet hit.

After a lot of screaming and whining, Tina managed to get to her feet.

Charlie supported her as best she could as they hobbled their way to the rock wall along the bank. Yazzie and Hatale joined them a moment later.

The shooter kept firing even though he could no longer see his targets.

Then two shots rang out in quick succession, followed by silence.

Chapter Eighty-Three

Lansing stopped his Tahoe and jumped out. "Mariah!"

"Oh, Sheriff! I'm so glad to see you."

Lansing was shocked. That was the longest string of words he'd ever heard from the girl.

"I'm glad to see you, too." He looked in the direction Mariah had come from. "Where's Tina?"

"She got sick. I had to leave her . . . but I didn't want to! Do you have some water?"

"Get in my car," he ordered. "There's a gallon jug on the floor."

Mariah obeyed. Lansing got behind the steering wheel.

"Is she far?"

"I don't know." Mariah took three quick sips from the plastic container.

"How long did you walk?" he asked after he put the SUV in gear.

"Two hours, maybe. It could have been three." She pulled a strip of jerky from her pocket.

"Where did you get that?"

"We met a man last night. He gave us food and water."

"Is he with Tina?"

"No. He left us last night. I don't know where he is!"

"You said Tina's sick. What's wrong with her?"

"She was hurting real bad. She said her stomach was bothering her, but I'm not sure."

"Why do you say that?"

"It looked like she was bleeding."

"She didn't fall, did she?"

"No . . . nothing like that."

Lansing didn't want to ask any more questions about Tina Morales. His imagination pushed him to think the worst. He would wait until they found her before he came to any conclusions.

They both rode in silence for five minutes.

Mariah finished her jerky, then asked, "Were you looking for us?"

"I was."

"How did you know where we were?"

Lansing explained Tina's car had been spotted by an oilfield worker. Mentioning the blood splattered RV didn't seem relevant.

"What about that man who kidnapped us? Did you arrest him?"

"This isn't my county." Lansing avoided mentioning that the man was dead. However, he knew now that the last time Mariah saw him, he was still alive. "San Juan County will take care of him.

"By the way, I heard the man had a gun. How did you two get away?"

"Tina . . ." she caught herself. "Miss Morales squeezed his knee and he dropped the gun."

"Squeezed his knee?"

"I think he hurt it when he robbed that store. When she got the gun, she threw it away and we left. He didn't try to stop us because he couldn't walk."

She pointed ahead. "There. That road . . . take a left. That's the way we went."

Lansing followed the instructions.

Everything was fresh in Mariah's mind. A half-mile later the road split when it reached an arroyo. They went to the right and soon crossed through the wash populated with the strange mushroom statues.

The high desert was warming nicely. Both driver and passenger rolled down their windows to avoid the stuffiness. What took Mariah two to three hours to walk, Lansing was able to cover in 30 minutes.

"We're getting close," the girl announced. "This is about where we saw the light from the campfire." She had him turn off the road, toward another wash.

A moment later, they both heard the sound of a gunshot. It was very close. Lansing stopped the Tahoe and looked at Mariah. "Stay here!"

"What are you doing?"

"I need to find out who's shooting . . . and at what."

Lansing got out of the SUV and pulled his pistol from its holster.

Another shot was fired, and the sheriff quickly pinpointed the shooter's location. He crept forward as quickly and as silently as he could.

Chapter Eighty-Four

Lansing approached from the south. To the west, 40 feet below him was the wash where Mariah left Tina.

The shooter's perch was a small, rocky outcrop ten feet above him. He was aiming at something in the arroyo. The sheriff looked as four people limped from the broad bed of the wash to the protection of the closest bank. He couldn't tell if Tina was among them.

Lansing hurried to come up behind the rifleman. The man finished reloading, then assumed a kneeling stance to get a better bead on his targets. So intent on his quarry, he never noticed the sheriff until he spoke.

"That's enough, mister! Drop the rifle!"

The man whipped around to find a .44 Magnum pistol pointed at him. He hesitated for a split second, then attempted to point his weapon and fire.

His bullet went wide.

Lansing's didn't.

The shooter fell backwards, dropping his rifle and clutching at his left shoulder. The sheriff kept his gun pointed at the wounded man.

"Mariah!" Lansing yelled. "You can get out, now."

A moment later the Navajo girl joined them. The man on the ground was trying to get up, cursing in Navajo.

"What's he saying?"

Mariah shook her head. "It has something to do with goats and your mother. I don't think you really want to know."

Lansing picked up the rifle, then holstered his pistol. "There's a first aid kit in the back of the Tahoe. Grab it and meet me at the bottom of the wash."

As Mariah left, Lansing grabbed the still cursing man by the collar and dragged him down the steep bank. The man, a Navajo in his thirties, struggled against the white man's firm grip but was in too much pain to offer much resistance.

Lansing found the four people he spotted from the arroyo rim. They had taken refuge along a rock wall. A Navajo man and woman were kneeling next to an old man who had been shot in the leg and . . . Tina Morales.

Lansing threw the gunman to the side and rushed to the teacher.

"Is she all right? Was she shot?" he asked frantically.

"No, she wasn't shot," Charlie Etsitty said. "But she's in a bad way. Who are you?"

"Cliff Lansing. I'm sheriff over in San Phillipe County."

"You're the rancher Tina dates!"

"Yeah," was all he said.

"Where do you think you're going?" Warren shouted. The gunman was attempting to sneak away. The former Navajo Ranger grabbed the man and threw him to the ground.

"Here," Lansing said, tossing Yazzie the rifle. "Check his pockets. He probably has more bullets. If you have to, shoot him."

"I will . . . gladly! By the way, I'm Warren Yazzie."

Lansing nodded. "Cliff Lansing." He looked at Charlie. "How long has she been like this?"

"I don't know. We just found her a few minutes ago."

Lansing knelt. "Tina, you're going to be all right." He brushed the hair from her face. "I'll get you to a doctor as soon as I can."

Tina's eyes fluttered open. "Cliff? What are you doing here?"

"I came to find you."

"Oh!" she exclaimed as she was wracked with another wave of cramps.

"What's wrong?"

"It's her woman's parts," Charlie explained. "I think she's bleeding out."

"Oh, my God." Lansing looked around frantically. "I need to get her to a doctor. My car's at the top of the bank."

Mariah scrambled down the embankment with the first aid kit. "Here's what you wanted."

"Give it to these folks," Lansing said, scooping the teacher up in his arms.

Tina tried her best not to scream in pain.

"I need someone to come with me!" Lansing had already started toward his Tahoe. "But I can't take all of you."

Charlie and Mariah looked at each other. Charlie wanted to be with her longest and dearest friend. The look on Mariah's face pleaded to let her ride with the sheriff.

"You go," Charlie said.

"What about this rifle?" Yazzie asked, calling after the sheriff.

"It's yours now!" Lansing shouted over his shoulder as he climbed back to the Tahoe.

"What about this guy?"

"He's one of yours . . . do whatever you want."

Charlie followed Lansing to his Tahoe. "My name is Charlotte Etsitty. Tina and I grew up together. Can you please call me and let me know how she is?"

"Sure."

She wrote down three phone numbers, assuring him she would be at least one of the locations.

A moment later, Lansing, Mariah and Tina were gone.

Chapter Eighty-Five

Tina Morales looked into Lansing's face as he carried her. "Cliff, you really came for me?"

"Yes," he said, trying to hide his fear for her life.

"I'm sorry," she whimpered. "I'm so sorry." She tried to bury her face in his chest.

"Mariah, get the back door," Lansing ordered as they got close to the patrol unit. He contained his impatience while Charlie wrote down her contact numbers.

Charlie waved at them as they left.

Mariah sat in the back seat of the SUV. Tina's head was on her lap. Lansing gritted his teeth every time he hit a bump. Tina responded vocally with each bounce, but it couldn't be helped. The Tahoe's speed was dictated by quality of the road . . . which was poor even along the best portions. It still took 25 minutes to get back to Tina's car.

All three were exhausted by the time they reached the Winnebago and the assembly of private and official vehicles.

"Stay with Tina till I can get help."

Lansing jumped out of the unit and raced to a San Juan Deputy Sheriff. "Listen, I'm Sheriff Cliff Lansing from San Phillipe. I have a very sick woman in my car. I need a Medevac, like, yesterday."

After establishing Lansing's credentials, the deputy contacted his dispatch. A Life Flight helicopter was dispatched from Farmington. While en route, Lansing answered questions from the on-board paramedic.

The best answer the sheriff could provide as to Morales' ailment was "It has to do with her lower abdomen . . . possibly her uterus . . . There's a lot of bleeding."

Not knowing much about Tina's medical history, he couldn't tell the paramedic when the last time the teacher had seen a doctor.

Before the helicopter arrived, the paramedic recommended not bringing the patient back to Farmington. The San Juan Regional Medical Center only had a Level Four trauma center. He recommended either CHRISTUS St. Vincent Regional Hospital in Santa Fe, or if Lansing preferred, the university hospital in Albuquerque.

Santa Fe was closer to Las Palmas. Visiting her at the University of New Mexico hospital would be an inconvenience. When he asked if Tina had a preference, she admitted she didn't.

From the deputy's call to the helicopter's arrival was 30 minutes. It took the flight crew less than 3 minutes to transfer Morales from Lansing's Tahoe to the transport. The Santa Fe hospital was less than an hour away. Unfortunately, there was no room for anyone to accompany her.

Lansing and Mariah could only watch as Tina Morales was whisked away. Lansing needed to decide his next action. Did he need to return to the canyon and retrieve the man he shot? Should he follow the helicopter to Santa Fe? What was he supposed to do with Mariah? She was still his responsibility. He could take her to Gallup or back to Las Palmas.

Stephen Clah had left to join his family at church. Being president of the Counselor Chapter House, Lansing was sure Clah could recommend what he should do with the girl.

Before he made a decision, he was approached by the San Juan Deputy.

"Sheriff, I just got a call from dispatch. The State Police are trying to contact you."

"What about?"

"I don't know. When they heard you were here, they asked if you could meet them in Lindsay."

"Yeah. Have your dispatch relay that I'm on my way." He looked down at Mariah. "Would you mind riding with me for a while?"

"I guess not. Where are we going?"

"Could you eat a real breakfast?"

She nodded.

"There's a café about fifteen minutes from here. We'll get you something to eat while I talk with the state patrol."

Chapter Eighty-Six

After years as a police officer and Navajo Ranger, Warren Yazzie had plenty of experience at first aid. While he worked on the wounded, Charlie retrieved the canteen near the campfire ashes. After that, she stood guard with the gunman's rifle to make sure he behaved.

Simon Hatale's bullet passed completely through his thigh. The only issue was to stanch the bleeding.

When the *hataałii* saw who the shooter was, he became angry. The man's name was Clayton Betoney. Originally from White Rock, at one time he studied to become a medicine man.

Hatale shook his head. "The man is evil. Everyone knows he follows the Witchery Way. You shouldn't help him . . . Let him bleed to death."

"I can't do that," Yazzie said. He had patched the man as best he could, but Lansing's bullet was still embedded in the shoulder. They needed to get him to a doctor. Both men needed medical attention.

Charlie surveyed Warren's handiwork. "I think you missed your calling." She poured water from the canteen so Yazzie could wash the blood from his hands. "I guess we'll look for those ruins another day."

"I'm afraid so," Yazzie agreed, standing. "I'll help Simon get back to the truck. Mr. Betoney can manage on his own. Just keep the rifle pointed at him."

"What are we going to do with him?"

"The nearest medical facility is in Crownpoint. After the docs see these two, we'll turn our new friend over to the tribal police. Let them decide what they'll do with him."

There was no short cut from *Kimbeto Wash* to Crownpoint. They retraced their route through Chaco Canyon and past the *Kin Klizhin Ruins*, eventually reaching Lake Valley. There, they contacted Hatale's daughter and told her to meet them at the Crownpoint Health Care Facility.

Once on State Highway 371, it was a quick 20-minute drive to the emergency room.

Insisting he didn't need an overnight stay, Simon was treated and released to his daughter's care. The Crownpoint hospital, such as it was, could only claim Level IV care status. Despite that, the doctors were no strangers to gunshots wounds.

While Betoney was in surgery, Warren and Charlie had a long talk with Navajo Police Sergeant Kenneth Chee. Chee and Yazzie had known each other for fifteen years, back to Warren's days on the force.

"You have no idea why he shot at you?"

"No," they both said. Charlie wondered if he was trying to keep them away from the *Kimbeto* ruins. Yazzie thought the same thing, but neither mentioned it. "His rifle is in my truck," Warren continued. "I'll get it to you before we leave."

"This Sheriff Lansing who shot the man . . . what do you know about him?"

"Not much," Charlie said. "I mean, he's a rancher in San Phillipe County . . . and he dates a friend of mine."

"But you don't know what he was doing in the Trust Lands."

"No," Yazzie added. "This friend Charlie was referring to . . . I think he was looking for her. In his defense if he hadn't shot Betoney, both of us would be dead."

"What do you know about Betoney?"

"Simon Hatale said the man is an *adiłgąshii*, a witch."

The sergeant frowned. Anything involving witches and the Witchery Way was bad news. That a Navajo witch was creating havoc in the Badlands wasn't a major news alert. However, catching one in the act seldom happened. Chee wasn't about to let Betoney slip through his fingers.

He got contact information from both Yazzie and Charlie Etsitty. He would call them if he needed anything else.

As he regained consciousness, Betoney discovered he was handcuffed to the bed railing.

"Why am I handcuffed?" he demanded.

"Because you're under arrest," Chee said. "And you'll stay like that until the doctors release you sometime tomorrow."

"No, no, no, no," Betoney pleaded. "I can't stay here! He'll get me . . . You have to protect me!"

"Who?" Chee asked. "Who's going to get you?"

Betoney didn't answer. Instead he begged, "If I'm under arrest, put me in jail. Lock me up. He can't get me if I'm locked up!"

Despite the medical staff's protests, Chee insisted on taking the prisoner with him . . . Betoney's idea, not his. Besides, *adiłgąshii* were notorious for escaping custody. Keeping a close eye on Betoney would be easier if he was in a jail cell.

Chapter Eighty-Seven

Lansing parked next to two State Police cruisers. Officer La Torre from Farmington stood talking with Segovia based Officer Larry Gaspar.

"It's hell trying to track you down, Sheriff!" La Torre groused as Lansing got out of his truck.

"I've been busy." He wasn't about to be intimidated by anyone. He turned to Mariah. "Go inside. I'll be right there."

"The SID guys aren't very happy," Gaspar started. "They went to the canyon about eight this morning with four tow trucks. The van they were taking to Farmington was gone."

"If you want to talk, come inside. I need coffee."

The officers followed the sheriff into the café.

"Did you hear me?" Gaspar asked impatiently. "Someone took that van."

Mariah had taken a seat at a table along the wall. Lansing joined her.

"So, someone stole the stolen van?"

"Do you know anything about it?" La Torre tried not to sound too accusatory in his tone.

"I don't have a clue, Frank." Lansing motioned to the waitress for coffee. "And, I might point out, it's not my responsibility. The big boys out of Santa Fe and Albuquerque took over the investigation.

"If they didn't think it was important to put a guard up there, that's not my problem."

"Why are you back in Lindsay?" Gaspar asked. "Isn't Las Palmas a two-hour drive from here?"

"I never made it home last night."

Ida approached with a cup and a fresh pot of coffee.

"What's keeping you here?" the officer pressed.

"I'm trying to help this young lady get home."

"Are you driving to the canyon to see if they need help up there?"

"No." Lansing took a sip of coffee punctuating the fact that the conversation was over.

Once Mariah ordered breakfast, the sheriff felt he needed her input on what she wanted for her future. He knew the girl's stepfather was sitting in jail for killing her mother . . . something Mariah didn't know.

"You've been through a lot this past week. I have to admit, you're not the same frightened girl I met last Monday. I don't know what you and Miss Morales discussed, but it seems to have helped a lot."

Mariah nodded. "Um-hm."

"Did you know she was taking you to Gallup?"

"Yes, but I'm still not sure why."

"You weren't talking at all last week. Everyone was worried. We all knew something had happened to you, but you wouldn't discuss it. Tina . . . Miss Morales was taking you to the Indian Hospital where professionals could help you recover from your trauma.

"Do you understand what I'm talking about?"

Mariah shrugged. "I guess." She looked depressed at the thought of going back to a hospital.

"I'm not saying you're going there, now. I think you're doing remarkably well." He studied her. "I also don't think people outside the Navajo Nation should decide what to do with you. So, what do you want?"

Mariah immediately perked up. "I want to go home. I want to go back to Chinle."

Lansing wasn't sure that would happen any time soon, but it wasn't his decision to make. "I know the President of the Counselor Chapter House. He doesn't live far from here. I would like to drop you off at his ranch and let him arrange to get you home . . . if that's all right with you?"

"You're going to leave me?" she whimpered.

"I have to. I can honestly say, though, I'm not worried. After you walked alone for nearly six miles to help Miss Morales, I'm not sure you're much afraid of anything."

Ida approached with Mariah's food.

"Are you going to the hospital where they took Miss Morales?"

"Absolutely."

"Can I call you and ask how she's doing?"

"Any time, day or night."

Chapter Eighty-Eight

Stephen Clah assured Lansing there would be no problem getting Mariah home. He would start making calls immediately. Though she seemed reluctant to be abandoned, Mariah gratefully thanked Lansing for all he had done for her. She reminded him she would be calling to check on Tina Morales.

Back on Highway 550, Lansing called dispatch to tell them he was on his way back to Las Palmas. He needed Sid Barnes to look up the number to St. Vincent Hospital. When he finally got cell phone reception, the sheriff called the hospital. It took two transfers before he found someone who knew about the woman Life Flight brought in that morning.

Morales was being prepped for surgery. The nurse said she knew nothing about the schoolteacher's condition or what was wrong with her.

Lansing thanked her and said he would contact her later to see what had developed.

Alone now with his own thoughts, Lansing tried to make a mental to-do list.

He needed to talk to the Medical Investigator's regarding the autopsy on the dead man he found that morning. Specially, he wanted to know how that death compared to Juan Pedro Garcia's.

Despite the SID's protests, he would assign a deputy, probably Jack Rivera, to act as liaison with the State Police to monitor their investigation. He had a good relationship with the patrol officers in his county. It was the idiots out of Santa Fe that gave him heartburn.

Fingerprints taken from Juan Garcia's truck were sent to the State Crime Lab for comparison with prints they had on file. He needed the results.

Then there was the issue of the man he shot at the arroyo. He was curious who he was and why he was shooting at people. The rifle he used was a Remington 700, popular for hunting. They normally used .243 caliber cartridges, the same caliber as the empty shells he found at the canyon.

He needed to contact Charlotte Etsitty and find out where the rifle ended up. It might be a dead end, but he wanted a ballistics comparison between that rifle and the bullet that killed the hiker in the canyon.

He would call Halley Basa, the school secretary, and tell her about Tina. The school needed to know why their only chemistry teacher was AWOL.

On top of everything else, he desperately needed a shower and a shave . . . maybe even a quick nap before he headed to St. Vincent Hospital. He wanted to be there when Tina woke from her surgery.

Chapter Eighty-Nine

Since the Skinwalker issue was far from resolved, Warren invited Charlie Etsitty to spend the night at his place. It wasn't as elegant as the Quality Inn, but he assured her it was clean. After picking up two KFC dinners and retrieving her car at the motel, they ended up at Yazzie's hillside home overlooking Window Rock.

Like many Diné homes, the stone structure was heated by a wood-burning stove. When they could, Navajos burned coal. It lasted longer and gave off more heat . . . plus the reservation seemed to have an endless supply.

It was early evening and the temperature had dropped to the low 40s. While Yazzie got a fire going Charlie made a phone call to Tuba City.

"Hi, Mom. It's Charlie."

"Ah, it's good to hear from you. The girls want to know when you're coming home."

"I'm not sure. Maybe day after tomorrow. I don't know if there's anything more I can find out here."

"Tina keeps asking when you are moving back to Phoenix. I don't know what to tell her."

Neither did Charlie. "Let me speak to her, please."

"Hi, Momma," Tina said. She sounded less surly than she had Friday evening.

"Listen, Baby, I'm trying to get everything wrapped up here in Window Rock as quickly as I can. I don't know when we'll be able to go back to Phoenix, but don't pester your grandmother. She doesn't know anything."

"Do you?" her daughter snapped.

"We'll talk when I get back in town." There was silence from the other end. "Put your grandmother back on."

"Yes?" Amanda Etsitty said.

Charlie told her mother about finding Tina Morales that morning in the Badlands. She was hurt and probably would have to be operated on. She had given Sheriff Lansing, Tina's boyfriend, Amanda's phone number. Charlie didn't know if the Window Rock cell reception was any good. If the sheriff called, she wanted her mother to provide him with the number to Warren Yazzie's house phone.

Warren and Charlie sat at the kitchen table eating the barely warm chicken dinners.

"I have to agree with you," Charlie said. "This is a clean house."

"It's nothing I do. I have a cleaning lady come in three times a week. Otherwise, I would never let you through the door."

"Were you ever married?" She noted the absence of a wedding ring when they first met.

"Once," Yazzie admitted. "A long time ago. How about you?"

"Divorced. In fact, that's how I landed my job at the Garcia's law firm." She took one last bite of chicken, then wiped her hands and mouth on a napkin. "Fortunately, I have two wonderful daughters, so, I'm hardly alone."

"Yeah, kids are great."

"Do you have any children?"

Warren shook his head. "No. Never happened."

His house phone rang. After answering it, he motioned for Charlie to come over.

"This is Charlie."

There was a slight pause, then, "Charlotte?" It was Lansing.

"I'm sorry, Sheriff. Charlie's my nickname."

"Oh, I see. I couldn't reach you on your cell, but your mother said you would be at this number. I wanted to update you on Tina's condition."

"Yes, please."

"They took her into surgery about one this afternoon. They gave her eight units of blood to stabilize her first."

"You mean she's been in surgery for five hours? Did they say what's wrong with her?"

"No. The doctor said they needed to open her up first and find the problem before they could fix anything."

"Do you know how much longer it will be?"

"I don't have a clue. If it gets too late, I'll call you tomorrow." In case he forgets to call her, he gave Charlie his cell number so she could call him.

"One more thing," he said, almost as an afterthought. "Where is the rifle we took from that shooter?"

"Warren left it with the police in Crownpoint. Why?"

"It may have been used in a homicide earlier this week. I'll coordinate with the Navajo police to get a ballistics comparison."

***

Another call came into Yazzie's place at 9:00. This time it was Sergeant Chee from Crownpoint.

"That woman you were with today . . . her last name is Etsitty, isn't it?"

Warren admitted it was.

"I have Clayton Betoney locked up at the station right now. He keeps babbling on about Skinwalkers. I can't make any sense of it. He thinks one of them is coming for him. He's scared to death. But the name Etsitty keeps popping up.

"Do you suppose you two can come back to Crownpoint in the morning? Maybe you can figure out what he's talking about."

"We'll be there!"

Chapter Ninety

"Sheriff?" the doctor said, softly. "Sheriff Lansing?"

Lansing woke with a start. The surgery waiting area for families had over-stuffed seats, and straight-backed chairs, but no sofas. He had pulled a chair over to prop up his feet while he made himself comfortable in a stuffed seat. He sat up and yawned.

"Yes?" he realized where he was. "Tina? Is she all right?"

"She's in recovery. We'll move her to the ICU when she comes out of the anesthetic."

Lansing looked around. It was still dark outside. "What time is it?"

"One a.m."

"My God, she was in there for twelve hours?"

"She was in bad shape."

"What was wrong with her?"

"In layman's terms, she had tumors on her ovaries. They had become swollen, then burst. That's where all the bleeding came from."

"Is she going to be all right?"

"We're hoping for the best, but it may be touch-and-go for a while. We'll know for sure in the next forty-eight hours."

"Can I see her?"

"I'm afraid not. Not now. Maybe sometime later today . . . once she's transferred to intensive care. I recommend you go home and get some rest."

As much as he wanted to stay close to Tina, Lansing knew he wasn't helping her or himself by remaining. It would be 3:00 before he got back to the ranch. A motel room in Santa Fe was a possibility, but he needed to be in his office the next morning anyway.

After he set his "to-do" list in motion, he would return to the hospital.

Chapter Ninety-One

After seven years as sheriff, Cliff Lansing knew the foundation of leadership was trust. He had to trust his deputies to carry out their assigned duties. They had to trust him to back them up when they carried out those duties. He could delegate his authority, but ultimate responsibility always fell on his shoulders. With that said, he had no problem turning over his daily duties to Jack Rivera.

"Jack, I have to take some vacation days," Lansing said. "You'll be acting sheriff."

Chief Deputy Jack Rivera now understood why Lansing came to work in civilian clothes. However, his boss never took time off. "Is something wrong?"

"Tina's in the hospital in Santa Fe. I want to be with her while she recovers from surgery."

The deputy raised an eyebrow. "I thought you two weren't . . ."

"She doesn't have any family that's close," Lansing said, cutting him off.

"Okay . . ." Rivera raised his hands as if to block his boss' words. "Is there anything I need to do?"

"The State Police took over the Lindsay homicide investigation. They've buddied up with the Feds. Have you talked to Jake Redwine yet?"

"No. I was on call this past weekend, but I didn't come in."

Lansing filled him in on what they found in Rockhouse Canyon, particularly the *Southwest Antiques* van. It had gone missing again. He needed Rivera to respectfully pester the State Police Special Investigations Division regarding their progress. He provided the business cards of the two SID Agents he met. The operation was being conducted out of Farmington.

Lansing then detailed his search for Tina and the Navajo girl, Mariah, after they were carjacked. He described finding the dead carjacker . . . Mariah taking him to the canyon . . . and his shooting the man firing a rifle. He wasn't sure if the San Juan Sheriff or the Navajo Police needed him to provide a statement, but he wasn't worried about being charged. The shooter was still alive.

"Where is Mariah? Did she make it to the hospital in Gallup?"

"Honestly, I don't know. I left her with a Navajo family in Counselor. The father is president of the chapter house there. He said he'd make sure she found her way home."

Rivera nodded. Sue would be asking him what happened to the girl. So, would Deedee.

"I need to make a few calls before I take off," Lansing said. "If I can think of anything else, I'll let you know."

Referring to his New Mexico Law Enforcement Directory, he found the number to the Navajo Nation Police Office in Crownpoint. He talked to Sergeant Kenneth Chee, the man who received the rifle the day before. Lansing explained his suspicion that the weapon was used in a shooting in San Phillipe County.

Chee was cautiously cooperative. Navajos were not treated kindly in the white man's courts. The sergeant admitted he had the shooter, Clayton Betoney, in custody. He would continue holding him if Lansing needed. Also, he would coordinate with the State Police to get a ballistics comparison.

Lansing admitted he shot Betoney. He offered to make himself available for a statement, if the Navajo Police needed one.

Chee already knew Lansing was the shooter but thanked him none the less. He would let him know.

Lansing's next call was to St. Vincent Hospital. Tina Morales had been moved to the ICU at 5:00 that morning. Her condition was still considered critical. She would be allowed one visitor at a time and only immediate family. Lansing thought "We'll see about that."

He called Las Palmas Middle/High School. After asking how the teacher was doing, Halley gave Lansing Tina's parents' contact numbers in Phoenix.

He kept his composure as he explained Tina's condition to her parents. He didn't go into great detail as to where he found her. He also informed them he would be staying in Santa Fe until she got better.

They thanked him for contacting them. They would be on their way to Santa Fe immediately.

Confident he had finished his call list, he said his office goodbyes and headed to Santa Fe in his personal truck.

Chapter Ninety-Two

"I am sorry . . . I am so sorry," Clayton Betoney began.

Charlie Etsitty couldn't believe how much the man had changed in less than 24 hours. Some of the change had to do with the fact that he had been shot. But the wound couldn't account for everything. His eyes were sunken and dark. He looked like he hadn't slept in weeks. When he walked, he shuffled like an old man.

She looked to see if he was wearing shackles . . . he wasn't.

"Sergeant Chee asked us to talk to you," Yazzie began. "He couldn't understand what you were babbling about last night."

Betoney shrugged.

"You were talking about the Etsitty family," Charlie interrupted. "That's my family."

Betoney stared at the woman but said nothing.

"Is that why you shot at us in that canyon yesterday?" Warren asked. "Because her name is Etsitty?"

"I didn't know her name . . . I wanted to keep you away. I didn't mean to shoot anyone."

"But you did, Clayton." The comment came from Chee, who stood along the wall of the small interrogation room.

"Keep us away from what?" Yazzie continued. "Something in the canyon?"

The prisoner shrugged again.

"From those old ruins?" Charlie asked.

He nodded.

"What's so special about them?"

"It is sacred ground."

"For the Diné people?"

He shook his head. "Not for all Diné."

"For *adiłgąshii?*" Yazzie asked. "Witches?"

Betoney hesitated, then nodded.

"Simon Hatale said you followed the Witchery Way. He said you are an *adiłgąshii.*"

"I am not!" The man screamed, jumping up lunging across the small table that separated him from the others.

Kenneth Chee scrambled to grab the man and secure him to his seat. He looked over to see Warren Yazzie in a crouching position. If the prisoner had touched either Yazzie or the woman, the sergeant was confident the former ranger would have torn him apart.

"I wouldn't do that again," the officer said, whispering in Betoney's ear. "If that man across the table doesn't kill you, I will."

It took a full minute before Betoney calmed down. Shaking his head, he said softly, "I am not a witch."

"But you wanted to be one, didn't you?" Warren continued his interrogation.

The prisoner turned his head and stared at blank wall, reluctant to look at anyone. "Once, maybe."

When no one asked another question, he understood he needed to explain. "I was apprenticed to Norman Keyanna. He was a great medicine man in White Rock, and I started when I was very young. I was with him a year, then he went away . . . I didn't know why.

"I tried to learn from other shaman, but I couldn't remember the songs. I was called stupid and worthless. I was told to go dig holes for outhouses. That was all I was good for.

"Then, ten years ago, Keyanna came back to White Rock. He knew what had happened to me. He said come with him. I would be his apprentice again. He would teach me more than the other medicine men ever knew. I didn't know it was the Witchery Way.

"For a year I tried to learn. I watched their ceremonies and listened to their words. Then one night, four of them threw animal skins over their backs, two wore coyote skins, one wore the skin of a mountain lion, the other a bear skin. They danced in front of a fire. They howled and barked, and after a time they changed . . ." He seemed to choke up. Clearing his throat, he continued. "They changed and were no longer men."

He looked at the others, his eyes wild. "I know you don't believe what I say, but I saw them change into the animals . . . then they ran away from the fire . . . into the darkness."

"We believe you," Charlie said. "I've seen them." She was tempted to reach across the table to touch his hand, then thought better of it. "Why did you think we wouldn't believe you?"

"Because Norman said I should tell no one what I saw. He said no one would believe me. He told me my mind was not strong, and every-one knew it.

"Deep inside, I was afraid. I told him I wanted to leave and go back to White Rock. He said I couldn't. I had seen too much. I knew too much.

"That's when he talked about *adiłgąshii* and *yee naaldlooshii*. I had heard about them when I was young, but I thought they were stories to scare me. But they are real . . . I saw them."

"Why didn't you just go back to White Rock?" Chee asked.

"I tried," Betoney said, hanging his head. "I had been gone a year. When I went home, my parents said I had gone with Norman to follow the Witchery Way. I was evil now. I could not live with them . . . or any Diné people.

"I had no choice. I had to go back with Norman and his people. He told me I could never leave again. I had to stay and do what the others told me to do. If I did try to leave, they would find me and kill me. Then they would kill my family. I stayed. I have been with them now for these past ten years . . . doing what they say.

"I know what they told me is true . . . but I am not going back. They will come to kill me now. They will kill my family just like they have killed other families."

"The Etsitty family?" Charlie asked softly. "Are they killing my family?"

Betoney looked at her with tears welling up in his eyes. "Yes."

Chapter Ninety-Three

Lansing parked in front of the Santa Fe County Sheriff's offices.

His visit to the hospital wasn't as long as he wanted. Tina was still in the ICU and the hospital was adamant only family members were allowed to visit. He tried to convince them he was her boyfriend/fiancé. That didn't change their minds.

He could see her once she was out of intensive care and moved to a regular room. They had no idea when that would happen. Her condition was still listed as critical due to low blood pressure.

It was an eight-hour drive from Phoenix to Santa Fe. He didn't expect the Moraleses to arrive till 6:00 p.m. at the earliest. He wanted to be at the hospital to greet them when they arrived. In the interim, he needed to busy himself for the next six or seven hours.

It was too early to check into a motel.

Round trip to Las Palmas would eat up almost three hours, but that was a waste of gas. Besides, he wanted to stay close in case Tina was moved out of the ICU.

Since he was in town, he thought he would give Sheriff Ed Moreno a courtesy call. The Santa Fe Sheriff's office was two miles south of town. It was across the road from the county correctional facility and less than a mile from the Penitentiary of New Mexico.

Santa Fe County was 1900 square miles. San Phillipe was three-times larger. But population wise, Santa Fe had 140,000 residents as opposed to his 40,000. Granted, the capitol city had a 155-man police force for its 84,000 residents, but that did little to stop the rising crime rates.

Santa Fe County easily had ten times the number of reported crimes as San Phillipe.

Lansing admitted to himself his force was supplemented by the Jicarilla Reservation Police, the Segovia Police, and the State Police. It wasn't as if they were some lonely outpost in the wilderness . . . though it felt that way at times.

He wasn't jealous when he walked through the door into Moreno's building. It was bustling. There were 85 sworn officers on the force with even more support personnel. It reminded him how much he didn't miss living in a big city.

Since he was in civilian attire, he had to show his credentials to prove who he was. Even so, he sat for 15 minutes brushing imaginary dust from his hat before Moreno was available.

"Hey, Cliff," Moreno said, smiling. He stood when Lansing entered. After shaking hands, he offered his counterpart a seat.

"What brings you south?"

"I'm taking some vacation days . . . visiting a sick friend in the hospital. I thought I would make a social call."

"Would you care for a cup of coffee?"

"No, I'm fine." He paused for a second. "Do you coordinate a lot with the State Police?"

"When we have to. What are you referring to?"

Lansing explained he had a murder investigation that the State Police Special Investigations Division had commandeered. They were working with the FBI. The FBI was involved with a missing persons investigation on the Navajo Reservation.

"The SID folks were going to place an outfit called *Southwest Antiques* under surveillance. I think *Southwest* vans are being used in human trafficking. The state, even the FBI, agree. I was curious if they said anything to you about a stakeout."

"Let me talk to the Patrol Division. They're the ones who would investigate suspicious activity. The State guys wouldn't want one of my patrols rolling up on their operation and alerting any suspects."

Moreno picked up his phone and talked to the lieutenant in charge of patrols. The conversation was short, but he did write a note.

"You're right," he said, after hanging up. "The state does have a surveillance operation going on."

"*Southwest Antiques?*"

"Yes."

"Do you know where the place is?"

"Let's go over to the briefing room. There's a wall map we can look at."

Moreno's note had the address to the antiques shipping center. "It's off Interstate twenty-five, outside the city limits." He pointed to a side road paralleling the interstate. "It's close to where Highway two eighty-five joins I-twenty-five." He pointed to a spot southeast of the city. "It gets hilly around there, so, I would suspect the state boys would pick a spot where they can look down at the complex."

"That's great. I appreciate your time, Ed."

"You're not going over there, are you?"

"Maybe a casual drive-by. I won't do anything to raise suspicion."

"I hope not," Moreno warned. "My guys have enough to do. They don't need to pull your bacon out of the fire if you cross the SID."

"Don't worry. I'm a big boy. I can take care of myself." He put his Stetson back on and headed for the parking lot.

Chapter Ninety-Four

"Why are they killing members of the Etsitty family?" Warren Yazzie demanded. He was not gentle with his question.

Betoney cringed. "Because the man who calls himself *Nizéé'* killed Norman Keyanna." *Nizéé'* was the Navajo word for "The Silent One."

"That tells me nothing," Yazzie snapped. "Why did this *Nizéé'* kill Keyanna? Who is this man?"

"Keyanna was chief among all the *adiłgashii*. He made the rules the others followed. He said who could and who could not become a witch.

"Three years ago, *Nizéé'* came to seek out Keyanna and his people. He was a shaman and said he was ready to follow the Witchery Way. He even had proof he had already killed a close family member.

"Norman welcomed him. *Nizéé'* dedicated himself to learn everything there was to know about the Way. Even Norman said the young shaman accomplished in three years what it took others, decades to learn. He had never seen a man become a *yee naaldlooshii* so quickly.

"Maybe it was four months ago that Keyanna held what he called a conclave. Over a dozen *adiłgashii* from across the Navajo reservation came to the Badlands . . . to the sacred ruins."

"You were there . . . even though you say you're not a witch?"

"I told you . . . Keyanna said he would kill my family if I tried to leave. Yes, I was there." He glanced at the other three with the look of a defeated man.

"Go on," Charlie said gently. "There was a conclave at the ruins."

"Keyanna heard among the Diné that they again wanted to claim the sacred ruins . . . just as they had seven years earlier. He began talking of other things but was interrupted.

"*Nizéé'* demanded to know what had happened seven years ago.

"Keyanna said a man wanted to claim the ruins for the Navajo Nation. He was warned many times to stay away, but he did not listen. Keyanna stalked him. The time came when Keyanna himself changed into a *yee naaldlooshii*. He caused the man's car to crash. It killed the man and his wife. After that the leaders at Window Rock forgot about looking for their place.

"*Nizéé'* asked who this man was. I could tell Keyanna was getting angry at the interruptions. He answered anyway. The man's name was Etsitty. Isaac Etsitty.

"*Nizéé'* screamed at him that Etsitty was his father. Before any of the conclave could react, he had thrown on his hide and jumped across the flames." Betoney became more agitated and louder as he spoke. "The two men struggled. As they fought, they changed. They both became Skinwalkers.

"*Nizéé'* was bigger, younger, stronger. Finally, he knocked Keyanna to the ground and ripped out his throat with his teeth.

"We were all stunned. *Nizéé'* stood over the old man and screamed. Before anyone thought to stop him, he ran into the darkness.

"Since then, *Nizéé'* has been attacking other witches. When he could, he killed them. Joseph Hernandez declared himself to be Keyanna's replacement. He gave me one job. I had to track down *Nizéé'* and kill him. Because of what he's done, the rest of the *adiłgąshii* have sworn revenge against him, against his entire Etsitty family, wherever they live."

"This *Nizéé'* said Isaac Etsitty was his father." Charlie pressed. "Do you know *Nizéé'*'s given name?"

Betoney nodded. "Walter Etsitty . . . he killed his brother, William, so that he could follow the Witchery Way."

"Walter's still alive!" Charlie exclaimed in disbelief.

293

"And he followed the Witchery Way to find the man responsible for killing his parents," Yazzie concluded.

"So, you weren't just shooting at us to protect the ruins, were you?" Charlie asked, upset at the news Walter had killed his own brother.

"Walter always knows when I'm close. I followed him to the canyon. I found his old campfire and the woman wrapped in a blanket. I thought he would return. I waited on a hill, but you showed up. I was afraid you would take the woman away and *Nizéé'* would not come back.

"I wanted to scare you away. I am sorry I shot that old man. I was only trying to get close."

"What do you know about a missing ranger from Chaco Canyon?" Chee interrupted.

"I don't know what they did to him." Betoney's face was a mask of fear. "They said he followed them to the ruins. I was told to drive his truck far away so it wouldn't be found there."

"Who told you to do that? Joseph Hernandez?"

"No, no. He's dead. *Nizéé'* killed him, too."

"No wonder they're so pissed at the Etsitty family," Yazzie said under his breath. "It sounds like a war of attrition."

"What does that mean?" Betoney asked.

"That means it's a race to see if the *adiłgashii* can kill off the Etsittys before they're all killed off."

"Where is Walter now?" Charlie asked.

"I don't know."

"He must live somewhere."

"If I had known where, I would have killed him already."

Warren motioned with his head for Charlie to join him in the hallway.

"Do you think he's telling the truth?"

She sighed. "How else would he know about Walter and William?"

"Maybe he was involved with both of their murders from the beginning?"

"But that wouldn't explain the vendetta against my entire family. His story fits with everything else we know."

Warren pondered the situation. "You came to Window Rock to find out what happened to your cousins. Are you satisfied with the results?"

"Not completely. I would love to contact Walter somehow. That would make this trip worthwhile . . . but more importantly, we have to find a way keep the rest of my family from being exterminated."

"Let's ask Betoney," Warren suggested. "He seems to know about everything else."

Clayton Betoney rocked back and forth as he considered Yazzie's question.

Finally, he said, "If there is proof *Nizéé'* is dead, I think the other *adiłgqshii* will let your family live in peace . . . but that would be the only way."

Chapter Ninety-Five

Lansing was surprised at how busy the *Southwest Antiques* shipping center seemed. Behind the sliding gate, the lot was filled with a half dozen private vehicles, two windowless vans and a paneled truck. The garage-like doors to the warehouse were up. Men moved in and out.

He tried not to stare as he drove past. He counted ten men and his guess was something was about to happen. A quarter mile past the compound was a dirt road that climbed into the low hills. He followed it, eventually passing a truck with a large camper shell.

Campers like that were common in New Mexico. However, they were seldom simply parked along the side of a road. It appeared to be abandoned, but he knew better. There would be at least two observers stationed inside, watching the activities below.

He passed the truck, pretending it was of no interest to him. When he found a convenient spot to maneuver, he turned around and retraced his route back to I-25.

***

Tina's parents arrived sooner than he expected. They were already at the hospital when he returned at 5:30. Their daughter was still in the ICU and Mr. and Mrs. Morales took turns sitting with her. There had been no significant improvement.

Lansing recommended the motel where he was staying if they hadn't found a place. It was reasonably priced and near the hospital.

He visited with them until 7:00. That's when he excused himself. They needed rest and he insisted he did, too.

He had no interest in heading back to his room. He had been a lawman for over 20 years and in that time had developed a sort of intuition that something was about to happen. Officers had different names for it – a gut feeling, a hunch, a sixth sense.

For him, it was an itch in his brain. It was an itch he couldn't scratch. It would keep on itching until he did something about it. In this case, it was getting in his truck and heading back to the *Southwest Antiques* shipping compound.

Chapter Ninety-Six

"Would you even have a clue where you would start looking?" Yazzie asked. "As soon as we turned north off I-forty, we entered the Badlands. Through Crownpoint, Lake Valley, even Chaco Canyon, we were in the Badlands . . . and I'll bet we saw less than ten percent of that territory. You could spend a year out there and never find Walter."

Charlie Etsitty stared at her cup of coffee. They had driven back to Window Rock and she was deciding what she should do next.

***

Sergeant Chee had reservations about releasing Betoney. Officially, his prisoner had not been charged with a crime. He was doubtful the man would return on his own to face attempted murder charges. There was also no guarantee he could contact the *adiłgąshii*.

"Can you find them? These witches. You know where they gather, right?"

The failed medicine man nodded.

Chee looked at the other two. "I suggest I take Clayton back to where you first met him."

"*Kimbeto Wash*?" Charlie asked. "Near the ruins?"

"Yes. Clayton, if I take you up there, will you contact the *adiłgąshii*? Tell them *Nizéé'* will no longer attack them as long as they leave the Etsitty family alone."

"You said I was under arrest."

"I will let you go if you do this for me . . ." Chee nodded toward the woman. "If you'll do it for Miss Etsitty."

Warren pulled the officer aside. "We can't guarantee that Walter will quit attacking them."

"Yeah, but maybe this will buy us some time."

Chee didn't mention his conversation with Sheriff Lansing. If releasing Betoney saved one Etsitty life, he felt his actions were justified. He would continue to pursue the ballistics comparisons. Even if Betoney's rifle was used in a homicide, it would be impossible to prove he had fired it.

***

"I would love to see Walter again," Charlie admitted. "But I have to get back to my girls." She paused. "I need to get back to my job in Phoenix."

"You were talking about staying on the rez. What happened to that?"

"When I was a kid and we came up to the family ranch, it was fun. I got to see my cousins, my grandparents. I didn't notice how terribly poor everyone was.

"It wasn't until my senior year when we had to move to Tuba City that I learned what poverty really was. And it was a thousand times worse after I was raped, and my daughter, Tina, came along.

"Mr. Garcia got me out of a terrible marriage. He gave me a job and hope for the first time since my father was killed.

"Sure, I put myself through a guilt trip about wanting to be a good Navajo parent. I thought it would be great for my daughters to grow up Diné, learn about their culture. I guess I'm selfish. I don't want them to grow up poor. I want them to have a chance in this world."

Yazzie nodded. "I understand what you're saying. But remember, there are different ways a person can be poor. There is the absence of monetary wealth and there is the absence of spiritual wealth."

Charlie looked up, frowning. "Don't go confusing me."

"Are you going back tomorrow?"

"In the morning."

"Don't you want to find out if Clayton talks to the witches?"

"I do . . . but that's something you can tell me about if it happens. I don't have to stay in Window Rock. I have my girls to think about."

"Then you're finished here?"

"I found out what I wanted to know."

"We didn't find Jenny."

"I'm afraid that will take more than a two-day trip to Window Rock. If Walter didn't find her after looking for five years, my chances are pretty slim."

"I'm not the fastest typist in the world," Warren admitted. "It will take me a couple of days to put my report together."

"When you're done, please mail it to the law offices in Phoenix. I want Mr. Garcia to know his money was well spent."

Chapter Ninety-Seven

"Boss, you're not going to believe this," the man said from the door-way.

Bud Baker looked up from the stack of papers on his desk. He was in his usual sour mood. "Now, what?" he asked, with his teeth clenching a cigar.

"Juan Pedro just pulled through the gate with the missing van."

"What?" Baker jumped up and looked through the window blinds. It was dark outside. The large lot had few lights, but he could see the van. The driver stood talking with two other men.

"Tell that son-of-a-whore to get in here!" Baker barked. "I want to know where the hell he's been for the past week!"

Baker parked himself at his desk. Instead of being relieved he had his missing van back, he was angry. In fact, the more he thought about it the angrier he got. Where the hell had Garcia been? Why did he dump those three girls back on the reservation? Why did he attack Roberto de la Cruz? Why did he kill him?

By the time someone finally knocked on his door, Baker had worked himself into a frenzy. He had already decided Juan Pedro Garcia was a dead man. He had opened the drawer containing his 9 mm pistol.

"Come in!" he shouted.

A man Baker had never met before came through the door, shutting it behind him.

"Who the hell are you? Where's Garcia?"

"My name is Walter Etsitty. I am looking for my sister."

"How'd you get in here?"

"Your people thought I was the other man." The Skinwalker had taken on Juan Pedro's appearance. "I tell you again. I am looking for my sister, Jennifer Etsitty."

"I don't know what the hell you're talking about!"

"You took her from our reservation five years ago."

"What reservation?"

"We are Navajo. My sister lived in Fort Defiance. You came and took her away."

"I got news for you, Geronimo. I've never set foot on the Navajo Reservation."

"Your people did. They came for my sister, just like the girls who were in that van. The girls I rescued."

"Oh," Baker said with sudden realization. "So, you're the bastard who highjacked my van."

"Where did you take my sister?"

"I don't have a clue where she ended up," Baker said. It was one of the few honest things to come out of his mouth. "Girls come through here all the time. I can't keep track of every place they go." He waved his hand toward the window. "They could be anywhere.

"I'm feeling generous since you returned my van. I'll give you a choice. You walk out that door and forget about this place and your sister . . ." He pulled the 9mm from his drawer and pointed it at the Navajo. "Or I make you dead, and my boys dump your body in a canyon somewhere."

Etsitty said nothing. Instead he tried to jump across Baker's desk and grab the gun.

Baker fired two quick shots into Walter's chest, and the attacker fell to the ground.

The door to the office opened immediately. One of the two henchmen that entered desperately asked, "Boss, are you okay?"

"Yes," Baker sneered. He walked around his desk and thought seriously about spitting on the dead man on the floor. Instead, he knocked ashes from the end of his smoke and said, "Get that trash out of my office. Toss it down a mountain somewhere."

He started toward the door. Over his shoulder, he said, "And clean up any blood."

"Sure thing, Boss."

Baker continued outside. He wanted to inspect the condition of the once missing van. He was only 10 feet out the door when he heard the screaming.

Screams of terror . . . screams of pain . . . came from behind him . . . from his office.

Others in the parking area heard the commotion as well. Baker pointed at a group of five workers, a mixture of Anglos and Hispanics.

"Get in there!" he snapped. "Find out what's going on!"

Not a man moved. No one was interested in confronting whatever was in his office.

"Dammit!" Baker shouted. "I said get in there!"

Two men took tentative steps toward the building.

"Now!" he yelled, pointing at the door.

More afraid of Baker than the unseen terror, they hurried to the entrance. The three remaining men reluctantly followed.

By the time they reached the door, the screaming inside had stopped. Initially, they all hesitated and looked at each other. The first two, Hispanic brothers, ventured into the building.

They were there for several seconds, then one of them shot back out the door. He waved his arms wildly and screamed, *"Monstruo! Monstruo! Escaparce! Ándele!"* as he ran into the darkness.

From inside the building, his brother was yelling, *"Salva me! Salva me!"* followed by one final scream of terror.

The other men didn't wait to find out what would happen next. Two ran to their cars. The eight-foot tall, rolling gate was closed. The first car slammed straight into it, knocking it askew . . . wide enough that he could escape. The second car sped through the opening.

The third man ran for the warehouse, yelling, "Somebody get a gun!"

Baker stepped further away from the entrance. He wished he had brought his pistol. A figure appeared in the doorway. It was a man, but it wasn't a man. It emitted an ominous growl.

Bud Baker didn't wait to find out what the hideous creature was. There were weapons in the warehouse if he could get to them. He started running toward the building. He could feel the beast almost on top of him. Evan Florin emerged holding an AR-15.

"Kill it!" Baker screamed. "Kill it!"

Florin raised the weapon and fired.

Chapter Ninety-Eight

The highway was dark. Lansing guessed he was 100 feet from the *Southwest Antiques'* entrance when a car knocked its way through the closed gate. With no headlights, the car skidded onto the road. Barely in control, the driver swerved to miss Lansing's truck, then sped into the darkness.

Lansing slammed on his brakes and hit his horn.

A moment later a second car hurdled through opening. If he hadn't stopped when he did, Lansing would have plowed into the second maniacal driver.

Then, from inside the compound, came three quick shots from a rifle.

Experience told him he shouldn't handle the situation by himself. He picked up his cell and dialed 9-1-1.

"Nine-one-one, what's your emergency?"

"Officer needs assistance! I'm on the Old Las Vegas Highway near Highway two eighty-five. Shots fired at *Southwest Antiques* shipping center. I repeat, shots fired."

"I copy, sir. Shots fired. What's your name?"

"Sheriff Cliff Lansing, San Phillipe County!"

"Where exactly are you located?"

"Just outside the gate."

"Help is on the way! Stay where you are, Sheriff."

"Like hell," he said under his breath. He popped open his glove compartment and retrieved his 9 mm backup and a flashlight.

Rolling through the gate, the compound was mostly dark. The lights of his truck gave some illumination . . . but it also made him a target. Knowing he wouldn't stay in his truck, he opted to leave the headlights on.

The office building was still lit inside. If the warehouse had lights, they were off. The large garage door was raised half-way.

Earlier in the day there were two windowless vans in the parking lot. Now there were three. Lansing guessed he had found the van taken from the canyon.

A body lay face up on the ground between him and the open garage door. He quickly stepped forward and knelt next to the body. He felt the neck for a pulse, noticing the throat had been ripped open. Next to the victim was an AR-15.

Inside the warehouse, men were shouting. There were gunshots.

Not interested in being hit, Lansing ran to the exterior of the warehouse and put his back against the wall. He stayed there and listened, trying to picture what was happening inside.

As many as four men were yelling. He could make out a few words. ". . . see it . . ."

"No, over there . . ." ". . . come this way . . ."

Two gun shots were followed by a man shouting, "I got it! I got it!" Then a scream.

The yelling, the screaming and the gunshots continued for five full minutes, though they became fewer and fewer. Interspersed with all the other noises were the screams and snarls of a wild animal.

To Lansing it sounded like a very large and a very angry animal.

Suddenly the warehouse became quiet. No more voices. No more weapons being fired. No more shouting. Even the animal sounds had stopped.

Lansing wished back-up would arrive. He wasn't sure he wanted to face whatever was beyond the door. However, he had to check and see if anyone needed help.

Turning on his flashlight, he stepped into the building. The interior was large. Half resembled an auto repair shop. There was nothing in there that remotely looked like an antique.

He could find no victims in the large room.

The other half of the building had been portioned off into a dozen small, cubicles. Some of the doors were peppered with bullet holes. Some were smeared with blood. As he inspected each small room, dead men started appearing. Three of them.

The bodies were torn and bloody, the throats shredded. Eyes remained wide open, testaments to the terror they witnessed.

From the last room along the cramped hallway came a muffled grunt.

Lansing carefully pushed the door open and pointed his light into the darkness. On a filthy, bloody mattress was the body of a man. Bud Baker had suffered much more damage than the others. Besides the shredded throat, the eyes had been clawed out. The victim had suffered mutilation while he was still alive.

The grunt came again. He pointed the light into a corner.

The beast turned its head and squinted from the light in its eyes. It stood erect like a man and was just as tall. The profile was that of a large cat . . . a mountain lion. The normally erect ears were pulled back flat, as if the creature was preparing for an attack. The limbs were long and muscular. The forearms ended with large claws with the sharp talons exposed. The white hair around the snout was stained with blood.

The entire body was covered in short, tan fur. The tattered clothes had splotches of blood where bullets had penetrated.

"I have no quarrel with you," the beast growled. "Step out of the way."

Lansing pointed his light in the animal's face. The eyes glowed red. "You killed all these men?"

"For what they have done to my people, to my family, death is not enough . . . but it's the best I can do."

"Who are you? What are you?"

"In my tongue, I am called *yee naaldlooshii*. To other Navajo, I am considered Evil. But there are greater Evils in this world than even me . . . and I have taken my revenge.

"Step aside, White Man."

Lansing hesitated. "People will ask what happened here."

"Tell them whatever you want. You know the truth. They can choose to believe you . . . or not."

Lansing backed through the door. In the hallway, the beast stepped past him. Without looking back, it dropped to all fours and ran into the darkness.

In the distance Lansing could hear the wail of police sirens.

He doubted if anyone would believe what he had just seen.

Chapter Ninety-Nine

The Santa Fe Sheriff's department was the first to arrive at *Southwest Antiques*. Lansing told them what he heard and almost everything he saw. He was reluctant to mention the beast. Later conversations confirmed what he suspected . . . he had encountered a Skinwalker. It was a secret he shared with few others.

He was asked who did all the killing. He honestly admitted he never saw the "man" who did it and that he probably escaped out the back of the building. When asked if he tried to engage the assailant, Lansing stressed the fact that a good officer waits for back-up.

A total of 8 bodies were recovered. They were all killed in the same manner. It looked like the damage was done by a wild animal, but that made no sense. Sheriff Moreno told his people to be on the lookout for a crazed slasher, though one never turned up.

The FBI and SID descended on the compound like vultures on a dead steer. Bud Baker's *Southwest Antiques* was a hub for one of the biggest human trafficking operations north of the Mexican border. Digging through the records, they discovered *S-A* specialized in abducting Native American girls, often for sexual pleasure. Some were sold to brothels. Some to private individuals. Some became domestic workers in homes and motels.

Locally, a dozen *S-A* associates were rounded up. Lansing was more than happy to point out Wanda Florin as the faux social worker who tried to abduct Mariah Tsosie from the hospital. Miguel Cuellar, Mariah's assailant in the hospital room, had completely disappeared.

It would be years before his car was discovered in a remote canyon along with his remains.

Raids were conducted as far away as Chicago and St. Louis. A dozen brothels were closed down and the girls, many of them young women now, were offered the chance to go home. Many did. Others, too ashamed of what happened to them, were afraid they would not be welcomed. Unfortunately, with no support systems, they tragically ended up back on the streets.

***

Two of the abducted Indian girls identified the Winnebago as the same RV used to remove them from the reservation. The bodies of the two kidnappers were never recovered, which upset no one.

***

The state forensics lab in Santa Fe did a ballistics comparison of the bullet taken from the hiker in Rockhouse Canyon and Clayton Betoney's Remington 700. It was a match.

The Special Investigations Division of the State Police was not happy with Navajo Police Sergeant Kenneth Chee. He had released Clayton Betoney, their prime suspect, into the wilds of the Navajo Badlands.

Chee assured them Betoney promised to turn himself in once he finished talking to the *adiłgąshii*.

No one was happy when Clayton Betoney's dead body was dumped on Chee's doorstep a few days later. He had been murdered. Chee passed on the news to Warren Yazzie who, in turn, informed Charlie Etsitty. They weren't sure if Betoney was successful in talking to anyone. Only time would tell if the Etsitty family was safe.

Lansing closed his file on the Rockhouse Canyon homicide. He considered the outcome unsatisfactory. He knew in his gut, as soon as he relinquished control of the investigation, someone would screw it up. He was surprised it was the Navajo Police and not SID.

***

Warren Yazzie led members of the Navajo Rangers and Police up *Kimbeto Wash* to the notorious "ruins." The site had the remnants of several bon fires. There were octagonal, stone outlines marking the foundations for three Navajo hogans. These were the ruins. Experts would estimate they were 200 years old.

Yazzie considered that interesting, but hardly worth the life of a single person.

Interest among the investigators turned to anger when they discovered over a dozen graves scattered along the canyon rim. Most were several decades old. One was fresh. The body belonged to Harry Miller, the missing ranger from Chaco Canyon.

Yazzie offered his opinion. Miller had chased the witches from Chaco Canyon, up *Kimbeto Wash*, until they reached the ruins. He was captured, judging from condition of the body, tortured, and killed. The *adiłgashii* were angry that he chased them. Maybe he was killed because he found their sacred place. Maybe they killed him simply because they were pure Evil.

Whatever the case, the FBI took over the investigation but was never able to arrest a single suspect.

***

The autopsy of Junior Kee proved Lansing right. He had drowned the same way Juan Pedro Garcia had, by breathing in the bone dust toxins. After detailed analysis by the Santa Fe Forensics Lab, it was determined the toxins were a concoction known to Navajo witches.

Made from the bones and dried flesh of corpses, the toxic spores, in concentration, were lethal. Once inhaled, the respiratory system was immediately overwhelmed, and the victims died in minutes.

Lansing could guess why Juan Pedro had to die. He was part of Bud Baker's operation. The Skinwalker had taken his revenge.

He also guessed that the desecrated grave in Segovia was the result of that Navajo witch needing to replenish his supply of human body parts.

No one would ever know that Walter Etsitty had killed Junior Kee because he threatened Mariah Tsosie. Etsitty had saved her once before . . . from being raped by Esteban de la Cruz. He was her guardian angel that night . . . and again when she and Tina entered the Badlands.

Chapter One Hundred

"Cliff, how long have you been sitting there?"

Lansing woke with a start. Ever since Tina Morales had been re-leased from the ICU Tuesday morning, he had spent 12 hours a day at her side. When he wasn't with her, her parents were.

She drifted in and out of consciousness for three days. It was Friday morning before she actually woke up.

"I don't know," he said, yawning. "Most of this week." He suddenly realized she was conscious. He jumped up. "You're awake!"

"What hospital is this?"

"You're at St. Vincent in Santa Fe."

"Oh, my God. Has anyone told my parents?"

"Don't worry. They know. They'll probably be up to see you as soon as they're finished with breakfast."

She knit her eyebrows, trying to remember what happened. "Why am I here?"

"You were in bad shape, Tina. They had to operate."

She thought, then said, "I was hurting. I remember I was bleeding." She looked at Lansing. "You came looking for me. Cliff, I remember you carried me out of that canyon." Tears welled up in her eyes. "You saved my life!"

"Not just me." He stepped closer and gently kissed her forehead.

"Cliff, I'm so sorry. On vacation, I thought I was getting sick. I didn't want to be a burden to you. That's why I pushed you away. I didn't want you to have to take care of me!"

Lansing took her hand in his. "You will never be a burden to me."

Ever since he saved her life in Cohino Canyon, he wanted to protect her. For two years Tina Morales had been his confidante, his sounding board, his lover. In his daily morning prayers, he thanked the good Lord for bringing her into his life. He was shaken to his core at the thought of losing her. When she was better, when the time was right, he would tell her how he truly felt.

"Mariah!" she exclaimed. "What happened to Mariah?"

"She's back in Chinle . . . living with her aunt and uncle. She calls every day to see how you're doing. Next time she calls, you can talk to her."

Tina's parents came in. There were hugs, tears and laughter. Lansing excused himself so they could enjoy the reunion in private.

***

Tina Morales was in the hospital for a week.

The doctor explained how serious her condition had been. Fortunately, the tumors they removed were not cancerous . . . but the damage was done. She would never bear children.

She and Lansing had long conversations about her condition. Through many tears, she confessed that she thought she would be less of a woman. He assured her that didn't matter to him. He just wanted her healthy.

Both Maria Tsosie and Charlie Etsitty called daily to check on her progress. Tentative plans were made for a Thanksgiving reunion.

Tina convalesced for three more weeks at Lansing's ranch. When she first arrived, she was thrilled to find her Chevy Cavalier waiting for her. Lansing had retrieved it, replaced the shredded tire and had Midnight repaired, detailed and waxed.

Oscar Vega pulled double duty as a ranch hand and health care attendant. During those three weeks, at Tina's request, Lansing moved all her belongings from her small house in Las Palmas to the ranch.

The future looked bright.

Epilogue

Charlie Etsitty stepped out of the ranch house, carbine in hand. Whistling had come from the darkness and she needed to protect her daughters sleeping inside.

This would be her last night at the old homestead. The last of the sheep would be picked up in the morning. Her grandmother had already moved to Lechee. Once the livestock was gone, she, Tina and Lizbeth would go home . . . to Phoenix.

"Charlie!" The voice came from the dark shadows. It was deep and gruff and unfamiliar.

"What? Who's there?" She masked her fear as best she could

"Walter."

"What?"

"It's me. Your cousin, Walter."

"Walter?" Her voice trembled. "Is it really you?"

"Yes . . . I came to tell you . . ." A shadow moved closer, but not close enough for Charlie to see him. "I am sorry for the pain I have caused. I only wanted to find my sister. I sacrificed my own brother. I did not know my actions could destroy our entire family."

"Walter, let me see you!"

"No," he said firmly. "Remember me as I was. The conclave meets tonight. I will go there. After tonight, no one will harm our family again."

"What are you going to do?"

"Goodbye, Charlotte Etsitty."

"Walter!"

There was no response.

"Walter!!" she yelled into the darkness. "Don't go! Come back! Please, come back!"

Tears stung Charlie's eyes. Walter left before she could tell him . . . the FBI had found his sister. Jennifer was coming home.

The Skinwalker was gone . . .

He had to face the fate that awaited him . . . in the Badlands.

Coming 2021!

CERRO GRANDE
A Sheriff Lansing Mystery
Book 10
By
Micah S. Hackler

A controlled burn by the US Park Service becomes an uncontrolled inferno. The lives of thousands of people are threatened. Creatures of the forest escape any way they can. The people of Santa Clara Pueblo fight the blaze to protect their homes.

An old hunting outfitter struggles to save his operations. A body in a remote arroyo may be linked to a robbery. Three teenagers disappear in the mountains when tracking a wild animal.

Complications mount for Sheriff Cliff Lansing as he faces the murders and mayhem once again engulfing San Phillipe County.

For more information
visit: www.SpeakingVolumes.us

On Sale Now!

Sheriff Lansing Mysteries
Books 1 – 8

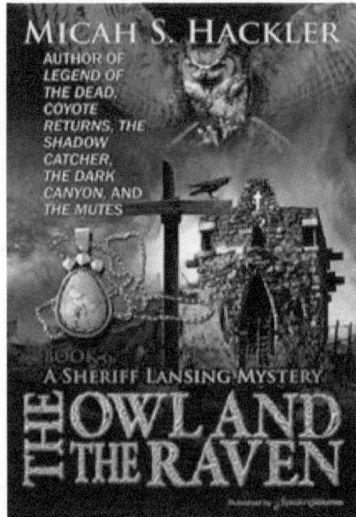

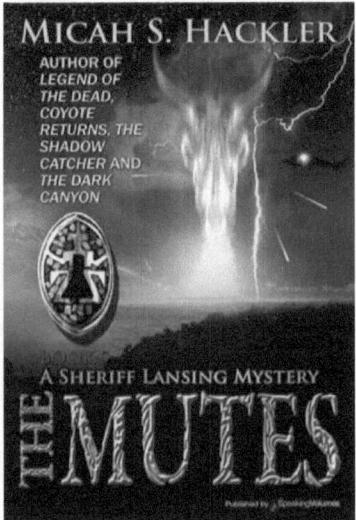

For more information
visit: www.SpeakingVolumes.us

On Sale Now!

Howard Moon Deer Mysteries
Books 1 – 6

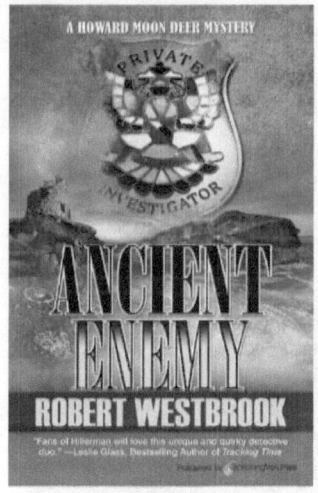

**For more information
visit:** www.SpeakingVolumes.us

On Sale Now!

AWARD-WINNING AUTHOR
MARDI OAKLEY MEDAWAR

For more information
visit: www.SpeakingVolumes.us

On Sale Now!